For

MW00940410

What if

WILD CARD!

A.J. PINE

AJ Pine

Entangled Publishing, LLC
2614 South Timberline Road
Suite 109
Fort Collins, CO 80525
Visit our website at www.entangledpublishing.com.

Embrace is an imprint of Entangled Publishing, LLC.

Edited by Nicole Steinhaus and Karen Grove
Cover design by Brittany Marczak
Photography by Shutterstock

Manufactured in the United States of America

First Edition December 2014

embrace

To anyone who's ever been afraid to take the road less traveled — what if?

Chapter One

MAGGIE

Where is it?

Shit. Shit. Shit. Where is it?

I always put my phone right back on the nightstand after I wake up. Step one is turning off the wake-up alarm. Step two—turn *on* bus alarm. But I can't freaking remember if I turned on the bus alarm because I can't find the phone, the one that should be sitting right where I'm looking.

It's not that I don't recognize the irony. Girl sets alarm on phone so as not to be late for bus. Girl can't remember where she put phone from the time she woke up until right this moment.

It's been a harrowing thirty minutes. Miles will feel like shit if he has to dock me a quarter-hour's pay again. Then I'll feel like shit for making him feel like shit. The usual.

I rifle through my drawers and medicine cabinet in the bathroom. Again. No luck. When I see the bus schedule I

What if

taped to the mirror, I flip it off for good measure. It doesn't matter now if I know the time because I can't leave without the phone. I am more than naked without it. I'm helpless.

In the kitchen, I half expect to find it in the freezer. Wouldn't be the first time. Instead all I find are my pills sitting on the counter with a sticky note reminder that reads: *Morning dose.*

I thought I took them already, but I'm going to trust the Post-it. I *always* trust the Post-it. And a girl and her blood thinners are almost as good of a pair as a girl and her cell phone.

That's when I hear the DEFCON 1-style alarm, the one specifically for my bus reminder, coming from my room. Here I thought the new alarm-tone would work in my favor, but I didn't take into account that it wouldn't matter if I didn't know where my phone was.

The sound is muffled, but I chose that alarm for good reason. Even if the phone was buried six feet under, I'd at least be able to identify the land under which it was laid to rest.

I follow the sound back to my room, to my nightstand, exactly where it's supposed to be. In the top drawer, under a small towel, is my phone, yelling at me that I'm getting close to missing the bus.

"I know!" I shout at it. "But *you* need to come with me, got it?"

Smooth move on my part. The towel triggers a memory from last night—Miles texting to say good-night as I washed my face before bed. I must have walked in here to return his text, patting my face dry with the towel that just stole most of my morning prep time. Shit. I may not remember my bedtime routine, but I do remember when towels weren't such a threat to my daily routine. I laugh, the bitter sound audible even amid the noise still erupting from the drawer.

I grab the rogue cell, turn off the alarm, and pivot to leave the room.

After two years of putting my life back together, I'm still startled, sometimes, when I see the bulletin board on my wall. It's the tool that keeps me going and also the reminder that in seconds—literal seconds—one angry blood vessel can alter the course of a girl's life.

I run the tips of my fingers over the miniature Polaroids—one of each of my professors, captioned with their names and the courses they teach. Many more are of customers, and for a few seconds the tension eases at the recognition of those who are now regulars—Amber from the movie theater, George and Jeanie—the ones who never roll their eyes when I mess up an order or hesitate before greeting them by name.

"Maggie?"

I step from my bedroom and yank the door shut behind me.

"Right here, Paige."

I give her a cursory wave as she stands in my open apartment doorway.

"Sorry. I let myself in when I heard the weird alarm. And the shouting. Is everything okay?"

I nod. "Just trying not to miss the bus. I'll be late for work if I do."

She glances behind her, down the stairwell, and when she turns back to face me, she cringes.

"What?" I ask.

What if

She shrugs and tries to force a smile. "Do you mean the bus that just drove away? I could hear it from my room. I wish I had a car, Maggie. I really do."

"Crap!" I grab my coat and bag, making sure not to let go of my phone, and push past Paige and down the stairs. Maybe I can catch it at the corner.

As I risk my life hopping down the stairs two at a time, I hear Paige yell from our hallway.

"Hey, Maggie! You forgot to lock up again! Want me to do it for you?"

"Yes!" I shout, and I'm out the door and running—for a bus that just turned the corner a block away and is now out of sight.

Shit.

• • •

GRIFFIN

Don't be late.

No *Hi* or *Hey* or anything other than an echo of my mother's words from last night's voicemail.

On the way.

I text back when I hit a stop light, shaking my head that Nat has stooped to Mom's level.

Don't they know? I'm a Reed. Anything less than ten minutes early is certifiably late, according to the family handbook. I've had twenty-three years of practice, going so far as being born a week ahead of my mother's due date. If there's one thing my family can depend on, it's a Reed being on time. In my case, that's about the only thing they depend on, except my sister's text tells me I might not even have that going for me anymore.

I'm already ahead of schedule, having given myself an hour to make a thirty-minute drive. I don't blame my sister. If she hadn't sent the text, Mom would have had Jen or Megan do it. Besides, once they see my face, the time of my arrival won't mean shit. Like I said—they can depend on me to be there, but the state I'm in when I show up is anyone's guess.

I laugh at the thought of my father's first glimpse of the swollen, purple skin beneath my right eye. *Ouch.* I wince, the laughter aggravating the still-developing bruise. I knew the girl was at the bar with someone, but she was a willing participant, which means she used me as much as I used her. Too drunk to truly feel the crack of her boyfriend's fist against my face, I retaliated only for show, leaving the asshole with a split lip and me with a split knuckle…and my face the picture-perfect image of the would-be mayor's son. Sometimes it's nice to feel something other than numb, and this morning I'm definitely feeling *something.*

I laugh again when my eyes fall to the fading ink on my hand. She still gave me her number.

At the next light I grab the water bottle from my drink holder and down the whole thing along with a few ibuprofen tablets. I may not be able to change the way I look, but I can at least get rid of the hangover and increasing pain. Coffee. I have time for coffee. I flip on my turn signal to head a couple miles off-course, step on the gas, and then just as quickly pause when I see her—a girl on the sidewalk, walking backward, thumb in the air.

Her eyes meet mine, and she smiles. It's not like she's the first girl to smile at me, but shit this girl is beautiful. Even with an intersection between us, that much I can tell. Instead of turning, I cross the intersection, flipping on my hazards as I pull over to the curb and open my window.

"Are you…hitchhiking? For real?"

She looks at me, eyes narrowed. "My thumb in the air didn't give it away?" She takes a step closer. "Is that what the last hitchhiker did to you? If so, I can understand your hesitation. I'm pretty fierce."

I smirk, followed by another wince. Shit. Her sarcasm doesn't faze me. But her auburn hair hanging in two long braids, freckles, and pale pink lips, those do. I'm officially

"But you're in suburban Minneapolis. And it's damn ng. Who hitches a ride out here?"

Better yet, who stops for a hitchhiker in the 'burbs?

When they look like this girl, I sure as hell do.

She steps off the curb and walks right up to my passen-r door. Her bravado falters as she struggles to rest her elbows on the window's frame, my truck taller than she seems to have anticipated. I smile but bite back the gesture as she regains her composure.

"It's thirty-five degrees in November, and I have two miles to go. Are you going to give me a ride or not?"

Her hands, covered in fingerless gloves, tap in anticipation against the door.

"So you're just going to get in the car with a complete stranger?"

She cocks her head to the side and fixes her gaze on me, then smiles.

"I trust your eyes."

I arch a brow. *Shit*. Gotta remember that hurts.

"Probably the most trust a girl has ever given me." I

smirk.

She isn't fazed. "Bruised or not, you can tell a lot about a person from his eyes. Plus…" She leans in through the window. "It's warm in here, and I'm still standing outside."

I glance at the immaculate interior of my Ford Expedition, at the buttons on the center console indicating the warmers for my leather seats. Then I look back and watch her eyes roll. Disdain? Impatience? Probably both.

"Crap," I say under my breath but not quietly enough.

"Excuse me?" asks this annoyed Pippi Longstocking hitching a two-mile ride. And there's something in that voice, in her I've-got-you-figured-out expression, that should warn me not to mess with her. But I give my judgment the morning off. Hell, I'm pretty sure I gave it extended vacation leave.

"I was just imagining your inner monologue. *Can't believe this asshole is making me wait in the cold while he cranks up his heated seats.* Something like that?"

"Something like that." But I see it; she's fighting the upturned corners of her mouth.

I unlock the door and reach across to open the passenger side.

"Ahhh, so Pippi knows how to smile."

She doesn't respond at first, her quick wit suddenly lost in her faraway green eyes. When she *clicks* her seat belt secure, the sound jolts her back from wherever she was, and she turns to me. "Nope. It's the eye," she says. "Must be distorting your vision."

"Ouch. Pretty harsh for the guy who just saved you from the cold."

"I don't need saving." Her words are calm, but her eyes are now focused and sharp. "But thanks. For the ride. I didn't know it was going to be this cold out today."

Then without warning, she extends her left hand toward my face, but I don't flinch when she rests it against my cheek. Her thumb sweeps across the swollen skin under my eye, and I suck in a breath, partly from the tenderness of the bruise and partly from the tenderness of her touch. My eyes fall closed when she doesn't pull away, and I hear her breathe in.

"This is new?" she asks, and I open my eyes and nod, impressed she didn't ask the obvious question: *Does it hurt?* Her gaze moves from my face to the broken skin on my hand, and she chews on her lip. "Let me guess. I should see the other guy?"

I shrug. "He threw the first punch. I threw the last." I don't mention that, with the combination of Scottish whisky and my eye swelling shut, it was nothing more than luck that I even made contact. And I sure as hell don't tell her it was because of a girl.

Nope. No mention of the asshole's girlfriend who kissed me anyway or that the kiss was merely provocation for him to introduce his fist to my face.

It's been almost two years since I said good-bye to the girl I never intended to fall for, especially when she was falling for someone else. Then the text came last night.

Jordan: *How's my favorite Minnesotan who used to live in Aberdeen? We're going to see you at the reunion Thanksgiving weekend, right? Please say you're coming! Miss you!*

We. A hard word to miss. Not *I*, but *we.* It's not like I don't know that she and Noah are still together, that they're the real deal. But I wasn't. Real, that is. I don't blame her. I never promised her a commitment. In fact, I offered the opposite—fun with no complications. And that's the only way she ever saw me. It's what I do best. I'm all about the fun.

I still haven't responded, at least not to Jordan. No, I saved all my responding for a bottle of Drambuie and some chick on a mission to piss off her boyfriend.

Mission accomplished.

I remove Pippi's hand from my face.

She reaches into her massive brown purse, emerging with a cotton ball and a small travel bottle filled with clear liquid. Flipping up the spout, she pours the stuff on the cotton ball and reaches for my face again. This time I do flinch.

"What the hell?" Before I can finish protesting, the cotton ball touches my skin, the cool liquid immediately soothing the angry-looking bruise.

Pippi smiles and then grabs my hand, gently guiding it toward my face so I can relieve her from cotton-ball duty.

"Witch hazel," she says. "Soothes the skin."

"And you happen to have it with you?"

"I happen to have a lot of things with me. Nothing wrong with being prepared. For whatever might happen. It's helping, isn't it? So don't knock my preparation."

She's got a point. I nod. "Thanks." I don't know what else to say or how else to respond. No one's ever taken care of me like this, let alone someone I barely know.

"You're welcome."

I'm vaguely aware of the cars honking as they pass us and realize we should get moving before they think we're in trouble.

Again she reaches into that magic bag and retrieves...a

What if

camera? Before I have time to react, she snaps a quick photo of me, and immediately it prints from a small rectangular opening.

"I didn't know they still made those," I say, hoping she's on the verge of telling me where I'm taking her.

Her fingertips grasp the photo, waving it lightly while she watches it develop.

"Wanna see?" she asks.

Our hands extend at the same time, and my fingers brush hers as I grab the photo. My skin against hers jolts something inside me. Again, that distant voice shouting its warning. And again, here's me ignoring it.

"Two things," I say as my eyes shift to the item in my hand. *Why the fuck am I smiling in this photo?* "What's with the camera?"

When I take a hesitant breath, she grabs the picture back from me and asks, "And the second thing?"

"Right. Uh, where am I taking you?"

I steal a glance at my phone. At this point I *should* panic at the time. But I don't.

She lifts her bag. "Preparation, remember? And you're taking me to Royal Grounds. The coffee shop. Are you late for something?"

Traffic is light now that I'm out of the city, so I back into the intersection, to the right turn I initially intended to make.

"No. I'm not late." The total lack of sureness in my voice says otherwise, but for some reason I don't care. "And you've gotta be shitting me. I was on my way to Royal Grounds."

She shifts, leaning her back against the door so her whole body faces me.

"I'm almost always late, to the extent that people would

probably be disappointed if I was on time." She regards the photo in her hand. "I'm glad I'm not taking you out of your way, but just in case…" She opens the window and tosses out the evidence of her photo ambush of me. "If you try to kill me in the next two miles, that picture exists, and someone will find it—with both our fingerprints on it."

I throw my head against the back of my seat and laugh, this time ignoring the pain. "Yeah, Saturday morning in the suburbs is prime murder-your-hitchhiker-on-the-way-for-coffee time. I thought you said you trusted my eyes."

She shrugs. "You never can be too safe."

Safe. I let the word hang in the air for a few seconds before responding. "And hitchhiking is safe?"

She sighs. "I like to think of myself as a creative transportation enthusiast."

I roll my eyes. "That's not a thing."

"It's a thing if someone does it," she starts. "I'm doing it, so it's a thing."

"Is it a thing you do on a regular basis?"

Her smirk fades. "No." Her eyes roam around the car. "Please tell me this is a hybrid or some newfangled electric beast."

Nice change of subject, Pippi.

I open my mouth to speak but first pet the dashboard lovingly. "Don't worry, sweetheart. She didn't mean it. You're not a beast." I glance at my passenger who doesn't share my affection for the vehicle that saved her from the early November chill. "No. It's not a hybrid. It's a car that gets me through Minnesota winters. Why?"

She taps her index finger on her pursed lips. "What you must spend on gas, not to mention your carbon footprint—"

What if

"Uh, says the girl who just tossed a photograph, probably loaded with less-than-environmentally-friendly chemicals, out my window," I interrupt. "Plus, *I'm* giving *you* a ride, and you trash-talk my girl? *Yes*, cars do have gender, and this one is most certainly a girl. *My* girl. Why are you betraying the *beast* that's getting you where you need to go?"

I fix my stare straight ahead and blow out a long breath. I never have to defend my truck. Everyone loves the truck. Girls *love* the truck, especially how roomy it can be reclining on a summer night, stars shining through the moon roof, and yeah. No one's ever complained about gas mileage or carbon footprint. In fact, I've heard nothing but praise. Plus, I can rattle off a list of people grateful for my *beast* towing their sedans from snowy ditches.

Her eyes grow distant. "My grandfather was a mechanic. He hated SUVs. Some things you don't forget."

Her voice bears an echo of sadness, and a small part of me wants to ask about her grandfather while the rest of me says, *Dude, get her where she needs to go before you're late.* I shake my head. Maybe I'm more hung over than I think.

"I didn't get your name," I say as we pull into the coffee shop's crowded parking lot. "I'm Griffin." I extend a hand to shake, the gesture awkward and unfamiliar now that she's already had her palm on my face.

When she doesn't reciprocate, I lean back and release my seat belt.

"What are you doing?" she asks, alarm taking over her features for the first time since she stepped into the car of a stranger.

I rub the back of my neck, brows raised. "Getting coffee?" The words are meant to come out as a statement, but the tenseness in her shoulders stops me in my tracks.

She lets out a breath and smiles, the expression forced. "My treat," she says. "For giving me the lift. How do you take it?"

"Double-shot cappuccino."

"I'll be right back, Fancy Pants." And she's out of the truck before I can protest.

Fancy Pants? Fuck. I look at my pressed khakis, the ironed-in crease down the middle, the freaking neon sign of who I am no matter how much I ignore it. I'm the same asshole I was before Scotland. What did Jordan call me? *A man-whore with heart.* I've done a good job since my return to lose the last part of that phrase. But at the end of this year I'll be exactly who my parents raised me to be, Griffin Reed Jr., MBA-bound and tied to the plan they set in place for me when I was a freshman in high school.

But I'm not that guy yet.

And for some reason I give a shit that this girl knows me for two minutes and thinks she has me pegged.

I watch her through the glass door, this stranger who has challenged me since stepping up to my car, her red braids spilling over her shoulders. She strides to the counter, letting her coat fall loose as she orders. I notice the exposed ivory skin of her neck, and wonder if it sports the same freckles that fall across her nose and cheeks.

I shift in my seat, forcing my thoughts from her possibly freckled, possibly not freckled neck. Grandma Reed. My third-grade teacher. My niece quizzing me on her thorough knowledge of Harry Potter. Exhale. Good. Crisis averted. For safe measure, I close my eyes, but my mind starts to recreate her image.

What if

Tap. Tap.

I jump to find her standing outside my window. I try to open it, forgetting I turned the car off, forgetting pretty much everything except what this girl is doing to me in the space of several minutes.

My hand fumbles with the key until the car is in accessory mode, the window finally obeying.

She reads the side of the to-go cup, confirming my order.

"Double cappuccino," she says with confidence, handing the drink to me.

"Thanks," I say, transfixed by her eyes, more hazel now than green. *Fucking hell.*

"I got you this, too." She raises her other hand, a plastic bag full of ice dangling from her fist. "Alternate temperatures. After about ten minutes of this, switch to a warm compress."

She hands me the bag.

"Are you pre-med or something?" I ask.

Her head shakes in response. "I've got…friends in the medical field. They've taught me some tricks of the trade."

"Where's your drink?" I ask.

Pippi looks over her shoulder into the shop and waves before turning back to me. "Inside."

"Oh." I nod. "Do I at least get your name before I leave?"

She shakes her head and then motions at my face. "You've got stuff to deal with, Fancy Pants," she says, backing away.

"It's Griffin." I groan, defeated, the rejection both new and familiar, and I'm compelled to keep her at my window for as long as possible. "Will I see you again, Pippi?" I ask, and she smiles, her gaze knowing.

"Probably not," she teases, and something in my gut

sinks. Then she reaches into her bag and retrieves the camera, snapping my picture once again without warning. "But I'll remember you, Fancy—"

"Griffin," I interrupt her.

"Griffin," she says, but the smile fades, and I hear a tinge of regret in her voice.

"Wait," I call, her back to me now as she makes her way to the door. She doesn't turn, though, but walks into the shop, blending into the Saturday morning crowd.

I'll remember you, too.

Chapter Two

Maggie

I duck inside the coffeehouse, weaving my way to the back room. My shift started ten minutes ago, so I don't bother to punch in. Instead I toss my shit onto the table, find a Sharpie in my bag, and fill in the white space underneath the photo.

Griffin/Fancy Pants

"How ya doing, Mags? And who's your ride?" There it is, the smooth, familiar voice of comfort.

I spin and thrust the photo at him.

"Who messed up his pretty face? Wait, is he for me?" Miles asks, and I snatch the picture back. "And it's not even my birthday."

I groan. "So it's still boys this week? I can't keep up because you asked the same thing when I showed you my lab partner's picture at the beginning of the semester."

"Uh-oh." Miles grimaces. "Addison. Uh. How is she?"

I backhand him on the arm with Griffin's Polaroid. "She's been a shitty lab partner since you stopped calling her back. That's how she is."

Miles bats his thick black lashes apologetically, and I kiss him on the cheek.

"Sweetie," I say, "I love you, but stay off my home turf, okay? After all I missed last year and being forced to take a part-time schedule this year, I can't afford to fuck up, which means you have to stop fucking my lab partners."

He winces, but doesn't argue.

"That means damaged J. Crew is off-limits, huh?"

I give my throat a dramatic clearing. "What about Andrew?" I ask.

Miles sighs. "We're just having fun. Doesn't mean I can't look at pretty things."

I roll my eyes.

"Oh, by the way, your gran called. She said she tried your cell, but you didn't answer. You know better than to make that sweet woman worry." He reaches into my coat pocket and finds my name tag, then waves it in front of the time clock. "It won't lock you out until quarter after, remember?"

I groan. "Actually, Miles, no. I don't remember."

"Mags…" His voice softens.

"Don't," I say.

I pull my cell from my bag, and there it is, the missed call and voicemail notification from Gram. Shit. I never miss her scheduled check-ins.

"My phone and I haven't been getting along this morning." I smile, my attempt at levity. "I must not have heard it while I was chasing a bus down the street or trying my hand at hitchhiking. I'll call her back in a minute."

What if

Miles crosses his arms and gives me a pointed look. "Honey, I have never heard of a hitchhiking story that ends with a pretty, broken boy picking up a pretty, broken girl and one of them not eventually burying the other's body. Instead you come in here flaunting that Polaroid but telling me I can't have him."

I let the tension out of my shoulders. "He gave me a ride, Miles. That's all. I have no claim on him. Pretty sure he's straight, though."

I turn to remove my coat and hang it on the rack. As I do, Miles wraps his arms around my midsection, resting his stubble-lined jaw against my cheek.

"Sexual preference is an evasive response to this situation, honey. You wrote down his *name*."

"I didn't give him mine," I say, the damning evidence of my hesitation still in my hand.

"Say it," Miles pushes. "J. Crew is off limits."

"It's Griffin. His name is Griffin. And pretty face or not, the boy's got issues if that's what he looks like on a Saturday morning."

It doesn't change the urge I had to fix it, to make him better. Control what I can to avoid what I can't — that's always a good distraction. But Miles doesn't need to know this. *I* don't need anyone new to deal with, especially someone like him.

"He'll forget me as quickly as I'll forget him." But my free hand clenches into a fist, the sensation of his skin on the tips of my fingers too fresh to be forgotten, the wish to touch him again too strong to be ignored.

Miles straightens, releasing his grip on me before he plants a kiss on top of my head.

"You wrote down his name, sweetie. Off-limits," he says

with a sureness I'll never possess. Then he turns me to face him. "And no one, Maggie, no one forgets you."

. . .

GRIFFIN

In the normal world of space and time, showing up at the top of the hour would be fine. No questions asked. I take one last look in the mirror and shrug. No way can I hide how my night went. I throw back the rest of my cappuccino and hop out of the truck, bracing for my mother's disappointment, or better yet, my father's silent condescension.

All three of my sisters are here, probably have been for the better part of an hour. I walk up the driveway past Nat's blindingly green Golf and chuckle. She always did make a statement. I'm sure she picked up Megan and Jen to make sure they weren't late. If there was room for me, too, in her pocket-sized car, I have no doubt she would have been pounding on my apartment door two hours ago. Never mind that I live an hour out of her way.

I breathe in, steeling myself for what lies beyond the door, and I enter.

"Uncle Griggs!" My niece, Violet, launches herself at me, and I forget everything other than this, holding the most beautiful eight-year-old girl in my arms.

I kiss her nose, and she giggles. "How's my Vi?"

"Good!" She shimmies out of my arms, patting out any wrinkles threatening to form in her blue dress. She learns quickly. Once free of my grasp, she gets a good look at me. "What happened to your eye?" she asks, her hands then covering her mouth. "Grandma's gonna be mad at you."

What if

I laugh. She's right to be more concerned about my mother's reaction than how I'm actually doing.

"You should see the other guy," I say. "Still Uncle Griggs, huh?"

She shrugs. "It suits you."

It suits me? This kid needs to slow down on the whole maturity thing. Other than her size, Vi calling me Uncle Griggs is the only evidence she's still a child.

Nat stalks through the foyer, her hands laden with packages of batteries.

"One thing I asked of you, Griff. One thing, and you're freaking late." Now she's close enough to see. "What the FRAK?"

I cover Violet's ears with my hands. "Hey. Don't taint my niece's vocabulary with gateway cursing. We all know freaking and frakking lead to fucking, and then what's left?"

"I can still hear you guys," Violet informs us.

"Shit," I say.

"Damn it, Griffin!" Then Nat's hand shoots up to cover her mouth as her eyes go wide.

Violet frees herself from my hands. She looks at both her mom and me and shakes her head. "*Merde.* You two are hopeless." Then she saunters off to the great room, presumably where Natalie was headed in the first place.

"What was that?" I ask, knowing exactly what my niece just said.

"She's learning French for our trip next month."

"I get in trouble for ear-muffing her, and you're teaching her how to say *shit* in French?"

"Well…" Nat hesitates. "I Googled some French slang for her so she wasn't only learning textbook speak. I may have stepped away for a minute with the window still open. What can I say? She's a quick learner. I mean, she used it in the correct context and everything."

I grab the batteries out of Nat's hands. "I take it the photographer isn't ready yet?"

She shakes her head.

"So I'm not *really* late, only in Reed time."

"Correct." She sighs, her eyes focusing on mine. "Honey, what did you do? When is shit like this going to stop?"

I cover my ears like I did with Vi. "Shhhh. Remember there are sensitive ears nearby."

She doesn't appreciate the joke.

"Griffin…"

"Natalie…"

She crosses her arms and gives me a pointed look. Though she's only twenty-six, the youngest of my sisters, the disappointment coming from her tears at something inside me. I was almost proud to walk in here and have Mom and Dad flip out at me. Not Nat. She's the one who roots for me, which means she's always the one who gets let down.

"Everyone's in the other room?" I ask.

This time she nods.

"Let's do this, then." I lean down to kiss her on the cheek. "Hi, by the way."

"Hi." She smiles, and I'm guessing it's probably the first time this morning she has. "Now get your freaking, frakking ass in there."

She marches ahead of me, and I follow. Mom and Dad may run the show, but behind the scenes, Nat's the one in charge, the one with true maternal instinct. She may have gotten pregnant young, but like everything else, she shines at the whole mothering thing. It's in her blood. In that we're so different. I love my niece probably more than any other human, but I could never do what Nat does. And definitely not alone.

The French doors leading to the great room swing open, and Jen and Megan burst out to greet us.

"Please save us," Megan says. "If Mom raises her eyebrows one more time, I swear she's going to break through her Botox."

"What about Dad?" I ask.

Jen answers this time. "He's doing that scary-ass silent thing where he stands next to the piano observing. I think he's saving the rage for you."

"Dad doesn't rage," I say.

"I know. The silence is worse."

Jen's right. There's nothing worse than someone who turns off everything rather than letting it all spill out. But that would be too messy for Griffin Reed, Sr. And Dad doesn't do messy. In that respect, I've learned from the best, leading a life free of any real complication, mild bar brawl notwithstanding.

"No one has anything to say about how I look?" I flash Jen and Megan an exaggerated grin, waiting for them to reprimand me as well. My plan backfires as I cut the grin short, a shock of pain reminding me of my physical vulnerability.

"Honestly, Griffin." Jen says. "It's getting harder to keep up with your bullshit." She turns to Megan. "Didn't he come with a busted lip to Dad's casino night fund-raiser last month?"

Megan shakes her head excitedly. "No! That's when he got drunk and started singing "Blurred Lines" in the Bingo caller's microphone. The busted lip was for family dinner the week after."

"Oh yeah," Jen says. "That performance was actually pretty epic."

"See?" I say. "I'm adorable."

"An adorable mess," Nat adds. "We thought you'd grow up in Europe, having to rely on yourself for over a year. But you came back no different."

I laugh, shrugging off her analysis to mask the twist in my gut, then head toward my mom. How do I explain that the year off was my best year, that I wasn't this guy over there? I gaze around the room. I love my family, and sometimes I think they do bring out the best in me—at least my sisters do. But it's not enough, not when family is defined by expectations and obligations. I may be my father's son, but I'll never be the Griffin Reed that he wants me to be.

"Hey, Mom." She stands, scrutinizing the frames and holiday-decorated vases adorning the mantle. Everything is tasteful and understated, of course. "Someone need some batteries?"

She doesn't look at me yet. With a flick of her wrist, she motions to the photographer setting up in the corner to her right. "They're for him. This is what I get for taking a recommendation from a neighbor. Someone young and fresh. I hope he understands this is coming out of his fee."

I hand off the batteries.

"Good to see you, too, Mom." I kiss her on the cheek, and she lets out a breath, one that makes it seem as if she's been holding it since this day began, and it's only ten o'clock in the morning.

She softens as she faces me, but only for a second until

What if

her hands find their way to my face.

She doesn't speak, but her fallen expression says it all.

"Mom, it's only a bruise. He can Photoshop it right off my face." I look to the photographer and point to my eye. "Hey, man. You can edit this out, right?"

Photo guy looks from me to my mom, and then back at me, before nodding.

"No problem, Mr. Reed."

I roll my eyes. "It's Griffin. And thanks."

Mom's expression doesn't change, her sad eyes saying more than she would ever let on.

She kisses my forehead. "You're here. Late…but here."

That's my mom, stating the facts. I close my eyes, trying to internally reboot.

"I'm right on time, Mom." I open my eyes and take in the activity going on in all corners of the room—Nat talking to the photographer, Jen and Megan finishing their coffee at the game table, Vi reading a *Harry Potter* book on the window seat, and Dad overseeing it all from his silent post. *This* is the photograph that would say it all, that would give the public a clear view into the life of a would-be member of political office. *This* is the *Happy Holidays* portrait people would believe, each member of the Reed family scattered around the room, maximum distance separating those confined to the same space.

But that's not the picture that will show up in all the local papers in a couple weeks. We'll all stand, pose, and smile like we always do, the dutiful children and their hard-working father. The headline will read something like, "Griffin Reed, Sr.—Business Man, Family Man…Mayor?" Below the headline will be the portrait of staged perfection.

I think of the Polaroid, the goddamn candid shot that caught me looking at a strange girl with a kind of need I don't acknowledge, a need to know more. Not much I can do without a name, but my mind wanders to thoughts of her anyway. It doesn't stop me from wondering if I went to Royal Grounds tomorrow, would she be there with friends again? Is she a student at the U? Because I'd totally be able to find a girl whose name I don't know on a campus of over thirty-thousand students. Fuck. My phone is filled with names, names that come with numbers. I'll call one tonight, give myself a reset, and forget this stranger.

"Time to line up, everyone."

For the first time since I got here, Dad takes notice of the photographer, of me, even. Only once we're all in place does he move toward the group, the last piece of the perfect-family puzzle.

"Griffin."

That's my greeting, an acknowledgment of my presence.

"Dad." We're one for one.

"Stay for dinner tonight," he says, the invitation unexpected. Despite my light class-load for senior year, I always lay on the homework excuse, but his tone tells me this subject is not up for discussion.

"Sure," I answer.

"Good. It's time we discuss the decisions you're going to make when the graduate school acceptances start coming in."

I hold back a laugh, remembering a similar *discussion* that went something like this: *Your mother and I would like you to take the January GMAT.* I should have seen it coming. Tonight's dinner is to remind me what my next step is on my obvious career path. I'm the one with his name, which

What if

means I'm the one with his plan.

"*Discuss* is a subjective word when it comes to us, isn't it?" I ask him, then wonder where the fuck that bit of bravado came from. I didn't come here today with the intent of arguing. The plan for today was to defend how I spend my free time, despite the evidence on my face, not rock the grad-school boat.

He leans closer so he can speak quietly, but we're all too close for no one else to hear.

"We can also discuss how your mother and I let you fuck around Europe for over a year without spending a penny of your own and how I called in a very high-profile favor to keep your spot at the university so you wouldn't have to withdraw. How about we discuss that condo you live in and the truck you drive?" His tone is mockingly pleasant. "We have lots to *discuss* tonight, son."

My jaw clenches as I swallow back my defense. Because he's right. I have no argument. I just have to do what's next, follow the path someone else set for me. That's who I am.

"Sure, Dad. I'd love to stay for dinner."

"Smiles, everyone!" The photographer has the floor.

The giant flash momentarily blinds me, but I know we all got it on one take. We always do.

Dinner. I just have to make it through dinner. Then a drink, or two, or seven. It's looking like a Scottish whisky kind of night—minus greeting anyone else's fist with my face. I make a mental note to check my phone for someone willing to join me. Whisky goes great with a late-night phone call.

Chapter Three

Maggie

I tamp the grounds down into the filter and brew, a perfect crema forming atop the espresso shot. The steamed milk is ready to go, and George, a Saturday night regular, waits and watches.

"What'll it be tonight?" I ask him, hoping he'll order something simple. Almost at the end of my double shift, my design skills wane as does my energy.

I glance at my row of sticky notes along the back side of the counter and find the one with George's name, just to get confirmation. I sigh, a satisfied smile taking the place of my worry. Ninety percent of the time, George orders a latte. The notes don't lie.

"Jeanie would love one of those tulips." I lift my gaze from George to find Jeanie at their usual table by the window. She winks at me, and I wave. In the time I've worked

What if

here, they've been steady customers, stopping by on Saturday nights after babysitting for their grandchildren. I like the regulars. They're patient with me as I learn their orders—and write them down so I can remember next time. Plus George and Jeanie are great tippers.

"A tulip for the lady. Absolutely," I say.

I tilt the mug forward as I pour the milk, watching it sink under the coffee. The volume increases as I lower the pitcher to rest on the rim of the mug. A white circle begins to form on top of the crema, and I lift the pitcher, stopping the flow. With the mug still tilted, the milk stream falls north. I repeat the process two more times, each movement forcing the circle narrower, longer, until the three pours morph into a budding tulip.

"Not bad for the end of a double shift, huh?"

George slides a ten dollar bill across the counter, more than twice what he owes for the drink, but he never asks for change.

He leans closer to me, lowering his voice to a near whisper. "Don't tell her I told you, but Jeanie keeps asking when you're going to stop working Saturday nights and go out with the other kids your age. Serving coffee to old farts like me and her or the off-campus drunks is no way to spend *every* Saturday night."

"Routine works for me," I say. "Plus, I get to draw for you and Jeanie. Drawing works for me too."

I smile and look over my shoulder at Miles, who stacks the freshly washed cappuccino mugs on the counter. George follows my glance, first to Miles and then to the framed sketches that line the wall above the coffee supplies. My sketches.

"We do love your drawings, Maggie."

George's voice is soft and sincere, but the sigh that follows mirrors my own thoughts. I swallow back the lump in my throat as I stare at my work, moments captured inside a coffee shop: a group of college girls in animated conversation at a sunlit corner table; a young couple with a toddler — locals most likely — looking tired and disheveled but at the same time happy. Then there's the guy and girl, a first date maybe, sharing a tentative kiss.

All my drawings are fictional, idealized versions of people I see here, images burned in memory where names may escape me — images of a life I might have had if things had gone differently. The art is my therapy, a place to live in moments that aren't mine though I wish they could be.

Miles turns around, his gaze meeting mine. I don't give him a chance to ask that all-too-familiar question. *How ya doing, Mags?* Instead I direct my attention back to George.

"Aren't you worried about him going out with kids *his* age?"

George waves me off. "Miles is a grad student. He's had his fun."

I shrug. "I like it here. I like spending my Saturday nights with you. Kids my age are overrated." I laugh at his choice of vocabulary. I'd go back to the *kid* version of Maggie in a heartbeat. Even the late teen years — I'd do those again. Teen me was so straight-laced, so careful. I did everything right. What did I learn? Careful doesn't mean shit. Careful didn't keep me from weeks of intensive care or months of learning to function like a human being again. I'd give anything to go back and tell that naive version of me that a night of reckless abandon — reckless within reason, because I am who I am—would do me some good. I chose careful then. Now? Careful chooses me, though I still manage to mess up. This morning's bus incident proved that. These days the only way things get out of hand for me on a Saturday night is if the foaming wand gets clogged. Riveting.

Miles grabs a hand, pulling me into an unexpected twirl that ends with a dramatic dip.

"Besides," he says, his words for George but his eyes bore into mine, "who would I dance with if Maggie wasn't here?" He straightens me up, kissing me on the cheek as he does.

"I don't feel like a kid anymore," I say quietly in Miles's ear.

"'Course you're a kid, sweetheart. Don't grow up on me so fast."

I hear the reassurance he tries to infuse into his words, but I'm unconvinced. My eyes leave his, trailing back across my secret stash taped to the counter. In addition to the sticky notes are photographs of some of my regular customers, many that Miles took when I was too embarrassed to ask. Each photo is captioned with the customer's name. Now, at least with the regulars, I'm more consistent with names *and* drinks.

"Mags…"

"It's just, before…this isn't where I would have spent *every* Saturday night. I used to do *some* stuff, Miles. Freshman year I finally started to let go with stupid things like drinking too much and staying out too late…even forgetting to study." He fakes a gasp. "I know that's hardly wild and crazy by anyone's standards, but it's stuff I took for granted that I can't do anymore." I huff out a breath. "It's fine. I'm fine."

Miles knows I'm full of shit, so he twirls me again.

"You're *you*." He presses his cheek to mine, chuckles in my ear. "Kid." Then he kisses that same cheek. "Plus," he says, "we're gonna do the thing tonight, right? One night of wild and crazy?"

I shrug. "Within means. My own brand of careful crazy."

"Careful crazy. Just the way I like it," he says.

The door opens in time with our movement, and I groan at the thought of new customers. It's after eleven, less than an hour before we close.

George slides the mug off the counter and heads back to Jeanie, and I watch with annoyance as the group of five, all guys, head toward the counter. Before anyone notices, I paint on my smile and greet the first one with, "What can I get for you tonight?"

Miles hip-checks me, knocking me away from the register and in the direction of the espresso machines. "You're pulling," he says. "You're faster than me."

"That's what she said," I tease under my breath.

He retaliates. "Or maybe he."

Miles begins to rattle off the orders, most of them regular coffees, which doesn't give me much to do. With my back to the counter, I pour the simple beverages. Then I hear the last order.

"Got anything stronger than espresso to put in those drinks?"

Miles laughs. "Sorry, man. Not while I'm on the clock, but if you want to wait around..."

He hesitates, and so do I. I put down the mug I'm filling, my hand finding its way into my apron pocket. My thumb rubs over the edges of today's photos.

What if

Fancy Pants. F, G…G…Griffin. His name is Griffin. Griffin who drinks a double cappuccino.

I slide the pictures out, thumbing through them quickly to confirm my guess, and I'm…right?

"On second thought," Miles starts as I turn toward the customer, "off-limits."

"I don't…" Griffin says, and then his eyes find mine.

"Fancy Pants," I say, my voice a little short of breath. I bite back my grin when I notice his worn jeans and hoodie peeking out from under his jacket. He watches me size him up, his eyebrows rising as I do.

"Not so fancy, Pippi. Am I?"

Miles, an I-told-you-so look in his glinting eyes, interrupts.

"Pippi? Oh, honey. So off-limits."

I suck in a breath, even though I know Griffin has no idea what Miles means.

"Black eye or not, the boy has got some serious swoon-making going on." Miles winks. Griffin laughs, and I wait for a hole to open up in the floor and swallow me. "I'm gonna let you finish out this order." He scoots past me to grab the regular coffees, passing them, one by one, to the other guys. Griffin and I watch as they make a beeline for a table, leaving him alone at the counter.

"Heading to the storage room to grab some more napkins," Miles says, his eyes darting from mine to Griffin's. "And while I kind of love the naughty innocence of the nickname"—he flicks one of my braids—"she also answers to Maggie."

This is the last thing he says before disappearing.

I pivot to face Griffin, my cheeks warm with—embarrassment? Anticipation? Whatever stirs inside me, I let it settle to the bottom.

Griffin chuckles before speaking. "Maggie." He says it with realization, as if he should have known the whole time. "Maggie," he says again, and my hands start to fidget.

"Yes," I say, ready to rush into some sort of action that will give my hands something to do, like pull a shot or steam some milk. Because when my eyes leave his, they go to his mess of sandy waves, and I want to brush them off his forehead so he can see better. So I can see *him* better, despite the livid bruise staring back at me.

No. No, no, no, no, no. I shake my head, willing away the thought that will be gone by morning.

"I take it you weren't in the mood for coffee tonight?"

His brows knit together.

"Asking for something stronger than espresso?" I remind him.

His hands find the front pockets of his jeans.

"Right. Yeah, no. I, uh… It's been a long day. I was hoping for a drink, but no one wanted to head back to campus with me. So, here we are."

This time I'm confused. "None of your friends are in school with you?"

He sighs. "I took some time off to travel. I'm a year behind. Means all my buddies are back here now, working. Apparently drinking coffee instead of something stronger."

"Griffin! Dude!" One of his friends stands up from their table across the shop. "What's taking you so long? She can't go home with you unless you stay until she closes the place."

Griffin's eyes close, and he mutters a "Fuck" under his breath. Then he lifts his hand, flipping his friend off without turning around to answer him.

What if

"Double cappuccino, right?" I ask, moving toward the espresso machine.

"What? Oh, yeah. Sorry about Davis. He's a dick."

I ready the shot and contemplate my words. "That's what you do?" I try my best to make sure there's no accusation in my question, but I ask it anyway. "I mean, if you'd made it to a bar tonight, that's what your plan would be. Looking for someone to take home?"

His eyes widen but only for a second before he relaxes into a smile. He rakes a hand through his hair, and I focus on the shot, on locking it in place before brewing. Because his answer doesn't matter. It shouldn't matter. I don't know him, other than he's the kind of guy who wakes up with a shiner and picks up hitchhikers, and he sure as hell doesn't know me.

"Yeah." He laughs. "I guess that's what I'd be doing."

I'm so prepared for him to explain his way out of the question, but he doesn't even try. He simply admits it.

"But I'm not at a bar," he continues. "And plans change. Davis is still a dick, though." He pauses, yet I can tell he wants to say something more, so I wait. "And if I knew I'd be seeing you again, I'd have gotten here sooner."

I laugh, loud, and my hand jerks the small pitcher of milk I'm trying to steam, spraying a good volume of it onto my apron.

"Shit," I say, giggling even more at what a complete mess I am in front of this guy, this stranger who wears pressed khakis and drinks cappuccino. A double shift, waves freeing themselves from my braids, milk sprayed across my apron, and the frayed hem of my skirt hanging over my tired-looking, sensible clogs—that's the mess he can see. What's going on underneath—inside—I can't clean up.

He peeks over the espresso machine. "You okay?"

His bruise will heal quickly, but me? I'm a continual work in progress.

I set the pitcher down and turn off the steamer, patting my apron dry.

"Perfect," I say. Then I pour the two shots I just pulled into the drain.

"Why'd you do that?"

"Because." I dump the brewed grounds and start the process over again. "They've been sitting too long already. By the time I do the milk, they'll be way past their prime." I look up at him. "Sorry. You don't need to wait while I make the new drink. I can ring you up and bring it over when it's done."

He glances behind him at the nearly empty shop, grabs a stool, and drags it to the counter. "I'd rather wait," he says, easing onto the stool and extending his long legs in front of him. "And I don't want a cappuccino. Make me your favorite drink. But make two." He nods his head toward the table of friends behind him. "Those assholes are fine without me. I'm drinking with you tonight."

That's when I see the frayed ends of his jeans resting atop a worn pair of black Converse.

Nope. Not so fancy at all.

"Pour one more," Griffin says, and I sigh.

"We're closing. There's no one here to even drink it."

Griffin's behind the counter with me now, and I'm not even sure how this happened. His friends left ten minutes ago, and he didn't feign an excuse for staying.

I'm gonna hang with Pippi for as long as she'll let me.

When I tried to protest, Miles somehow put him to work straightening the counter.

"What's all this, Pippi?" he asks, eyeing the sticky notes and photographs that line the back of the counter. *My* sticky notes and photos. I collect them quicker than he can read, stashing them in my apron pocket.

"Trainee," I lie. "But she shouldn't need these anymore."

He shrugs, hopefully thinking nothing of it, while I work to steady my breathing as he infiltrates my safety zone. Leaning in closer with a lazy grin, he asks me to make one more latte so he can see how I draw with the milk.

"Last one?" I say, half questioning, half telling.

"Last one."

"You want to try it with me?" I ask, and he perks up, brushing his hands on his jeans, though there's nothing to brush off them.

He nods, and I ready the espresso and start the milk steaming. When the shot is pulled, I pour it into the cup and explain.

"The light brown stuff is called the crema, and if you don't have that, then you don't have your canvas." I raise my brows, waiting for him to tease me, but he doesn't. "Then you have to make sure the milk is ready." I point to the thermometer that's nearing one-hundred-forty degrees. "You have to lift the steam wand out so it's close to the top of the liquid."

I have him grip the pitcher, keeping my hand wrapped around his so we froth the milk together. His skin is warm under my own, and I attribute it to the temperature of the pitcher. That's all it is.

"Good," I say. We lower the pitcher together, slowly as the foam takes form. "We're ready to pour."

I let go of his hand long enough to turn off the steamer, then ask him to grab the cup.

"Tilt it away from you like this." I show him first before he takes it. "Then we add the milk."

I pick up the pitcher to hand to him, but instead he mirrors my earlier action, placing his hand over mine, the size of it dwarfing my own, the rough texture of his skin sending a shiver through my fingers, all the way up to my neck.

His touch is light, leaving me freedom to move as we pour the shape into the waiting espresso. It's a little messy, but still recognizable.

"It's a leaf!" Griffin's deep voice startles me in its child-like excitement. "We fucking made a leaf!" We set the cup down gingerly, and he stares at it, a goofy smile spread across his face. An adorable, goofy smile I can't look away from. Every minute I spend with him reminds me that he's the kind of guy a girl remembers, that I might not be able to forget despite the tricks my brain plays on me. But he's also the kind of guy that easily forgets because, God, look at him. He's punch-you-in-the-gut beautiful even with a shiner, and if he wasn't here by default, he'd be on his way home with someone else. But stupid as I am, I can't look away.

Miles joins us behind the counter after straightening the last of the tables.

"Nice job, darlin'," he says, his lips finding my cheek again. "You still need a ride home?" He winks, an exaggerated effort, and I know he's referring to the fact that we aren't heading straight home, that I have my crazy-within-means plan for tonight. Even if Miles is just humoring me, my heart swells knowing he's willing to do this, to give me a night where I actually want to forget—forget how careful I have to be.

A *whoosh*ing sound diverts our attention to the door. I'm ready to tell the tall blond in a black leather jacket we're closed until his eyes meet Miles, and they both grin in a wordless *hello*. Miles skirts around the counter to meet him, each guy's lips greeting the other's in a different sort of silent salutation.

Griffin's interest in our artistic creation vanishes as his head volleys from Miles and Andrew back to me.

"I can drive her home. *You* home. I mean, Maggie, can I drive you home?" He grins. "Looks like Miles has plans anyway."

Sure Miles has plans, *our* plans. But when I look at my friend standing side-by-side with the guy he's *just having fun with,* I wonder how much more fun he'd have without my planned antics.

Then Miles nods, an encouraging smile giving me silent permission to cut him loose for the rest of the evening. The decision is mine, and it all comes down to how crazy I really want this night to be.

I purse my lips in contemplation, thinking of George calling me a kid. I want to be a kid again, someone who doesn't have to think or plan. Okay, so maybe tonight was a planned night of crazy—within means. But Griffin was never part of that plan. Nothing about him is *within means.*

Griffin breaks the silence. "I meant what I said before, about Davis being a dick and plans changing and all that. I didn't come here with the intent… I didn't know you worked…"

But I cut him off, fisting his hoodie in each of my hands as I pull him to me. He doesn't falter, not one bit. Instead he falls into the kiss with such ease I almost don't believe that I'm the one who initiated. His lips are soft and strong, his late-night stubble scratching my chin, but all it does is make me want this more. *This*. What is *this*? It's me, parting my lips and him doing the same. It's the warmth of his breath on my skin, the taste of him on my tongue. His hands cup my cheeks, and a sigh escapes my lips, filling the space between us when we separate only out of the necessity to breathe. *This*. Something I haven't done in months. Something a little reckless, even. But mostly, something I've missed. A connection—albeit physical—but I feel it in the pit of my stomach and the tips of my toes. Dizzy... He makes me dizzy, and I'm a girl who needs solid ground.

As quickly as the kiss began, I push him away but smile as his expression starts to fall. I think about tending to his eye in the car today, the touch of his skin under mine, proving he's exactly what I need to help me forget—forget who I am now and be who I could have been, the girl he might have met if circumstances were different. He needs this, too. I see it in his gaze, a mirror of the soft expression when he let me take care of him earlier. We can be alternate versions of ourselves tonight, taking care of each other.

"You're trouble, aren't you?" I ask, my thumb grazing his bruised skin.

"Probably," he says, the glint in his eyes melting all the brain cells that know this is a bad idea. "But I get the feeling you might be, too."

He's right. Trouble seeking itself out, that's what we are.

"Then you can give me a ride," I say, "on one condition."

"What's that?" His brown eyes gleam.

"We don't actually go home. I'd like to cause a little

trouble, together, first."

He grins wide, and it's as beautiful as it is terrifying. It's the kind of grin a girl falls for, but something tells me he doesn't easily fall back. He is all beauty, and risk, and everything I need for a few hours of being the old Maggie, the version of her I should have been. I was so worried about control when I could have been freer. Losing control now means hitchhiking to work or forgetting someone's name. But for a night—for a few reckless hours, I want to be lost.

"You did say I'm *not* taking you home, right? Is there another kind of trouble I should know about?"

No. You're not taking me home, not to my place. There I can't hide. There I can't pretend to be the girl I am tonight.

"Trouble comes in all shapes and sizes," I say. "I was thinking more of an adventure." My smile is coy, and I hope it's enough to convince him.

"You got yourself a deal, Pippi." Griffin leans in for another kiss, one hand firm on the small of my back, the other cradling my neck. I let him take control, surrender to it, and for this short moment, I don't worry about what comes next. Instinct tells my mouth to open and let him inside. My palms splay against his chest in need, and I taste the coffee as I let his tongue tease its way past mine. I know we have an audience and at the same time don't care one freaking bit, not if it means putting space between my hand and the thundering beat of his chest; not if it means I can't savor him, sweet like candy on my lips. We're Pippi and Fancy Pants, miles away from the crap that makes us Maggie and Griffin. And damn if it isn't just a bit delicious.

"Shit," Miles says through soft laughter, his fingers threading with Andrew's. "Like I said. Off. Limits."

Chapter Four

GRIFFIN

"Just drive." That's all she says after we get in the truck, nothing about why she kissed me—or why she let me kiss her back. And for the fucking life of me, I don't know why I care.

I lick my bottom lip, still tasting her on it. *Oh, genius. That's why you give a shit.* This isn't like last night. No selfish agenda. But the whole time I sat with her while she worked, I didn't expect the night to move beyond the café, nor did I expect the undeniable relief when I realized it would.

My phone *buzzes* with a text, and I glance down just to check the name. I let out a sigh.

"Someone special?" Maggie asks.

"No." The word comes out too quickly, but I'm not fast enough to keep her from seeing.

"How would *Stacy from Poli-Sci* feel about you saying

that?" She gives me a pointed look.

My jaw clenches. "We were partners for a project early in the semester." And maybe some late-night work sessions turned into overnighters, but I don't tell Maggie this. For some reason I want this stranger to see me as something other than I am. As much as I don't want it to, and even more can't explain it, the opinion of a girl I've known for mere hours matters. And I'm pretty sure a midnight text says all she needs to know. "Can we turn off the judgment now? *You* invited *me* on this little adventure, right?"

"Yes. Shit. I'm sorry. You're right. Turn here," she says, the strain in her voice unmistakable as the words sputter from her lips.

Things would have been different if the guys weren't assholes and came back to campus with me. I'd have done exactly what they said I'd do, what I always do. That text would have been enough. But now it's not. I don't want this girl to write her number on my hand so I can wash it off when I get home, forget her name by morning. Because she's not the type of girl I'd forget, which also means she's not the type of girl for me. But she kissed me. And I kissed her back. Now here we are.

As soon as I make the turn, I know where we're going. "A movie?" I ask, the tension easing as I realize we might still salvage a night that hasn't yet started. "But it's, like, midnight. Everything has already started." I offer a tentative smile and wait.

She nods, biting her bottom lip as she responds with a grin, and it takes everything in me to keep my hands on the wheel, to *not* pull her toward me or think about climbing in the back of the truck and tasting her again.

"We're sneaking in." Maggie pauses for a second, her smile fading. "I am sorry, Griffin. I had no right to judge."

I nod toward the theater. "Lead the way, Pippi."

She beams and then throws open the door, barely waiting for the car to be in park before she hops out.

I laugh, trying not to be disappointed that she wasn't looking for a place to simply park. When I join her, she faces me, camera in hand. The corners of my mouth twitch into a grin, helpless against her inexplicable whimsy.

"Smile!" she yells, my only warning before the *click* of the instant camera. "You, while you're still on the right side of the law," Maggie says, waving the developing photo in the air. "You are on the right side of the law, Fancy Pants, aren't ya?"

I smile to let her know I am. But that tiny mention of the law brings me right back to where I was this evening, when dinner with my parents left me needing something stronger than coffee. I know enough about rules and expectations. And obligation. Would finding myself on the *wrong* side of the law be enough to release me from mine? It's a theory I haven't tested yet, one that might be too far even for me.

"What's wrong?" she asks. "You too good *not* to pay?"

This makes me laugh, her teasing obliterating thoughts of anything that came before the café. From the second she raised a caring hand to my face this morning, I knew she was different—unlike any girl I've met before. She may have an agenda, but it's more than physical, or we wouldn't be here right now, sharing this experience. I'm all for having a good time, but if she thinks she sees more than that in me, she's setting herself up for disappointment.

"I'm just second-guessing what I'm getting myself into

here. You might be more trouble than I am."

She walks around the front of the truck to meet me, brandishing the now-developed photo.

"*This* guy *is* trouble," she insists, looking at the photo before grabbing my hand. "But I do consider myself a worthy adversary."

I let her lead me toward the theater's entrance, but before we make it to the front door, she skirts around the side of the building to a place where a metal door with no outside handle greets us.

She lets go of my hand, but instinct makes me squeeze hers tighter, and I tug her close, looking down at her lips, her teeth grazing the bottom one again. I dip my head toward hers, but she leans back, only slightly, though enough to halt my movement.

"Okay, we need ground rules," she says, her voice shaky and a little breathless. Momentary thoughts of rejection are replaced by intrigue. She may have pulled away, but we're both still here, her voice admitting her nervousness.

"Ground rules?"

"Yes. The first one is a definition. Of tonight." She pauses as her eyes search mine. She must trust that I'm following her because she continues. "The definition of tonight is *not a date.* It's nothing personal. I'm just not the dating type."

Again she tries to back away, her expression composed, but when I hold my ground—and her hand—something in her eyes softens, and her fingers curl around mine again.

"Funny," I say, hoping my smile will coax one from her. "I'm not the dating type, either."

"Yeah, I kind of got that from your buddy."

And from an incoming text. I wonder how much of her

declaration is truth, how much of a reaction to a name on my phone. Either way, it's self-preservation, and if anyone can appreciate that, it's me.

I shrug. "You knew what you were getting into with me. How about you give me all the ground rules and let me know what I got into with *you*. So far *doesn't date* and *steals movies* are all I have."

I pull her hand around my waist, letting go only when I feel her thumb hook into a belt loop. My hands cup her cheeks, and she closes her eyes. A street lamp casts enough light to illuminate her face. And I stare, her freckle-dotted lids and auburn lashes hypnotizing me for a few seconds. Then I remember my question. I lower my head toward hers and kiss each eyelid. "Is this within the boundary of the rules?"

She nods, a slow smile spreading across her face.

"What about this?" I kiss the tip of her nose, and she giggles. Fucking giggles, the sound of it doing shit it shouldn't inside of me.

Another nod.

Not sure I have enough in me to ask permission again, the only word that makes it out is a questioning "This?" before my lips find hers again.

She falls into me…right as the handle-less door swings open. Maggie jumps back at the sound while the heavy edge nails me in the shoulder.

"Fuck!" I yell, my hand flying to the point of impact.

"*Shhhhh!*" I look up to find both Maggie and the door-wielder, a girl with long, black pigtails and matching black-framed glasses, in shushing unison.

"You're fucking kidding me, right?" But my question comes out as a strained whisper, a clear sign that I'm on board

What if

with the whole *shhhhh* business.

"Thanks…" Maggie hesitates, like she's about to say the girl's name, but she just stops mid-introduction. A strange silence hangs in the air until pigtails fills it.

"I'm Amber," she whispers. "Royal Grounds regular. And I'm pretty sure you aren't Miles."

Maggie laughs, finding her voice again. "Amber, yes. Amber." She lets out a breath. "This is Griffin. He's a first-timer."

Amber winks at Maggie and shifts her eyes to meet mine. "Sorry 'bout the door, dude. Rookie mistake. Maggie should have known better than to let you stand so close. Something must have distracted her." She grins and winks at Maggie again, and in the pale streetlight I see Maggie's cheeks turn pink. Totally worth the bruised shoulder.

Maggie squeezes my hand and leads me into a dimly lit hallway, Amber disappearing without another word as soon as she guides the door closed behind us.

"Emergency exit," I say. "Nice. How did she know you were coming, though? Were you supposed to be here with Miles?"

She purses her lips, hesitating before she nods.

"But you cut him and his boyfriend loose for me?"

"Excuse me, but you were pretty insistent on giving me a ride home. Were you not?"

I watch her pale flesh turn pink again, enjoying the sight.

"Touché, Pippi. I guess we're both busted."

We make our way into the main hallway lined with movies already in progress.

"So she's kind of on-call for you?" I tease.

"Something like that."

"Top secret information?"

"I could tell you…" she starts.

"Yeah, yeah. But you'd have to kill me. I got it. We all have our secrets." I'm only partially joking when I say this, and the brief faltering of her expression confirms I'm not alone. I don't know this girl, and she doesn't know me. That doesn't change the ease of clasping her hand, of teasing her, of wanting to kiss her again. Whatever this night is feels different from any other night with any other girl, and it should paralyze me, make me run as far from this place as possible. Instead I move forward, her hand in mine. And when I read the marquee above the theater door, a stupid grin takes over any expression of doubt.

"You've got to fucking be kidding me. *Gladiator*? They're showing *Gladiator*?"

She mouths a *shhhhh* as she yanks open the door, but she's grinning as big as I am, pleased with her choice of films—pleased, I hope, that I feel the same.

I behave myself for what's left of the film, a full hour, but once the credits roll, I'm right back where we were before getting nailed in the shoulder by the emergency-exit door.

"About those ground rules…" I say as she turns to face me, and without another word, my hands cup her cheeks, and she grabs my hoodie without hesitation. And shit, she still tastes so good, so much that I crave her even when my lips are on hers, when her tongue tangles with mine. She's right here, yet I can't get enough, and it's this realization that has me pulling away, panting, a smile forced to disguise the fear.

"What's next, Pippi? Still too early to take you home?"

Her expression mirrors mine, a smile that doesn't quite reach her eyes.

"Not until daylight...if you're up for it...in which case we have a few more hours."

She doesn't hide the hesitation in her voice, and I pause before I answer, knowing the best thing for both of us would be to end the evening right now. Because I'm buzzed on her presence already. If I stay with her till dawn, I'll be downright drunk, which means any decisions I make at that point will be far from what's best for either of us.

But it's too late. I've had a taste, am already impaired. Even on a good day, I don't necessarily do what's right, but I do what I want. And I want her.

"I'm up for it."

This time her smile is real, all the way to those gorgeous hazel eyes that keep their secrets, but I don't give a shit. We're all hiding something. Tonight I want to be the one who makes those eyes smile.

Tomorrow I'll force myself to forget her like I do all the others. It's what I'm good at. But for the next few hours, I'm a fucking goner.

Chapter Five

I can't stop kissing him. Admitting the problem is half the battle, right? Then I can take the steps needed to cure myself. I scoff out a laugh under my breath.

Right. Because healing happens so quickly.

"What's so funny?" Griffin asks, catching up to me.

I guess I have to work on my timing. His wide-eyed expression made me think he'd sit there in the driver's seat, stunned or too nervous to join me as I hopped out my door, wandered around the block, and into the alley. But here he is, next to me. It's been his M.O. all night—being there. It's what I asked him to do, and him saying yes, that made me kiss him, that taught me I don't want to stop kissing him, even though I should. I have a hard enough time keeping drink orders straight. Someone like Griffin is a disruption to my routine, and routine gets me through the day.

What if

I didn't come here with the intent…

I couldn't let him finish, couldn't let him say something about me being different than whoever's phone number was on his hand this morning. It doesn't matter that I see him trying to figure me out when he looks at me. It doesn't matter that one kiss has turned into…I'm starting to lose count. Because I don't want to be different, not tonight. I throw my rules and routine out the window. For the next few hours, I welcome the disruption.

"You," I finally answer, still walking until I find the right spot. "Why aren't you scared?"

"Of what? Haven't we already determined I'm trouble?"

I stop, and he follows my lead. When I turn to him, I'm pulled back into his orbit by that contagious smile.

Admit the problem. Admit the problem!

But my body betrays my brain as I bring a hand to his face, rubbing my thumb over his bruised flesh.

"Can I ask why this happened?"

He leans his cheek into my palm and sighs, the smile falling as he does.

"You won't like me very much if I tell you, but I will if you want me to." He makes a sound, something like laughter, but he closes his eyes and lets out a long breath. When he opens them again, he holds me in his stare. "You know, I spent the entire day with my family, and you're the only one who's asked."

I swallow the knot in my throat, the hurt I feel for this stranger in front of me mirroring the same hurt I hear in his voice.

He shakes his head, freeing himself from my hand.

"On second thought, forget it. That's not what this night

is about, right?" The smile is back, but the bite in his tone gives him away. "I mean, unless you want to share a deep, dark secret of your own, Pippi? We could go all slumber party and shit and, I don't know, talk about our feelings."

I narrow my eyes at him. "My name is Maggie. And do you always go from zero to asshole in less than sixty seconds?" I don't wait for an answer and instead spin on my heel, stalking farther into the alley. I stop where the glow of the streetlight provides illumination to see what I'm doing but is dim enough to keep us hidden. I drop my bag to the ground and take out supplies, all the while hating myself for being such a hypocrite, for getting angry at him for doing exactly what I set out to do when we left Royal Grounds.

When I walked out the door, I left the Maggie he met this morning back inside the shop. She'll be there waiting in the morning. Didn't I give Griffin the invitation to do the same?

"I'm sorry," we both say. He squats next to me, and our words intertwine in a chorus of regret.

"Maggie…" My name on his lips threatens to knock me over, and I sit down all the way before he can tell he's thrown off my balance. He sits, too, facing me, his legs crossed like a pretzel, as if we're about to play pat-a-cake in preschool.

"Griffin…" His name is new, my voice hoarse as I speak it. Have I called him nothing but Fancy Pants all night?

He scoots forward so our knees touch, and the chill that runs through me has nothing to do with the frigid Minnesota November. And when his head dips down, his forehead resting on mine, I triple-dog-dare the temperature to drop further, to plummet, and freeze us right here so this moment never ends.

What if

I watch the rise and fall of his chest as he breathes, not moving—not speaking—so as not to rock the boat that is our tiny pocket of now.

"Another ground rule," he says, and I sigh. Because here it comes. He's going to stop this train before it crashes, as well he should. I only wish I knew that last kiss was the *last* kiss.

When I don't say anything, he continues, backing away so his eyes meet mine. I force myself to keep them open, to hold his stare. We've already had a fantastic few hours. If we call it a night, I'm still grateful for that.

"No back story," he continues. "We aren't the dating types. So we don't need to go through all the bullshit that happens on a date. Because this isn't one, right?"

"Right." Never mind that it feels like one, and far more than a first date at that. Stupid kissing.

"So tonight we have no past. No future. Only a present. Does that work for you?"

How do I willingly forget when I've spent the last two years fighting to hang on to the shards of what I can't remember? But Griffin's brown eyes shine with possibility. Regardless of anything I might regret tomorrow, I can't help wanting to prolong this night.

"Works for me." I mask the hesitation in my voice by extending a hand, ready to shake on the deal. Griffin grabs it but lowers it gently, the contract unsigned.

"I don't shake on deals, Pip…Maggie."

"How do you seal a deal, then?"

My words challenge him, and his raised brows and mischievous smirk say, *Challenge accepted.*

"I think you know the answer to that."

And he scoops me up, dropping me into his lap. I yelp with laughter and shush myself just as quickly.

"What are you doing?" I whisper-yell. "We're going to get caught before I do what needs to be done!"

But it doesn't matter. My arms drape around his neck, the warm air of our breath the only thing hanging between us.

"Then I better shut you up and seal the deal."

We close the space of our breaths, and I taste him again. But instead of getting lost in the feel of the kiss, this time it's in the intimacy of his arms, of letting someone hold me, something I haven't felt in so long. I sink into his chest, the warmth of his body mingling with the growing heat of mine. We stay that way until the sound of a car driving by jolts me back to reality. I need to do what I came here to do and then get as far from here as possible.

• • •

GRIFFIN

I'm not even surprised when I see her take a can of spray paint out of her bag. She had witch hazel for my face. Why wouldn't she be more than prepared for a little early-morning graffiti? What does surprise me, though, is what she does with merely a can of paint.

Yes. The latte foam shit was impressive, but I never would have guessed she could do this. I want to ask her how or how long or *why*? But all I can do is watch as she, according to the law, defaces public property. I don't see it like that, though. What I see is beauty. Grace. A fucking ballet of words and emotion spilling from her hand.

What if

It's only words. Two. *What if?* But the depth, shadow, illusion of color change when she only uses the one can of blue paint—it's stunning. *She's* stunning. And when she turns to face me, cheeks red with the cold and eyes shining with the threat of tears, she smiles.

My first instinct is to run, to get the hell out of Dodge and do anything but remember the stagger in my pulse at the sight of this girl. And if I could run, if it didn't mean abandoning her in an alley before dawn, I'd be gone already because this isn't what I signed on for, this...this...*need.*

"Are you...okay?" She clears her throat after croaking out the words, somehow swallowing whatever it is that powered her through what she just did, taking care of me when *I* should step in to take care of her.

When I don't answer, she holds out the can to me, the corners of her mouth turning up in encouragement.

"You wanna try?"

The tips of her fingers match her cheeks, but when I reach for the can, my skin brushing hers, I feel nothing but warmth.

"Anything I write," I start, instinctively shaking the can, "will ruin what you have up there. I can't do... Maggie, you're a fucking artist. The latte, this? I mean, who *are* you?"

A flash of something streaks across her eyes, but she covers it with a smile.

"Just a girl whose two little words don't want to spend eternity alone."

I grin. "Eternity?"

She shrugs. "Okay, fine. The owner may repaint the wall two days from now, but don't hang me out to dry, not even for two days."

Her voice teases, but I hear the plea she's trying to hide.

"Tell me what it means?" I ask. "What can I write that will fit?"

She wraps her arms around her torso in a lonely embrace, her eyes focusing on her shoe as it toes the pavement in front of her.

"Anything," she says, facing me again. "As long as it helps me remember tonight."

"Okay." I shake the can again, approach the wall, and write.

Souvenir.

Memoria.

Cuimhne.

My penmanship is no match for her art, but my words scattered around hers don't look half bad. Somehow they fit.

I set the can down on the ground and attempt to brush the already dried flecks of paint from my jeans. Maggie moves to my side, but her eyes stay trained on the wall.

"I know the French one, *souvenir*, because we use that one, too. It means *memory*, right?"

I nod. "The second is Spanish. And Italian. I kind of cheated there. And the third is Gaelic."

She pivots to face me now, her eyes widening as she interprets the meaning.

"I wanted your words to have some memories." I nudge her shoulder with mine. "So they won't be all alone for eternity." I skim my fingers along her hairline. "I want *you* to remember tonight."

She bites her lip as tears well, and I don't know if I've said the right thing—or the wrong. She opens her mouth to say something, and that's when we see the approaching headlights.

Fuck.

"Fuck!" Maggie yells. I reach for her bag, not forgetting to throw the paint back in it. And then I reach for her hand already extended and waiting for mine.

And then…we run.

"This alley dead-ends at another one, but I think it leads away from the car!"

I trust her knowledge of the block's layout and pull her away from the oncoming car, which I see, as I look over my shoulder, is of course a cop car.

When we hit the end of our alley, we head left down the intersecting one, and I assume we're being taken to another that will lead us back to the main road and to my truck if we don't end up in cuffs first. I can't help but laugh at the thought of my father having to bail me out. Even for me, that would be a first.

But when we get to the alley I predicted would be there, any semblance of laughter stops when we face the one thing standing between us and, hopefully, freedom — an eight-foot-high, chain-link fence.

Fuck.

"Fuck." Again. "We don't even know if the cop saw us," Maggie says, radiating an unusual calm.

"Yeah, but if he or she or whoever did, we're caught unless we climb."

Maggie looks down at her long skirt and then up at me.

"You got this, Pippi. I'm right behind you." I throw her bag over my shoulder and across my body, nodding for her to climb. And she does.

I'm behind her and then next to her when we reach the

top, my fingers numb against the cold metal, Maggie's maybe surviving better in her cut-off gloves.

"What if my skirt…" She trails off, but I know what she's thinking.

"I'm not gonna let you get stuck, Maggie. Okay? Do you trust me?"

She nods, hoisting a leg over the pointed top of the fence while trying to maintain her modesty. And if I didn't glance back and see the beam of a flashlight approaching the end of graffiti alley, I might have thoughts of sneaking a peek. Now all I want is to keep her calm, keep myself calm, and, for reasons far different than the ones I felt nearly an hour ago, get the fuck out of here.

When Maggie makes it over the top without incident, I'm more than confident I'll do the same, which is why when the front of my hoodie catches on the intertwined spindles of metal, lifting it and my shirt up to my chest, I panic. Haste clouds any rational thought as I slide my torso up the fence, flush against the metal, freeing my clothing but leaving a tiny bit of me as a souvenir.

Fucking hell. I make my way down the rest of the way, wincing at the sting where the topmost point of the fence grazed my skin as it gave me back my clothes. *That's gonna leave a mark.*

When my feet hit the ground, Maggie says nothing but holds out her hand, and we run once again toward the street, only to look in the direction of my truck and see, far beyond where we parked, the cop car fading in the distance. When I turn again toward the fence, I find the flashlight's owner — a woman walking her small dog, and bark out a laugh.

"What?" Maggie asks as we slow to a walk, both of us

breathing hard.

"Nothing," I say, stopping to catch my breath and shaking my head as I laugh even harder. I take her bag off my shoulder and hand it to her.

She laughs, too, a sound full of relief, as she backhands my stomach.

I wince.

"Hold it there, Fancy Pants," she says, grabbing the hem of my hoodie and lifting it slowly to reveal what looks like an attempt to slice me open with a serrated knife.

"It's a scratch," I say, because it isn't much more, aside from the few locations where the metal took a bit more skin. The blood is already drying, but yeah, it stings. And I'll be lucky if I don't wake up with tetanus spasms.

"I'm sorry," she says, my skin still exposed to the chilly air. "This is my fault. If I hadn't brought you here, this never would have…"

"Hey…Maggie…" My hand covers hers as we ease my sweatshirt down together. And while I'm careful not to pull her hand too close, her fingers trail over my skin, and tetanus or not, I feel nothing other than her touch.

"I am a willing participant in this entire evening—morning—whatever you want to call it. I panicked at a goddamn flashlight some lady was using to walk her dog. So unless she is some sort of pawn in your evil scheme to end the night by drawing my blood, *this* is all me."

A corner of her mouth quirks in an attempt to smile, but the guilt still hangs on her expression.

"I guess this would be the end of the night," she says, backing away from me and heading down our original alley. Questioning my sanity every step of the way, I follow her until she stands in front of our wall, instant camera in hand. Her flash won't illuminate the picture completely, but I hope it will be enough.

I wait, letting her have her moment with our creation, and a minute later she's back by my side where the alley meets the street.

"A memory of our memories," she says, handing one of two developing pictures to me. As I take it she asks, "Will you take me home, Griffin?"

I nod, the finality of the request causing an unfamiliar ache in my throat.

"Sure," I say. "Where do you live?"

We're at the car now, and she waits to answer until we're both inside.

Her eyes find mine, and she makes the request again, only this time it isn't a question.

"Take me *home*, Griffin."

And I understand.

"Maggie." I brush an auburn wave behind her ear. "I wasn't lying when I told you I didn't know you worked at the coffee shop. What Davis said—I didn't plan to take you home with me."

"I know," she says, filling the impending silence before it has a second to occur. "I know it wasn't your plan, but it is what you do, right? This is what I want, and I think you want it, too."

It's what I do, right? I silently thank her for the reminder. But she's right. I want it. I want *her*, and I'm not good enough to let logic cloud my judgment. So I turn on the grin, the one that reminds whoever I'm with that this *is* what I do.

"Okay, Pippi." I put the truck in gear. "Let's go home."

What if

But when she reaches for my hand, I think maybe she sees right through me. And while I don't flinch from her touch, willing her hand to linger, I decide to give her a reminder, too.

"We aren't the dating types. We already talked about this."

She nods, but her eyes tell another story, their longing so familiar I fight not to look away. "No. We're not." Her words are flat, but it doesn't matter. We both need to convince ourselves that if she comes home with me, it doesn't change who we are. Tomorrow we'll go back to being strangers.

I glance down at the picture on the center console, now fully developed.

Strangers, I remind myself, and know my only choice is to trash the picture once she's gone.

Chapter Six

GRIFFIN

We don't talk for the short ride to campus, and while it's not so much an awkward silence, there is a weight to it. The weight of me *not* waking up in my room at my parents' house, where I'm supposed to be in a few hours for brunch. The weight of how much I want this girl tonight, and of how tomorrow—shit, it already is tomorrow—the want will still be there, was there already the minute I picked up a strange and beautiful hitchhiker. Where's the fucking sense in that?

"Here we are," I say, entering the heated parking garage.

Maggie raises her brows. "I don't have to step out of the car to know that this is not what one would consider *campus* housing."

Her comment comes with a smile, and I don't try to suppress mine, grateful to get the hell out of my head.

"It's amazing what my parents will do for me if I attend

the right school, choose the right major. Following someone else's path does have its perks."

Her brows fall, and the moment of lightness leaves her eyes.

"Come on, Pippi. Just trying to tease another smile out of you. Looks like it backfired." She chews her bottom lip, gearing up to chime in, so I don't let her. "I'm a big boy. It's not like it wasn't my decision, too."

I throw the gear shift into park and hop out of the truck, but Maggie sits there, arms crossed. She doesn't move, only waits. When I get to her door and open it, I make no attempt to silence her. Whatever she wants to say, I can handle it.

"Are you happy with your decision?"

Her eyes hold steady on mine.

"Well, you don't pull any fucking punches, do you?"

Clearly not satisfied with my lack of an answer, she doesn't respond. So I open the door wide, angling my head toward hers. And when I hear it, the tiny, sharp intake of breath that tells me I've caused enough turbulence to knock her off-kilter, I kiss her, and she melts into it so quickly I almost forget what I intended to say because I could "talk" to her like this for the rest of our time together.

I back away and watch her eyes flutter open. "I'm happy right now, Pippi."

"That's not what I—"

This time I don't let her finish, covering her mouth with mine again. She doesn't argue, her lips parting in a smile over mine as I maneuver to unclick her seat belt and guide her out of the truck and up against it. My hands pull the rubber bands out of her braids, tangling in her wild waves while her arms wrap around me, fingers resting above my jeans. In seconds they're moving, climbing up and under my jacket, my hoodie, and then my T-shirt. My breathing grows ragged as the aching need, the one I keep trying to ignore, grows. And when her hands make their way to my chest and down my torso, I gasp—and flinch.

"Shit!" Maggie slips out from under me, her eyes wide with recognition. "I'm sorry, Griffin. I totally forgot!"

All I can do is bang my forehead against the door of the truck. Her beautiful, amazing, soft hands are on me, and I flinch from a goddamn scratch. Okay. Maybe it's a little worse than a scratch.

Maggie's fingers trail through my hair. Then she rubs my back, the small gesture caring and intimate.

"Can we get you cleaned up and then maybe continue with our...um...discussion on happiness?"

"I'm fine." I groan, stepping away from the truck to face her.

"I know," she says, lacing her fingers through mine and giving me a reassuring squeeze. "But there's nothing wrong with making you better."

I look down at our hands, not hesitating to squeeze my assurance back. Though what I'm assuring her of, I have no idea.

"Okay," I say, and I lead her inside.

• • •

MAGGIE

"Oh thank God," I say as we step through his apartment door. "I was half expecting lots of black leather, clean lines, maybe even a remote-control picture of a fireplace."

What if

Griffin laughs, tossing his keys on the kitchen counter.

"Okay, I spoke too soon. Granite countertops?"

I survey the rest of the space, which is smaller than I expected—a modest living room with dark hardwood floors, a plush red couch…and a leather recliner replete with drink holder. A flat-screen TV and coffee table strewn with textbooks and PlayStation controllers, and a small galley kitchen, with stainless appliances and granite counters. None of it is obnoxious. In fact it's…warm.

"It was a model unit." Griffin's voice comes from behind, and I realize I've been giving myself a small tour, walking around the sparsely decorated room to stop at an end-table cluttered with picture frames.

"Those are my sisters—Natalie, Megan, and Jen. They said the couch *had* to be red, and I said the recliner *had* to have a cup holder." He shrugs, and his whole face lights up with his grin. "Everyone wins."

I watch him take off his coat and hoodie, then glance at my own body, still bundled in my wool coat, fingerless gloves covering my hands.

"They're beautiful, your sisters." All of them with the same sandy waves as Griffin in varying lengths. "You're close with them?"

He nods.

"If it's okay with you, I'm going to grab a quick shower, wash all the poisonous bacteria off my, uh, little injury, here. Grab whatever you want from the fridge if you're hungry or thirsty. Or whatever." He strides toward me, taking a picture frame I'd picked up from my gloved hand and placing it back on the table. Then he peels off my gloves, throwing them on the couch. "Just—don't go anywhere, okay?"

Something in my gut twists at his request, as if he knows I might leave if he takes his eyes off me. Because that would be the smart thing to do.

But in his presence, rational thought escapes me, and I say the only thing I can. "Okay."

He disappears down the short hallway to the bathroom. I reach in my bag for my phone to check the time, and the sight of the numbers reading half-past-four hits me with a wave of exhaustion. Our *non*-chase from the cops pumped me so full of adrenaline, I had no idea how wiped out I was. Collapsing on the couch, my eyes close, blinking back the threat of a headache. Of course. Why should this day be different from any other? Miles will give me shit about it tomorrow, not just the friendly teasing kind of shit for leaving with Griffin, but if I stave off this headache and actually make it to work by one o'clock, he'll see the fatigue anyway, remind me of my limitations, that I can't do what I used to do before…

He gave me an out. Goddammit. Fancy Pants gave me an out. *I* asked *him* to take me home, something I'm sure happens to him too many times to count, and now he's going to play the gentleman card by leaving the room? Despite him asking me to stay, this is him letting me go—if I want to. But what I want to do and what I should do isn't quite matching up. Something flutters in my gut, and I silently curse the feeling because I can't want him to set me apart from the countless others. I can't look for meaning in this gesture, in his ignoring his friends the whole night to fail miserably at creating his own foam art. In his giving my words, my wall, me—memories.

I should tell him. Then I'll go. I should march into that

bathroom and tell him none of this can mean anything, that in the sixteen hours I've known him, thinking about him more than sixteen times is crazier than, well, me. And I'm pretty sure I have some paperwork to back up the latter.

I snatch my gloves and stuff them into my pockets, making sure my bag is slung securely across my body. I can find my way home from here, but first he should hear what I have to say.

In a few easy strides I'm at the bathroom door, the echo of the water's spray giving me the final boost of confidence to walk in because at least I won't have to look him in the eye. But when I throw open the door, Griffin stands facing the mirror in only his gray boxer-briefs, his face contorted in pain as he dabs a cotton ball down the jagged scratch that lines his torso—the scratch that clearly, at some points, went deeper than the first layer of skin.

Shit. Like, the shittiest shitterson of shits. What is it about this guy that compels me to take care of him? And it doesn't help my resolve that he's practically naked because I full-on gawk for several seconds before finding my voice. *Get a grip, Maggie. The boy is in pain.*

"What are you doing?" I ask.

He braces himself on the counter, letting out a long exhale.

"You could have gone by now."

"I know." I should be gone, but instead I'm lifting my bag off my shoulder and tossing it to the ground. Next, my coat.

"You should go, Maggie. We both know that's how this night should end." He lets out a short, bitter laugh. "If you stay, I turn into exactly the guy you think I am. It won't matter that I didn't come to Royal Grounds looking for this.

I'll be that guy, the one Davis said I was."

"Do you want me to leave?" I ask.

His answer is instantaneous. "No." He sighs. "But I don't want to be that guy. Not for you."

"You don't have to be anything you don't want to be," I say, stepping toward him and grabbing a clean washcloth from a shelf next to the counter. Isn't that what I've been doing for two years? Fighting to get my life back, to *not* be helpless and dependent. Maybe that's what connects us, not wanting to be defined as others see us. In one day, this stranger hasn't once seen me as lacking. And despite all the signs that point to him being every bit of trouble he believes he is, that's not who I see. I see someone lost, like me.

That's why I stayed.

Steam pours from the shower, thickening the air between us, and I slide open the glass door to reach inside and wet the cloth.

He faces me now, his back to the sink, and I step in close, only enough distance between us for me to see what I'm doing.

When I see the bottle on the counter, I wince. "Rubbing alcohol? That's hard-core."

"Yeah, well, I just Googled *tetanus* on my phone. I don't recommend clicking on *Images* if you ever get around to Googling it yourself."

"Noted," I say, my hand and the hot, damp cloth making contact with his chest under his neck, right above where the injury begins. "But you should clean it first before trying to disinfect it. Otherwise whatever contaminants were on that metal are still there unless you use enough alcohol to soak it. Plus, this stings a little less. I hope." My hand drags the washcloth down the cut, gently as I can yet with enough pressure to wash away the dried blood—and feel the hard muscles of his abdomen.

When I reach the top hem of his briefs, I restart at the top.

"Thank you," he says, his hand joining mine.

Instead of *You're welcome* or some other appropriate reply, a giggle bubbles up from my throat.

With a furrowed brow, he asks, "Is that how your people respond to declarations of gratitude? Because around these parts, laughter is not the socially accepted norm."

This does nothing except get me to laugh harder.

"Okay, now I'm developing a complex."

I shake my head. "I'm not laughing at you. I'm laughing at me."

He narrows his eyes.

"I was ready to leave," I tell him. "I should have left."

"But…"

"But you weren't supposed to be standing here, looking like *that*."

My hand motions up and down his body, but that's not why I'm still here. I'm selfish, because I don't want this night to end if it means *not* feeling special anymore. With Griffin, I find snatches of a Maggie who doesn't rely on outside help to keep her day-to-day activities straight, a Maggie who takes pictures to preserve a moment rather than remind her brain what happened when it can't recall on its own. From the minute he picked me up on the street, to walking into Royal Grounds, to now—not one second of our interaction have I forgotten.

But when sleep comes, and at some point I will surrender to it, the slate will be wiped clean. Maybe not all at once, but enough for me to lose the feeling I have right now, the one that won't let me walk out the door.

I drop the washcloth on the counter and watch as his eyes follow my hands, as they lift my Royal Grounds T-shirt up and over my head. Next I slide my skirt over my hips and let it pool on the floor around my feet, toeing off my shoes and socks before stepping over the skirt and back to Griffin.

"You're not laughing anymore," he says, his voice hoarse and strained.

I can only shake my head while I watch his hands now. They find the front clasp of my bra, the straps falling over my shoulders as the cups open, removing the last barrier between his upper body and mine.

Griffin's palms slide over my ribs and around to my back, pulling my chest to his. If he lets go, I have no doubt I'll fall to the floor in a puddle, my legs too weak to support me.

I expect urgency as I wait for his hormones to kick in, but he just holds me, his head lowering to my shoulder until his lips are on my skin.

"Thank you," he says against me, but this time I don't laugh as my arms wrap tight around his neck.

"You're welcome."

I back toward the shower door, not brave enough yet to completely bare myself, and he walks with me, our bodies entwined. It's still open, so we step through together, Griffin closing us inside.

He looks at me, a silly grin spreading across his face, and then his eyes skim the length of my body. Mine do the same to his, and that's when I understand.

I laugh, looking at his soaked briefs as they mold even closer to his shape, no question as to whether or not he wants what we're about to do. "I guess we should get you out of those."

"I guess."

His face grows serious as his hands skim down my sides until his thumbs hook inside the seam of my panties.

"Are you sure?" he asks, and I answer him by guiding his hands with my own, then stepping out of the garment so nothing is left to hide behind.

If I had to answer him with words, I wouldn't have the right ones. *Am I sure?* No. I've never been less sure about anything else. But I've given myself until daylight, when I'll have no choice but to turn back into a pumpkin. Though the ache behind my eyes threatens to grow, the need for his hands on me overpowers the risk.

I help him out of his boxers and marvel at the beauty of the boy before me—black eye and all—a boy who looks like a man but is just as lost as me in some ways, a child still needing a hand to be held but not trusting anyone to do it. I should be nervous, showing every bit of myself to him. But he only sees what I let rise to the surface. We may be naked, but I'm far from bare. So we hold each other, the hot water washing away the armor for a little longer.

"Does it still hurt?" I ask, stepping back to get a better look at his scratched-up torso. With the blood rinsed away, the wound looks better, but the deeper cuts stand out, the skin a tender pink. Then I kiss his neck, his collarbone, and feel him breathe beneath me.

"No." I can barely hear him above the flow of water, above the thrumming of my pulse in my ears.

My lips trail across his chest to his shoulder, the other side of his neck, the line of his jaw. When I'm standing straight again, Griffin turns me gently so my back is to him as he reaches over my shoulder to the wire shelves hanging from the shower head. He grabs a bottle of apple-scented shampoo, pouring a generous amount in his hand before depositing it on my head.

I can't suppress the moan of pleasure that leaves my lips as his fingers massage my scalp, chasing the idea of a headache to the far reaches of my mind. He's hard against my back but does nothing to indicate his intentions go beyond washing my hair, which is fine by me for now.

"That feels amazing," I tell him. Never mind that what he's doing right now is far more intimate than anything I anticipated. When his soapy hands massage their way down my neck and shoulders, finding a path to my breasts, my arm shoots out to brace myself against the wall, my legs threatening to lose all ability to support me.

"You're beautiful, Maggie," his ragged voice whispers in my ear. "So beautiful." I want to tell him there's no need for flattery, that I couldn't want him more than I do right now. That is, until the water rinses the shampoo away and his right hand skims across my stomach, hesitating for only a second. Then he dips lower, a finger brushing me at just the right spot, and I suck in a breath as he parts me, enters me, and I almost come undone right there.

Has it been so long since Miles and I gave this a try, since I felt the pleasure of someone else's hands on me?

Of course I know the answer. It has nothing to do with when or how long. It has to do with *whom*. I know why I should have gone, why I should run as far from this guy as possible. It's not because he's trouble, not the way he claims he is. He somehow allows me to see past that, which is how I

What if

know — he could steal my heart. If I had enough to give back, I might even let him.

That's why one touch, one night of coffee and crazy, can bring me to this.

"Griffin…I…" His fingers keep moving, and my thoughts and vision begin to blur. He must be holding me up now because I'm not sure I still have legs to support me. "Griffin…" I say again, not wanting to burst at the seams, not alone. "Together." I press my back against him, and he groans. "Not alone."

I don't think I'm making any sense until his fingers slip out, and he spins me toward him as I gasp.

"Not alone." He repeats my words, his brown eyes dark with need but also with understanding.

Somehow the water turns off. Did he do that or me? A warm towel over my shoulders, and Griffin's hand in mine, he leads me through another door. I sigh, noting the rumpled sheets and blanket, items of clothing strewn on his floor, grateful for some visual reminder of the disorder that is his life — that the image doesn't hold up past the cozy living room. I ignore thoughts of why the bed may be in said condition, deciding not to let nameless, faceless others intrude on this moment.

I drop my towel, and my hands instinctively go to my hair.

"It all rinsed out while I was…" He grins, answering my unasked question, and his pause only makes the heat inside me build.

I grab his hand as I back up toward the bed, and he pauses at the nightstand, retrieving a condom from the top drawer. This, for me, has always been the awkward part, the pause for safety, but when I watch Griffin roll it down his length, I realize there's nothing safe — or awkward — about this moment.

He follows my lead, letting me guide him down on top of me, and when he's inside, there are no words, nothing that feels right to articulate what's happening, so I respond with my hands splayed on his back, my lips connecting with his. In the shower I was overwhelmed, overcome with how it felt to be touched by him, but now my urgency is replaced with a tender ache, the knowledge that whatever this is will be over the second our bodies separate. Griffin must feel it, too, because he takes his time, uses gentle care as he rocks back and forth, my hips mirroring his rhythm. As the gray dawn threatens through the window, we try to outrun it, our pace growing as the euphoria consumes us.

In case I wasn't already on the verge, Griffin slides a finger between us, and my back arches as we erupt in a chorus of each other's names.

"Stay," he says, handing me a T-shirt and a pair of clean boxers. "At least until your underwear dries."

He smirks as he strides back to the bed in a fresh pair himself, the threat of sleep already softening the cocky expression.

I want to argue, but I want sleep more. Besides, tomorrow doesn't really begin until I've gone to sleep and waken up to the new day, right? I've always been good with that brand of logic.

"You don't need to be anywhere this morning?" I ask,

What if

giving him the out this time, but I'm already wearing the T-shirt, sliding on the boxers.

"Not early enough to matter." He lets out a soft sigh. "What is it about a woman in men's underwear?"

I roll my eyes but secretly enjoy the compliment. Somehow what happened between us is still—happening. And here I am in his shirt and freaking underwear, postponing the inevitable for as long as I can.

"I need my phone, then," I tell him. "It has my alarm already set for work."

Griffin changes direction, heading for the bedroom door rather than the bed.

"I'll get your bag."

Seconds later my phone sits charging on his nightstand while I lie in the crook of his arm, as if we've done this hundreds of times before.

"Can I give you a ride to work?" he asks, his voice lazy as he starts to drift off.

I kiss his chest, at the same time trying to ignore thoughts of what it would be like to fall asleep like this every night—cared for, wanted.

"Sure," I say, and he doesn't say anything more.

Sleep comes for Griffin quick and easy, but instead of finding the same peaceful end to our evening or morning, the headache returns quickly, the throbbing relentless, and only an hour after we settle in together, I find myself rummaging through my bag searching for the prescription bottle I never let too far out of sight. In the bathroom I cup water in my hands to wash the small pill down and then crumple to the floor, eyes squeezed shut against the early morning light, my only comfort the cold ceramic tile.

Twenty minutes. If I can make it through the next twenty minutes without him finding me like this, I can make my way home once I get to a main street.

Breathe, I remind myself. So I do, silently counting my breaths and waiting for them to slow to an even rhythm, one that lets me know the prescription is kicking in and Griffin won't wake to find me heaving over his toilet only steps from where we did things that were so much better than heaving.

Eyes squeezed shut. Cheek on tile. Breathe in. Breathe out. Repeat.

I make it to the point where the throbbing stops. Shaky and spent with exhaustion, I stand and find my clothes in a heap at the opposite door. I throw on my skirt but shove my shirt and panties in my bag. The T-shirt, maroon with the word *Aberdeen* printed across the chest, will have to be a casualty of the evening because it's coming with me.

I sneak back into the room to grab my phone, and I can't resist the urge to stop and look. Asleep, he really *is* such a boy, the peacefulness of his features painting him far younger than what must be his twenty-two or twenty-three years.

I allow my lips one last brush of his skin, the bruise beneath his eye. Not the lips. I'm toast if I kiss the lips.

He doesn't stir, and a minute later I'm out the door.

I text Miles as I approach the first intersection I can find. *Not gonna make it in today. Can you please cover for me?* Thank the gods, I know this street. I'll be home in ten minutes.

Headache? Miles texts back, and I don't know whether to feel like shit for waking him or promise to kiss him next time I see him for knowing me so well. And for not asking about Griffin.

What if

Yep. A doozie. Took my meds but am wiped. I owe you.

His response is immediate. *No worries, sweetheart. I'll come by after closing.*

I smile, welcoming the visit since I know it means he'll bring me the leftover pastries for us to polish off while watching *Gilmore Girls* DVDs. Royal Grounds closes at nine on Sundays. That gives me fifteen hours to get my shit together and come up with a story, because if I know Miles, and I do, his reprieve won't last past then.

Chapter Seven

GRIFFIN

Don't be late.

My life is fucking *Groundhog Day* this weekend. While yesterday I woke up hung over, alone, lucky to see out of my right eye, today I'm sober, the remnants of an asshole attack by a chain-link fence hidden under my shirt. Again, I'm alone. The difference?

Absence.

I knew she'd be gone, but I wasn't expecting to feel this—her absence. If she would have left when I gave her the chance, I may have had a *What if?* or two. But the second she led me into the shower, that was it. Now I can't turn it off, the need to see her again.

This morning I ignore Nat's text and drive. I'm already late, so a quick detour won't matter. I half expect to see Maggie on the same corner, for us to start over again from

What if

our first meeting. Knowing the shape I'm in now, would I let it happen again?

I know the answer when I find myself throwing the truck into park in front of Royal Grounds.

"Good *morning*, J. Crew," is the greeting I get as I walk through the door, and I realize I have no idea what to say to Maggie if she's here. I can't let last night be the last time I see her.

"Hey, man," I say. "It's Miles, right?" He nods, stepping out from behind the counter, making no attempt to hide that he's checking me out, slowly, head to toe.

"I'm Griffin. We met last night." For a second I consider extending my hand to shake, but his growing smirk, fueled by my discomfort, tells me he'd leave me hanging just to watch me try to recover. "Is, uh, is Maggie working this morning?"

His brows pull together. He thinks I should know the answer to my own question, but when I don't say anything else, he says, "No. Not today," his tone flat and dismissive, a total one eighty from his initial greeting.

"Does she work on other Sundays?"

He leans against one of the breakfast bar stools, arms crossed over his chest. Another barista glares at Miles from behind the counter, clearly not enjoying taking care of the morning rush by herself. But Miles's eyes stay trained on me.

"Why do you want to know?"

The edge in his deep voice aims to intimidate me, but Miles doesn't know he's talking to an emotional fuckup who got himself punched in a bar just so he could feel *something*.

I swallow the irony of why I'm here. Because for the hours I was with Maggie, I wasn't drinking myself numb or waking up with a phone number on my hand, unsure who it belonged to. I wasn't numb at all, and when I woke up, I hadn't forgotten a thing. Not one thing.

There is where my problem is. Remembering her—knowing what I'm missing.

"Forget it," I say, turning toward the door. "You're right. I don't know why I'm here."

"Wait," he says, resignation in his tone, so I stop and face him again. "It's not like I didn't hear what your buddies were saying last night, what a typical Saturday night is like for you. I mean look at you." He tilts his chin up in a nod of recognition. "A perfect, pretty little package you either abuse or use for evil rather than good."

I clench my fists at my sides, trying not to react. But the guy smiles. He fucking smiles because he thinks he has me figured out, and I can't help it. I play defense.

"Maggie knows that's not why I came here last night. And it's not why I'm here now."

Miles adjusts himself so he's now sitting on the stool, and he crosses his arms again. Regardless of him checking me out, his muscles grow tense, and I get the feeling part of him wants to kick my ass. I'm taller, but he's solid enough to do some damage. He wouldn't be the first.

"Now we're getting somewhere," he says, satisfaction in his voice. "She got to you. Maggie does that." His voice softens with those three words.

Confused, especially after he left with another guy last night, I ask, "Are you two…"

"No…no." He laughs, but the sound is forced. "Maggie and I would never work. I love her, and I'll do anything for her. You and I…" He gestures between us. "We're not so different. Only my inability to commit probably comes from a

What if

much less self-destructive place than yours."

I run my hands through my hair and sigh. He's right. When it comes to relationships—shit, the word is so foreign even in thought—I am anything if not honest that if things go beyond a day, a week, whatever, it's only until it stops being fun. Or it starts becoming work. On one rare occasion, I started investing and trusting. That's what gets me in trouble—trust. After last night, I don't trust myself to stay away. I *can't* stay away, and that scares the shit out of me. But here I am, talking to a dude who seems half attracted to me, half ready to level me, and admittedly in love with Maggie on some level, even if it's only as friends.

"Is this where you ask me what my intentions are? Because I don't have an answer to that."

Miles rubs his jaw, thinking. "Did she tell you she doesn't date?"

I nod.

"And you don't date. Not really. Am I right?"

I nod again.

"Then don't date each other. There's obviously something between you, and you've both got your fucking issues with labels." He waves his hand in the air as he says this. "Call it whatever the hell you want until neither of you is chicken-shit to call it something more." His eyes narrow. "She's special, more than you know, and she can use another person in her corner. If you're the guy, I can handle that." He exhales, long and hard. "And if you hurt her, I'll handle that, too."

I don't doubt him for a second.

"Does Maggie get a say in any of this?"

He laughs, and though it's genuine, I don't second guess

his fierce protection of Maggie.

"Of course she does. It's all Maggie's say. But if she puts her faith in you—if she trusts you, and you betray that trust—I'm the one who'll be there when you're not. That's all I'm saying."

He hops off the chair and heads back around the counter, so I turn to leave, letting his words sink in. If it didn't make me happy to see someone so protective of her, I'd think he was a douche. I laugh to myself, thinking of Scotland, of Jordan, and how she earned the same fierce protectiveness from her roommate, Elaina. Elaina would have kicked my ass without question if I hurt Jordan. Lucky for me, Jordan kicked my ass instead. And fuck that I'm still thinking about it two years after the fact. "If she's not in class or at the campus library, she's here." I hear Miles over my shoulder, so I pause at the door. "That's pretty much her routine, working there or working here. But not today. She'll be okay by tomorrow."

As soon as he says those last words, he curses under his breath. "Fuck." I open my mouth to ask him what the hell he means, but he nudges the other barista out of the way, taking over with the line of customers at the counter. I guess our conversation is over.

"Really?" Nat asks when I walk in fifteen minutes late. "You're killing me here, baby brother."

I push past her to the kitchen where I can see the pitcher of mimosa calling me like a beacon to the counter. "Nat, you're barely four years older than me. It'd be nice if you'd give it a rest sometimes."

She follows me until I stop, arms braced on the cool granite surface. "I'm sorry," I say, eyes trained on the floor.

"For what? Being late? Making it harder and harder for me cover for you so Dad still thinks you're worth investing in for this whole eventual, business-partner thing? Or is it for being a dick to me just now?"

This last one gets me to smile, and I pull her in for a hug, planting a kiss on the top of her head.

"I'm going to go with A and C for now. I'm still thinking about option B."

She sighs, defeated, of course, by my brotherly charm, and returns the hug.

"You could tell them. That's an option."

"They could take away the car, the apartment. Those are options, too."

She pushes herself from me, leaving her hands on my shoulders. "And you can grow the fuck up, do something that makes you happy, and support yourself financially. That's my favorite option."

"Mom! Earmuffs!"

Violet has impeccable timing. I scoop her into a hug, and she squeals with laughter.

"We have to do something about your mother's language."

"Tell me about it," she says before kissing me on the cheek. "Grandma wants more juice," she says, brandishing an empty crystal champagne flute, save for the bits of orange juice pulp clinging to the sides.

Nat grabs the glass from her, rolling her eyes. "Well, I guess Mom won't care if you're late."

"*She* never does," I say, filling my mother's glass and

then one for myself.

"Ugh," she says. "When do you get to stop being the favorite simply because you're the baby? Because it's been annoying the crap out of me for twenty-three years."

I raise my eyebrows and look down at Vi, who crosses her arms and stares at her mom.

"What?" Then the recognition registers on her face. "Damn it. Gah!" She slaps me on the shoulder. "This is your fault! You make me go all frustrated mom on you, and I lose any ability to censor myself. Violet, please tell him I don't talk like this at home."

Violet grabs the flute back from her mother and then turns to me. "Fine. She's better at home. But let's get one thing straight." She eyes us both. "*I'm* the favorite."

With that the little brat exits, and Nat and I both lose it.

"What'd we miss?" Megan and Jen brush past Violet as she exits, Jen holding her flute out for a refill and Megan nearly plowing into me with her eyes trained on her e-reader rather than where she's walking.

"Eyes on the road there, Rory Gilmore." She bumps into me anyway.

"Huh?"

"Haha!" Jen laughs. "I doubt you'd ever catch Rory reading *that*!"

"Huh?" Megan asks again.

"I don't even think she knows we call her that," Jen adds.

"We've been calling her that since the episode where Rory was reading *Ulysses* the same time *she* was." Natalie turns to Megan. "Not quite *Ulysses* today? Tell your baby brother what you're reading."

Megan's eyes narrow. "Tell Mom and Dad who your

What if

sperm donor is."

"Oooh, I like where this is going." Jen hops up on the counter next to the pitcher. "Are we ever going to find out?"

With her successful deflection, Megan's head falls back to her book, and she sidesteps the counter for the kitchen table and sits down. I follow her without notice and start reading over her shoulder.

"Careful, Megan. Or Griff's gonna read your porn." I guess Jen lost interest in Nat's baby daddy.

Megan's head shoots up, and my eyes go wide.

"Porn? Rory reads porn now?" I ask.

"It's not porn," Megan says, an eerie calm taking over her voice before her lips turn up in a wicked grin. "It's male-male shifter porn, and it's freaking fantastic."

I look at Jen, her shoulders shaking with laughter. My eyes switch to Megan who does the same. "Male-male? Girls like that?"

Megan's eyebrows shoot up. "Uh, yeah? Romance is romance, Griff. And shifter romance? Hot."

"Shifter?" I ask, trying to piece it all together.

Nat finally joins in with a sigh. "They're werewolves."

"With weredicks!" Jen shouts before all three of them burst into laughter.

Stunned for the moment, I check both entrances to the kitchen to make sure Vi's not hiding out, listening in for more evidence that her mom is, in fact, a potty mouth. Instead I find my mother lingering in the space between the kitchen and great room.

"Hey, Mom."

Her smile is inviting as I approach and kiss her on the cheek. Like I predicted, she doesn't care that I'm late.

"Come out to the porch with me," she says, leading me to the heated three-season room that separates the kitchen from the backyard.

I glance over her shoulder and see my father playing chess with Violet, not sure what surprises me more—an eight-year-old who can kick my father's ass in chess or the warm, easy smile on his face whenever he's in Vi's presence. I was too young to remember if he was ever like this with my sisters.

Mom rocks on the bench glider, patting the space beside her for me to sit. She looks cozy in her leggings and over-sized sweater, her sandy hair streaked with the finest bits of silver that she ties back into a messy bun. But her smile fades before I even sit.

"Sweetheart, you could at least pretend you're not laughing in his face, make a show of it for a bit?"

My feet planted firmly on the ground, I rock us back and forth but look straight ahead instead of at her.

"You think I'm laughing?"

She's tried to hint before she thinks it's all an act, each thing I do to tarnish my image in my father's eyes. How do I explain going to Europe to find myself only to come back the same as when I left—lost? I want to be the guy I was when I wasn't here. But that guy can't exist in real life. In my life.

"If not laughing, then what, Griffin? What are you do-ing to yourself?" She sets a ballet flat-covered foot on the ground, slowing the motion of the glider as she looks at me while I still stare straight ahead. "You have everything a guy your age could want, plus a secure future. So what is it with the drinking, the fights?"

I stand and cross the small enclosed space, doing what I do best—creating distance.

"First…" I raise my glass in her direction while she keeps hers noticeably cradled in her lap. "Let's not do the whole hypocrisy thing, okay? I don't think two little bar mishaps can be construed as *fights*." *Especially if I welcome the occasional split lip or black eye.*

Her regal shoulders sag, and for the first time in years I see a crack in my mother's armor and wonder if she's hoping to peek through mine, too. Then my thoughts shift to Maggie, to last night. What did she see when she looked at me? *Who* did she see? And did I ever get a glimpse of the real her, or was her mask even better than mine? I think of Miles and the words that were so obviously not meant for me to hear. *She'll be okay by tomorrow.* She hides herself as well as I do. Problem is, I don't know who I'd be if I came out from behind the curtain.

Now here's my mother, inviting me to be candid.

That's not what she really wants, though. She wants me to be who I'm supposed to be—to be grateful for the gift my family has bestowed upon me. So I throw on my easy smile, the one that says everything's going to be fine.

Perfect timing, too, because Vi leads Grandpa through the porch door, and even though the room has a table that seats eight, the space shrinks in my father's presence.

"Good morning, Griffin. Glad you could join us."

The edge in his voice is only enough to let me know of his disappointment—for being late. For being me instead of him. Who knows? I've grown too used to it to bother figuring it out.

"Morning, Dad."

I give Violet's hair a good ruffling before attempting to trade places with her and my father and heading back into the kitchen. "Food smells great. I know you, your mom, and your aunts went all out," I say, looking at my niece. "I'm going to see if Nat needs any help before we eat."

"Give us a minute, will you?" My father looks at me and my mother, and I know which one of us he's asking to leave.

My mom kisses me on the cheek and stands up, no words of encouragement. Not even a prayer for my safe return. I may get away with a lot when it comes to her, but at the end of the day, she's Dad's better half, supporting his endgame regardless of what it means for mine.

"Come on, Violet. Let *us* go see if your mom needs our assistance."

Vi grabs my mother's hand and skips out the door without another thought.

My father sits at the table, motioning me to join him.

"I'm good right here," I tell him, and he leans back in his chair, crossing his foot over his knee.

"You left in a hurry last night before we'd finalized your choices. You need to start signing up for interviews, so I know where I might have to call in a favor."

I laugh. "Call in a favor? Jesus, Dad. Here you want me to help run your business, but you don't think I can make it through a damn interview. Thanks for the vote of confidence."

He stands.

"This has always been the plan, Griffin. Whatever you've been getting out of your system these past few months, it ends now."

The finality in his tone tells me this isn't open for discussion. I know my place, to simply stand and listen, so I do, my

What if

teeth clenched so hard I feel my pulse in my temples.

"This is more than *your* future we're talking about," he continues. "It's the future of the company, the one you swore up and down four years ago you wanted to run. I didn't get a thing handed to me growing up, so I made sure things would be different with my children. We've given you everything. Now it's time for you to give back."

Give back? I want to ask. I don't remember signing a contract at birth saying I owed my parents for whatever they *handed to me* growing up. Who knows, though? The kid I was, hell even the teen I was, probably would have signed it anyway. It's not like I haven't enjoyed the perks, but I'm beginning to understand what it is I might be getting out of my system—*that* guy. The one who would have signed on to that deal.

He doesn't say anything else. After a few long moments of holding eye contact, he pivots and leaves the room.

Finally, I'm home free, back in the kitchen where my sisters are putting the finishing touches on Nat's spread, and I paint on the smile everyone expects me to wear. I snag a piece of bacon off a tray, and Nat slaps my hand, not before the food is in my mouth, though.

"Everyone's supposed to contribute a dish, Griffin. This is the second brunch you've come empty-handed, which is shitty considering you cook better than those two." She points a spatula at Jen and Megan who are already at the dining room table, mimosas in hand, ready to dig in.

"Earmuffs," I whisper, stealing one more piece and stuffing it in my mouth, then donning the oven mitts to grab Nat's famous egg soufflé to bring to the table.

"Fuck off," she whispers.

Violet calls out from the half-open door to the porch, her voice a sing-song accusation. "I heard you!"

Nat's shoulders slump in defeat, and I do my best to rein in my laughter, if only to save the soufflé.

My sister rolls her eyes, bested once again by an eight-year-old.

"I blame you, *Uncle Griggs*," Nat calls after me, but I don't turn around, don't take the bait. My smile is no longer forced when I think of my precocious niece, when I hear Natalie mumble to herself:

"*Merde.*"

Chapter Eight

Maggie

I should be used to it by now, that leaving for the day is more like packing for a weekend vacation. But my upcoming exam and paper translates to extra supplies, which means an overloaded bag. Books? Check. A myriad of Post-its, colored note cards, and highlighters? Check again. Camera and my planner. I pet the top of my planner with sincere affection before fitting it into my bag. I was resistant at first to handwriting instead of putting my notes in my phone — until I saw how much more I remembered from the act of writing everything down. Now I'm a convert, or at least a hybrid.

My phone alarm sounds with my second reminder. If I don't leave for the bus now, I'm going to miss it. And I'm thinking I should lay off the hitchhiking for a while.

Coat on, *luggage* over my shoulder, and I'm out the door and down the hall when I hear my name.

"Need me to lock up, Mags?"

Shit. Again? This weekend threw me off. *He* threw me off.

"Thanks, Paige!" I call over my shoulder to my neighbor. Why she's always up when I leave is beyond me since she usually works nights, but I love her for it. Can't imagine what I'd do if someone had easy access to my place. Never mind if something gets stolen, but mess with my organization or make me deal with change in the one place I never have to? I don't think I could handle that.

I'm down the stairs and at the bus stop with minutes to spare, so I lean inside the covered depot and text Miles, apologizing for sleeping through our pastry-gorging *Gilmore Girls* session last night.

Me: *What time did you leave?*

Miles: *Only stayed for one episode. Feeling better, sweetie? You were so out of it last night.*

I barely remember answering the door to let him in. It's been a while since a migraine like yesterday's. Even after the meds kicked in, I was too wiped out to function, which also means I was too wiped to tell him about Saturday. Miles didn't push, just let me doze while he popped in a DVD and hung out.

Me: *Miss you. We'll try again next Sunday?*

Miles: *Always , sweetie…but one thing I need to tell you…*

What if

The bus eases around the corner, and I scramble to find my bus card in my bag while not letting go of my phone. While Miles has a flare for drama, he's not one to use it on me. But when the bus stops in front of me and he hasn't followed up his previous text, I'm guessing he's allowing for a dramatic pause.

I get on the bus, swipe my card, and fall into the nearest seat. Still no text, and I have no patience.

Me: *WTF? What do you need to tell me???*

Miles: *Shit. Sorry. Had to say good-bye to my guest.*

I roll my eyes even though he can't see me.

Me: *You had a bootie call after you left me? It must have been midnight. Who ARE you? And tell me Andrew doesn't say yes to you at that time of night?*

I picture him laughing. It's not like this is the first time we've had this conversation, because this is Miles. Miles loves everyone, and everyone loves Miles. It's biologically impossible not to. There have been studies. His non-answer *is* the answer. I know he and Andrew are just having fun, but I find myself wanting to live vicariously through Miles, for him to find a happily ever after so I can sort of have one, too.

Me: *Guy or girl? Wait. I don't care right now. WHAT DO YOU NEED TO TELL ME?*

This time his response is immediate.

Miles: *He came to Royal Grounds yesterday looking for you.*

I don't need him to clarify. I do need to catch my breath and focus before I miss my stop. But my haste gets the better of me.

Me: *Do I want to know more?*

Miles: *Do *I* need to know more? You left with him after closing and he shows up looking for you the next morning. Details, girl.*

Me: *Later. Tell me what he said. Plz.*

Miles: *Not much. But I think you did a number on him…and I think you should think about seeing him again.*

I don't date. I can't date. Miles knows this. It's too much right now. I have him. I have Paige. Everything nice and neat and uncomplicated. Griffin—God, just thinking his name is enough to throw off my concentration. I shake my head, trying to erase the lingering thought of *What if?*

It's too late. I've already missed my stop.

Shit. I gather my stuff from the seat next to me and hurry off at the next corner, only a block from where I need to be. I stop on the sidewalk to respond one more time to Miles before I miss my biology exam.

Me: *Missed my stop! Mention of a guy I spend a single crazy night with, and I can't even get off a bus. That was me, thinking about seeing him again. Decision=no.*

What if

I pick up the pace as I approach campus but keep checking my phone for Miles to respond.

Miles: *He did a number on you, too, sweetheart. It's been two years. I think you're ready for more.*

Me: *Love you*, I text, so he knows the conversation is over.

Miles: *Love you, too. Good luck on your test.*

Wanting more and being ready for more are two completely different things. Miles can only pretend to understand, and he does it well. But he doesn't really get it, what it would be like to *be* with someone like me. It *has* been two years, and *I* have a hard time being with me most of the time.

I got to be someone else Saturday night. Griffin gave me that. We played our parts for each other, and for a few spectacular hours, I didn't think of alarms and planners. I got to take care of him instead of worrying I would need the caretaking, until I left. I did so well letting him see the old Maggie, not the one whose brain can't multitask, whose body fights fatigue, food additives, and alcohol consumption with debilitating headaches, whose risk for a repeat of what happened two years ago increases simply because I'm still alive. Yeah, throw all that on the table for a guy who doesn't do complicated—for a girl who can't handle more complication.

My stomach twists at the thought of him seeing me yesterday. Or maybe it twists at the thought of seeing him. Period.

Fancy Pants has enough baggage of his own. He doesn't

need to add me to the list. And I sure as hell don't need to add him to mine.

Biology. I'm going to focus on biology, my exam, and researching this afternoon for my psychology paper.

Biology. Not Griffin. Yeah. That's a good mantra. *Not Griffin.*

If only my brain would obey. But I've had two years to learn that when it comes to my own thoughts, I'm not always in charge. I've learned to compensate for short-term memory loss, kept my life organized and manageable through maintaining routines. Even though, little by little, I've established some semblance of normalcy, Griffin is anything but normal. When I'm still trying to get my life back, I can't afford a distraction like him.

• • •

GRIFFIN

The same girl sits at the information desk from the last time I was here an hour ago. She was also there the time before that. Doesn't she have a class to go to or something? She gives me the fucking side-eye this time, and I don't blame her for being suspicious of a guy who comes into the library, takes a couple laps of each floor, and leaves. I decide this is the last trip before side-eyes calls security on me.

I find her on the sixth floor at a table by herself. Her back faces me, but I could pick her out of a lineup with that gorgeous red hair pulled over her shoulder, the freckles I now know are splattered across her pale neck.

I freeze for a second in the entryway, realizing I didn't prepare for what would happen if I found her. Never mind

What if

I don't have a Monday class and have been hanging out on campus all morning anyway. So, here she is. In the real world and not in the fantasy we created Saturday night. I guess it's time to take a shot at reality.

Her head bobs slightly as she reads something out of a large reference book, her hair blocking her peripheral vision, but when I pull the chair out next to her, she doesn't flinch. I smile as I sit, seeing the phone next to the book and the earbud cable running up and into her hair.

She's dancing in her chair, and it's probably the goofiest, most adorable thing I've ever seen, but my staring must give me away because her head jolts in my direction and she gasps.

"Shhhh!" A patron to her right must not be one for gasping.

"Sorry," Maggie whispers but doesn't take her eyes off me, and I grin as heat colors her ivory neck and cheeks.

The table is covered with books, colored note cards, but everything is organized, has a specific place, nothing like the table would look if I was working.

"Come downstairs to the coffee shop with me," I say, knowing we can't have any sort of conversation here. This also buys me time to figure out what, exactly, I'm going to say.

"I'm researching," she says, but there's almost no resistance in her voice, and I let out a breath of relief. There are so many ways she could have reacted to seeing me, especially since she left without a word yesterday. But she's already gathering her note cards, paper-clipping them by color, a Post-it on top of each one detailing the subject of the pile. When she picks up her planner, a photo falls out of a guy who looks around our age. Something is written in the white space below his unsuspecting face, but Maggie grabs the picture as quickly as it falls.

"Who's that?" I ask, hating that I sound like I'm accusing her of something.

"No one," she says, her words pinched.

Because I know what I came here to ask her, I have to make sure I didn't misread what I felt Saturday night.

"You don't owe me any explanations, so…"

"No, Griffin. I don't owe you anything." Her voice shakes, though, as she says the words, and I see myself as she must—the way I see my father when he speaks to me.

I lean in my seat and let my head hang back with a groan. When my eyes meet hers again I say, "I'm sorry, Maggie. You *don't* owe me anything, and I'm a dick for insinuating that you do."

Her posture relaxes, and though she doesn't say anything else, she finishes packing up her books and study materials.

I raise my brows at her obvious activity. "So that's a yes, then, to my coffee request?"

I let out a long, hopeful breath and wait for her to return my smile, but instead she chews on her top lip.

"I don't want to give you the wrong idea, Griffin. But we can't talk here. So, yeah. It's a yes, but only to explain why *we* are a no."

Baby steps. She's not telling me to fuck off. I guess that's a start.

I buy her coffee, hoping I have at least as long as it takes her to drink it to figure this out.

She sips her latte, and I decide to wait, let her say something first.

"I'm sorry," she finally says, "for not saying good-bye yesterday. I figured a clean break would be easier than an

What if

awkward farewell."

Something in her tone doesn't add up. There's a strain to her words, and I don't believe her. I think back to Miles and his slipup, and I'm sure she's hiding something, but I don't push it. Baby steps.

"It's okay," I tell her. "I get it."

I hesitate, not wanting to bombard her with the plan I've got forming.

"Look, Griffin. Saturday was… It was wonderful. Spectacular, actually. But I thought I was clear. I'm not the dating type. *You're* certainly not the dating type."

I steel myself at her words, hoping she doesn't see my slight wince. She's right. I'm not the dating type. My friends made that clear. I made that clear. But here I am, ready to state my case.

"You're right. I don't do well with relationships. They're messy and complicated, and I want nothing to do with any of that. But what if things didn't have to get that far? What if we mutually agree to *not* date?"

Her brows furrow, and I have to concentrate on not leaning over and kissing the wrinkled skin between them. In a little over twenty-four hours, how did I forget how beautiful she is, how every little shift in her expression lets a tiny bit of the person she's hiding seep out and into view?

"I don't understand," she says, but she's listening—interested.

I lean forward on the table, hoping to convince not only by words but by proximity.

"You're right. Saturday was…" I don't have the words because I've never had a night like that, but telling her this will scare her away. Hell, it's enough to scare me away.

"We weren't dating, right?" I ask her, and she nods. "We made it clear we weren't looking for anything more, but shit, Pippi. Why deny ourselves that kind of fun because we don't want the baggage?"

I lean in closer, close enough to hear the tremble in her exhale, my lips a breath from hers. "No baggage," I say. "Just more of this."

I let my lips touch hers, waiting for her to pull away. She doesn't. Instead she kisses me back, and everything about the feeling of her mouth on mine again tells me that neither of us believes the lie, but I'll hide behind it if she'll do it with me.

"No baggage." Her voice is airy as she nods her agreement. "And when we think it's getting complicated… not dating?"

"A clean break. No bad feelings. We just walk away." I have to force the last sentence. Three trips to the library to find her are enough to prove I'm full of shit, but she doesn't need to know that. When she's ready to walk away, I'll let her. Because it will be what's best for both of us. All I know is that the need to see her again overpowers my logic. Or at least gives me the ability to ignore it.

She licks her bottom lip, and I'm ready to complicate things right here in the coffee shop, but I restrain myself, waiting for her to take the lead.

"The picture," she says. "I'm not explaining, but do you believe me that he was no one important?"

"Who could be more important than me?" I ask, giving myself an internal fist pump. She doesn't have to explain because she already told me all I need to know.

"I knew you were going to be trouble," she says.

"The best kind, Pippi." And I kiss her again.

Chapter Nine

MAGGIE

Straighten the mugs on the back counter. Organize the display on the front counter. Refill any missing pastries. Repeat.

This is my Friday night. Oh, and Miles giving me the one raised brow every time his eye catches mine. When I can't take it anymore—the anticipation of what he's going to say or ask or accuse me of—I crack.

"What?" I hop up on the back counter and cross my arms, and for a minute Miles continues to busy himself wiping down the espresso machine, even though we still have an hour before closing, and George and Jeanie are only one beverage in. With their late-night caffeinating, I doubt either of them sleep. But I love their company—and their business—so I don't complain. There are also the two girls who ordered our bottomless pot of coffee, though I don't know what for. One's had her nose stuck in her tablet all night while the other keeps getting up to walk and talk on her phone each time it rings.

I think I recognize one or both of them but realize that's how I feel about pretty much everyone after I've met them, so I don't dwell on whether or not I'm being rude by not going to say hi. Other than ordering their coffees from Miles, they haven't glanced my way at all.

Miles wipes the crusted milk off the foaming wand and gives the counter a once-over before finally turning to face me.

His expression is...wary. He's only ever looked at me with ridiculous, unconditional love and merriment. That's the best word for his personality—merry. His ever-present grin and lack of taking anyone or anything too seriously— that's my Miles. At my worst, his eyes smile, regardless of his expression. Even when he's the picture of concentration, the devilish mischief in his baby blues never quite disappears.

It doesn't matter that we made the horrible mistake of pushing our friendship beyond its boundaries. We came out of it laughing. A little embarrassed. A little disappointed. But with the laughter and love of the best friends we were before and still are today.

"What?" I ask again. Any trace of accusation fizzles from my voice, which instead is laced with concern.

Miles scans the coffeehouse, which, other than our Friday night regulars, is starting to empty. I guess he deems the crowd worthy of ignoring because he slides onto the counter opposite me, his back to the patrons.

"I've never pushed you, right?" he asks, and I'm not sure of his meaning. My hesitation must relay the message because he continues. "We've known each other since your

What if

freshman year, through everything that's happened in the past two years, and I've never pushed you to tell me anything you didn't want to, to share anything outside of your comfort zone. Am I making sense?"

I nod, aware now of where this is going, aware of the texts I didn't ignore but brushed off with countless excuses, somehow feeling the need to keep whatever happened with me and Griffin last weekend and then on Monday private. Even now when I have to tell him *something*, I want to tuck it away, keep it safe, because saying it will make it real.

I can't stop thinking about him. For once I want to forget, and I can't. He's in my head, in my not-so-innocent dreams, and I haven't seen him or heard from him since he left the library Monday afternoon.

Which shouldn't matter because we're *not* dating. It was my idea not to exchange phone numbers. Why would two people who are nothing more than that—two people—do something as permanent as program each other into their phones? I hold back a laugh, at the ridiculous thought of permanence in my life, in someone like Griffin's life.

Someone like Griffin. Because I do know him, right? I know his type. Yet he let me glimpse the hint of something more. He brought me to his place, showed me photos of him and his sisters. He gave me an out, but I didn't leave, not until I had to.

Permanence.

Neither of us wants that. We were clear. But I can't help reading between the lines and the hours and days it's been since we last spoke, since we made our crazy agreement, since I would have agreed to anything he'd asked once he showed up at my table in the library. When he left I headed back to the sixth floor to research, but not before the girl working the information desk asked me if I was okay, that she'd watched the guy I was with come in and out of the library three times that day.

"Was he bothering you?" she'd asked, and I'm not sure if I gave her any more of an answer than the goofy grin on my face.

He came looking for me, again and again until he found me.

I've been a shitty friend to Miles this week, and he's calling me on it. But I can't help the smile taking over my features, for a few seconds forgetting that for all of Griffin's charm—and talents at convincing me to do what I know will hurt us both in the end—I haven't heard from him since that day.

So I straighten the mugs on the back counter. Organize the display on the front counter. Refill any missing pastries. Repeat. But I have to come clean now with Miles, admit to spending tonight waiting and hoping for a twenty-something college guy to choose coffee over more obvious Friday evening options.

"You're right," I start. "You've never pushed me, and I appreciate your patience."

"But?" he asks, anticipating my next word.

I sigh. "But I want you to be patient for a little while longer. Until I figure this out." Whatever *this* may be.

Miles hops off the counter and crosses to where I sit. He leans his forehead against mine and rests it there for a few seconds.

"Ya gotta start living again." His deep voice is gentle, and his shoulders slump. "I'll admit it." He straightens to meet my gaze. "I used to worry what life would be like for you after the whole almost-dying thing. But you came back, Mags. And you're kicking ass at being alive. I just want to see you *live.*" He nods to my drawings on the back wall. "You're hiding in there," he says. "And in here." He taps my forehead lightly with his index finger.

"I'm okay," I tell him, and it's as close to the truth as I can be. I'm as okay as I may get. That much is true. If I could get okay-er? If I knew that was a possibility, I might do something foolish. I might allow myself to hope.

"I almost believe you." He backs away, the lull of the dwindling patrons interrupted by the *whoosh* of the door opening, the threat of the impending Minnesota winter evident in the wind gust as it enters along with the person at the door.

"Huh," Miles starts, as we both lock eyes on Griffin Reed, who as soon as he enters is flagged down by the occupants of one of the few tables of people left. The two girls with the bottomless pot of coffee. He kisses each of them, on the cheek, but still. My insides riot at the sight of it. He hasn't even looked at me yet, but it's not like he doesn't know I'm here, right?

Miles grabs my hand and squeezes it, a sign that I have not mastered the art of caging my reactions when I'm thrown emotionally off kilter.

But something shifts when Griffin's gaze turns in our direction—his and those of the two girls at the table. The familiarity. The *resemblance*. Maybe it would have clicked if there were three girls instead of two. If I had seen a smile on either of their faces before Griffin's arrival. Because they share it, that smile. All three of them. Not to mention different shades of the sandy hair that, at least for Griffin, offers the perfect contrast to his deep chocolate eyes.

I exhale, long and shaky, but my stomach no longer threatens to leap out of my throat. My hand relaxes in Miles's grip.

"You okay?" he asks, and I nod as I watch Griffin leave the two girls behind, their eyes trailing after him as he makes his way to the counter.

"Uh-huh," I say. "I think so."

Miles leans in close to whisper in my ear. "Remember," his voice both teases and pleads. "Remember how to live."

He lets my hand go and greets Griffin with that raised chin thing guys do, and Griffin responds with a, "Hey, man." Then Miles is gone, busying himself with the preliminary closing routines.

Griffin sits on a bar stool, and I stare at him for a second, noting the difference.

"Your eye," I say. "It looks good." The lack of evidence of a night gone wrong transforms him into someone else entirely, if only by appearance.

"Managed to stay out of trouble *this* week." His grin lights up his face, lights up the whole goddamn room because this revelation seems to mean something to him.

My hand fidgets in my apron pocket, but tonight it's free of any requisite photos. No reminders needed, not of him. I haven't forgotten the touch of his skin on mine, or our kiss in the library coffee shop, one that dripped with possibility. I can't remember if I locked my apartment door this morning, but I remember him. And there's nothing more terrifying than the strength of this memory because with it comes ideas I've trained myself to live without: *Want. Need. Hope.*

What if

"Can I make you a drink before we shut everything down?"

He shakes his head. "I didn't come here for a drink, Maggie."

My cheeks burn. The use of my name instead of Pippi throws me. It lacks the playfulness of the nickname, evokes a strange intimacy. I hesitate longer than I should to respond, and Griffin fills the silence.

"I didn't know if I should come here tonight," he says. "I sat in my apartment, ignoring texts from my buddies about where to meet them because all I wanted to do was see this girl who didn't want to give me her number."

From anyone else this would sound like an admission, but not Griffin. In the short time I've known him, he hasn't held back. What he thinks, he says.

I find my voice again. "This girl...she sounds like a pain in the ass."

He laughs, and I feel the tension melting between us. We can do this. Our *non* this.

"She is, now that you mention it. I wasn't even sure if she worked tonight, but there was no way to ask her."

I grab a stack of sticky notes from my apron and jot down a phone number, then slap it to Griffin's chest. His brows rise.

"Not my number. The coffeehouse number. You know, so you can call and check who's working on any given day or night."

He opens his mouth to respond but is interrupted as his female counterparts approach him on either side.

"We won't creep on your visit any longer," the girl to his right says as she starts spinning back and forth on the stool next to him.

"But glad we got to see you for a few." This from the other girl who, although still standing, barely matches Griffin's height where he sits.

The corners of his mouth quirk up before he says anything to confirm what I already know.

"Maggie, this is my sister Jen." He nods to the girl on the stool, and her hand juts in my direction, strong and eager.

"So, so great to meet you. You have no idea," Jen says.

The other girl, the one still standing, rolls her eyes. "What she means is…" She extends her hand as well, and we shake. "…we don't meet many of Griffin's…friends. So this is kind of a treat. I'm Megan."

His sisters. Two out of the three I saw in the photos on his table.

His *sisters*. He introduced me to family. This is so not part of the deal. "I'm Maggie." The plan is to plaster on the fake smile I use for any customer I don't know well, but the plan is averted when I can't help but get caught up in the warmth that spreads between the three of them, the affection. It spreads like an airborne contagion, and I'm all but willing to let myself get infected by this foreign experience—this connection.

"Well," Megan says, looking across Griffin to Jen. "We should go."

Jen nudges her brother in the shoulder with her own.

"We'll see you Sunday?" she asks, and Griffin nods his reply.

"See you then," Megan says, mussing his hair, and I let out a small bubble of laughter.

Miles sits across the room with George and Jeanie at their table. His eye catches mine, and the grin I wear falls

What if

on him now.

He shrugs, questions me with his dark brows.

I shrug back, not sure how to respond or what the right answer is. I'm starting to remember what it's like to let go of the fear, to simply live. The old Maggie could have done this. Miles can vouch for that. He has such faith I can be that girl again.

Then there's this guy in front of me—who doesn't want complicated but who makes me feel like I might be more than the complications I bring to the table. In his presence I feel like that other girl, the me I could have been, the one who's fought so hard to get back and steal center stage from the one who took her place.

As Griffin's sisters head toward the door, his focus comes back to me. He runs a hand through his tousled hair, and my palms itch to do the same.

"So, yeah. I didn't quite mean to ambush you like that. With Jen and Megan."

This is my moment where I either encourage him or don't. Where I take a chance at making room for more, for however long I can keep up.

My deliberation lasts only seconds before I step around the counter, around our metaphorical safety zone, and take over the seat Griffin's sister vacated.

"If that's an apology," I tell him. "It isn't necessary. They're lovely."

He peels the sticky note off his chest and slams it down on the counter.

"Megan texted to ask me a question, and when she said she and Jen were here, I figured I had to ask."

"Ask what?"

"If there was a gorgeous barista working tonight — and, of course, I first had to read a few of Megan's thoughts about Miles that I can never un-see."

Sweaty palms. This fluttering in my stomach. It's too much. *He's* too much, but I can't back away.

"Soooo…you came here to see Miles?"

Griffin laughs, and this sound is more contagious than anything yet, not because it makes me laugh, too, but because of how it feels to be the one to cause this reaction in him. The bitter edge that hung off his smile that first day we met is long gone, replaced by something far better.

"I came here to *not* ask you out on a date." He pauses, but his tone makes it clear he's not done.

I cross my arms, hoping to hide the thundering of my heart against my ribs.

"Okay," I say, drawing out the last syllable.

"Because we're not dating," he continues. "Which is why you won't give me your number…and why I have to *not* ask you out in person."

"Makes sense," I admit, playing along, while hoping not to give away how much the anticipation is killing me.

"You work tomorrow?" he asks.

"Early shift!" Miles calls from behind us, the freaking eavesdropper.

I roll my eyes, acknowledging our audience. "I'm off at four."

"Four it is," he says, and then he stands up, glancing at the note still stuck to the counter. "I think I've done okay finding you without that so far," he muses and backs toward the door.

What?

What if

"Good night, Pippi." He turns his attention to Miles. "Miles."

Stunned silence. That's my response as I watch him leave, but when the door bangs shut, I'm all words.

"What the hell was that? Miles, what do I... I don't even..." Okay, maybe I'm all words, but I never claimed they were coherent.

Miles watches the door with me as he approaches the bar.

"Do you want control of your life, Mags?"

I nod. Everything I do is an attempt to regain control. Of course that's what I want.

"It's up to you, sweetheart. If you want my opinion, that was some romantic shit he just pulled, but if you want a say, if you want to be a part of this decision, then *be* a part of it."

So I spring up from the stool and race outside to where Griffin sits, already behind the wheel of his truck. Thank God because I didn't think this through. No coat.

I yank open the passenger-side door and climb in. Wide-eyed but grinning, Griffin waits for me to say something.

"I *don't* want to date you," I say, repeating what I keep telling him, keep telling myself.

"I know. We have an agreement. I was there when we made it." His confidence doesn't falter, but his words are painted with a slight edge he means for me to hear.

I rub the chill from my arms, and Griffin starts the truck.

"For the heat," he explains.

"I know about our agreement, but that doesn't mean you get to waltz in here with this sort of anti-grand gesture and knock me on my ass."

He lets the mask fall, and there he is—*him.*

"Knock you on your ass? Maggie, I didn't mean…"

"I know. This is uncharted territory. So you know what that means."

He sighs. Because he knows.

"Ground rules?" he asks.

"Ground rules."

"Lay them out for me," he says. "Let me know how this works."

I maneuver to my knees, my hands fisting in his jacket.

"Rule number one. Never, ever say good-bye without kissing me."

His brown eyes darken almost to black.

"Did I knock you on your ass?" I ask.

"Yeah, Pippi." His voice is low and gravely. "You did."

"Good." I run a hand through his hair, my itching palm finally getting its fill. "We're even."

He waits for me to come to him, and I press my lips to his, taste what I've been hungry for all week. But it's more than just him. I taste his hunger, too. So we linger while the truck heats up, while his warm breath mingles with mine. For a few moments, it is the perfect kiss good-bye.

If only I knew what came after rule number one.

Chapter Ten

GRIFFIN

I call the coffeehouse at three and recognize her voice as soon as she answers.

"Royal Grinds, may I help you?" she asks, her voice rushed and breathless, and I have to shake my head to remind myself that she's at work and not half naked in my bathroom.

"Uhhh, don't you mean Grounds?" I ask. "Though I'm kind of thinking I like your version better. I mean, who doesn't want a royal grind?" So much for burying the naked thoughts.

"Shit. I'm sorry. Shit! I didn't mean to swear. I mean, can I help you?"

Shit.

"Maggie. It's okay. I was a dick. I shouldn't have corrected you."

For a few seconds, nothing but silence. Then, "Griffin?"

My name is a question but one filled with relief. "Maggie?"

A sigh, and then, "Oh, thank goodness. Miles knows I hate to answer the phone. I never get it right, but the line is so long. Some weird afternoon rush, and I've already messed up four drinks. But he's with the last person in line now, and I grabbed the phone so he could finish. Anyway, I'm kind of just vomiting out words now, so yeah."

I lean back on my leather recliner, happy to listen to her flustered verbal vomit for as long as it takes. In the silence that follows I remind myself why I called in the first place.

"Hi," I say.

"Hi."

"So. We don't have a date tonight."

She laughs, a quiet sound but not hidden. "No. We don't."

"Which is good," I tell her. "Because if it was a date, I might be worried about what we should do, make sure I get everything right."

Another laugh, this one not muted. "And I might be worried about smelling like a bottomless pot of coffee, or that I'll fall asleep in middle of the evening because I've been up since five."

"Oh," I say, realizing I've only been thinking about to-night from my perspective. But shit. I didn't consider this. I think about giving her another out, but she speaks before I can offer it to her.

"So what are we *not* doing tonight?" she asks, keeping up the game, which gives me the confidence to jump back in.

"That's exactly why I called. I need a short inventory. If this *was* a date, what kinds of things would be deal breakers, which would guarantee you'd say no to a second date?"

"Oooh!" she says. "This is good. Um, how about, guy

asks me out only to take me to his apartment to play video games. And for dinner, a frozen pizza."

"This deal-breaker dude sounds like a cheap asshole."

"Hey, I'm all for a good pizza," she says, "but the frozen ones are full of additives that can really mess with your system."

"A girl who's careful about what she puts in her body. I see."

"High maintenance, right?" she asks. "Good thing you're not dating her."

This time I laugh, but her answers already start to rearrange themselves into a plan. For our *non*-date.

"Video games are a deal breaker?" A guy's gotta double check.

"Totally." Her one word is a challenge, one that I eagerly accept. But now I'm pressed for time and need to get moving if I'm going to make this work.

"See you in an hour, Pippi."

"Fifty-five minutes, Fancy Pants. Not that I'm counting."

I am.

When she gets into my truck, I take in the aroma of the coffeehouse, the warmth and familiarity of the place that once held little meaning but now makes me think of nothing but her. I realize we haven't established a ground rule for how we're supposed to greet each other. I wait for her to slide to the edge of her seat, to take my coat in her hands like she did last night, but she's a picture of caution, her body close to the door, seat belt clicked into place seconds after she sits down.

"Where to?" she asks, a slight tremor in her voice, and my pulse quickens at the sound of it. Because whatever label we give tonight, it's *something.*

Then I think, *fuck it,* and I unlatch my seat belt so I can close the distance.

My plan is still to play it safe, to just let my lips touch her skin, but she turns to face me as I make my move, and my mouth is on hers. When she doesn't push me away, I make full contact.

She's warm, her cheek heating my palm. She tastes of caramel, espresso, and…mint? This observation gives me all the confidence I need as I let my head dip to her neck, my lips finding the freckles under her scarf. I smile against her, breathing her in, not registering any other scent but Maggie.

"Brushed your teeth for me, did ya?" I tease, and her gasp is her admission.

"Ground rule," I say, my lips trailing over her throat as she swallows her acknowledgment. "I always kiss *hello.*"

• • •

MAGGIE

I don't know what I was expecting, but I'm relieved when Griffin pulls into the parking garage of his apartment building. Too much tonight is new, out of my comfort zone, and despite what happened between us the last time I was here, there's a certain safety in being somewhere I've been before.

"You approve?" he asks, noting my smile.

"So far. Yes. I was afraid you were going to take me somewhere and get all…date-y on me."

We exit the vehicle and head inside. I eye the ingredients

strewn across the counter as I unbutton my coat. Fresh mozzarella, tomatoes. A jar of red sauce reads, "Organic pizza sauce. No additives." Next to it is a pizza pan with dough kneaded into a circle. Homemade crust.

"Not frozen pizza," I say, swallowing hard against the overwhelming need to throw my arms around him and kiss him senseless. It was a game, everything we said on the phone, but he listened in a way I couldn't expect.

"Oh, shit, I forgot one thing," he says.

He strides to the window on the far wall of the living room where he plucks leaves from a small potted plant. When he gets back to the kitchen, he drops the leaves on the counter next to the rest of the ingredients.

My jaw drops, and then my eyes meet his.

"You grow your own freaking herbs?" I ask, and if I wasn't so impressed I'd want to smack that self-satisfied grin off his face. No, scratch that. I want to kiss him until I can't remember my own name—the one thing I never forget—for surprising me at every turn, for letting me see all these little nuances I hope he doesn't share with just anyone.

My eyes dart to the living room again where I remember the PlayStation and the giant flat-screen. Griffin's coffee table is tidied now, no remotes in sight, and he follows me as I make my way to the couch, sitting down as I examine the stack of board games. Monopoly. Clue. Othello. Connect Four. And on top of the pile, a small red card-box that I pick up, my eyes pricking with unexpected tears.

"Uno. I played this a lot with my grandmother when I..." I catch myself before I go down that road, the one that will show Griffin just how complicated I can be. "Whenever I was sick," I tell him, redirecting my thoughts. "She would sit with me in my room and play Uno for hours."

Griffin sighs, and I want to ask him to rewind our entrance, to let me try it again. I should thank him for the most thoughtful date that wasn't and do what I'm supposed to do—smile and laugh at his reversal of my worst date idea. Instead I swipe a tear from under my eye before it has a chance to fall. Because everything is a reminder of why I shouldn't be here, why it's too much too soon.

But when his arms wrap around me, bringing my back to his chest, I let my body fall against his, breathing out the tension.

His chin rests on my head. "You and your grandmother were close?" he asks, his tone hesitant but curious.

"You don't have to do this, Griffin. *We* don't have to do this, the whole getting to know you, sad family history thing. We said no back stories, remember?"

His head falls so his warm breath tickles my ear. "That was for last week. This is tonight. We don't have to do or say anything you don't want to. I'm instituting another ground rule." His lips brush against my temple, and I squeeze my eyes shut but to no avail. Another tear escapes, this one not so much from what I remember but from what I know I won't be able to forget. *Him.*

Stupid, stupid hitchhiking idea. If I had called Miles last week and told him I forgot to set my phone alarm, what would have happened? He could have sent one of the regular patrons to pick me up. Jeanie's done it before. But I didn't want to disappoint Miles again. As understanding as he's been about my slow recovery, about whether or not I'll ever fully recover based on my own standards, every friend has his limits. What would happen if I became too much, even for him?

"What's the rule?" I ask, letting my head slide down his shoulder so I can see his face. His eyes stare back at me, dark and intent.

"That we keep making the rules up as we go, until we figure this out."

I don't ask him what *this* means, needing to leave any sort of definition of *us* unspoken. My rule, but one I keep to myself.

I slide back against the arm of the couch, out of his grasp but facing him, my knees to my chest.

"My mom died when I was really young, before I turned three. I never knew my dad. Not even sure if my grandparents did. It's not something they liked to discuss, and I never really asked much. My grandparents raised me, so I always felt like I had a complete parental unit, you know? I didn't need to know any more because I was happy with what I had."

He doesn't interrupt. I could stop now, but I don't. Regurgitating what I do know, the parts of my life that are solid in my memory, feels good even if the memories are painful ones.

"My grandparents were big on board games. My friends used to come over for family game night when I was younger. Uno was our thing. My grandpa was fiercely competitive. It was pretty funny to watch him play." I pause, the memory of him as clear as glass. What would those first weeks, or months, of recovery have been like if he was around to help Gram out, if she could have had a break from the repetition, the monotony of teaching me the rules of the game over and over again, when I'd known them all my life? Would he have been able to let me win like she did, watch me make the same mistakes in the same hand because I couldn't retain the information?

Griffin pulls my ankles so my legs straighten and drape over his lap.

"You okay?" The skin between his eyes crinkles with concern, which means I must have been hanging out in my head for longer than it felt.

"Huh? Yeah, sorry. Just thinking."

"Are they still around? Your grandparents?"

His hand gently strokes my thigh, up and down, the movement soothing, reassuring.

"My grandma is." I sniff back any more tears. This is *not* going to be how this night goes. I've let him see as much as he needs to, as much as I can handle him seeing. "But she's in Florida now."

"I don't blame her," Griffin says, not pushing the issue, letting his unasked questions go unanswered. "It's fucking cold out there." He nods his head toward the window.

I laugh, and so does he, the mood shifting for now.

"You hungry?" he asks, and I nod. "Well, then we better get to work. You okay being sous chef?"

I swing my legs off his lap and stand, offering him a hand to pull him up after me.

"It's only pizza, right? Is there really that much to do?"

Griffin's eyes widen, and he staggers back in mock horror, clutching at his heart.

"If at the end of the evening you still feel that way, I will have failed you. Now go wash your hands. You're in for a treat."

I know. You don't have to convince me.

Chapter Eleven

Maggie sprawls on the recliner, her bottle of water resting next to her in the cup holder. I offered her one of my IPAs, but she doesn't drink. Something else about additives. I didn't press the issue, and only now that I pick at the last piece of pizza do I notice I've barely had a sip of mine.

"So you cook," she says, shifting to her side to face me on the couch. "Like, you made me pizza from scratch. *This* beautiful pizza. With basil that you *grew.*"

She retrieves her mini Polaroid from the side table, providing photographic evidence that the two of us put away an entire pizza.

"I cook," I say. "Usually only for myself. Or on rare occasions, my family."

"Why only rare occasions?" She asks the question still looking at the photo. "They must love it."

I start gathering our plates from the coffee table. "Because sharing food with my family means spending more time with my family."

She yawns and stretches, her arms reaching above her head. Her Royal Grounds T-shirt moves with her, revealing a patch of porcelain skin above her jeans. I cough and clear my throat as I move toward the kitchen.

"Let me help." Maggie lowers the footrest of the recliner, but I shake my head.

"Haven't you been doing shit like this all day? How about you shuffle the deck?"

This request somehow revives her, and she springs to life as she reaches for the pile of games that were moved to the floor so we could eat.

"What's wrong with spending time with your family?" she calls across the room. "I was raised by my grandparents, but I've always had this romanticized notion of a big family, all these people to love." She laughs. "People who have no choice but to love me back."

Her words sound like she's making a joke, but the wistfulness in her voice says otherwise. How do I tell her about my family without shattering her vision?

I pile everything in the sink, deciding to ignore the mess until morning. Back on the couch, I grab the bottle of beer I've been ignoring and allow myself a nice, long swig before answering.

"Your sisters seem great. Looks like you guys get along," she adds.

"We do," I say. "Things are different, though, when we're all together in the same place. The big family thing—it does have its perks. More people to love, sure. But it also means more people to judge your every move. With me and my sisters, it's like a game of deflection. Someone asks Natalie a question about my niece's dad—deflect to Jen. My parents want to know when she'll be done playing the role of student and ready to be an adult. She'll pass the torch to Megan, who's missed more than her share of family gatherings this year for a guy no one has met."

I lean back, draining more of my bottle in a few hungry sips.

"And you?" Maggie asks. "What do you need to deflect?"

My head tips back and bangs lightly against the couch.

"You don't want that laundry list," I tell her.

She slides off the edge of the recliner, Uno deck in hand, and takes the seat on the couch next to me. Sitting cross-legged and facing my direction, she shuffles the deck, then spreads it like a fan.

"Pick a card," she says, and I laugh.

"I'm pretty sure that's not how the game is played."

She hums her amusement, a grin playing on her lips. "Deflecting already, I see. Just pick a card."

"What happens when I do?"

She huffs out a breath. "Whatever number you draw, that's how many questions I get to ask you, and you have to answer *sans* deflection."

"You're sexy when you speak French."

She rolls her eyes, and I laugh again.

"What happens if I get a WILD card?" I ask, reaching for the deck and thinking of ways to make Uno much more fun than anticipated.

She slaps my fingers. "It's not that kind of game, mister."

I hold up both my hands in mock surrender, waiting to

hear the rest of the rules.

"If you draw a WILD card, you get to ask me one question." She pauses. "Anything you want," she continues. "And I have to answer honestly."

"Let me get this straight. I have to answer any number of questions, one through *nine*, depending on what card I pick, and you have to answer *one*, and only if I draw a WILD?"

She shrugs. "I don't make the rules."

With mock grudging I pick a card. "Yeah, actually. You do."

Maggie bounces with excitement when she sees my card. A green four.

"Okay, okay. I'll go easy on you the first time. One — what's your middle name?"

I smirk and answer proudly, "Caldwell."

She snorts with laughter, and I raise my eyebrows at the sound.

"Griffin Caldwell Reed? Does the name come with a Rolls Royce?" She drops the cards long enough to mime rolling down her window. "Pardon me, would you have any Gray Poupon?"

I nod my approval. "Old school. I like it. And it's Griffin Caldwell Reed the second, if that helps." She laughs even harder. "It's my grandmother's maiden name."

"And if you have a son, he gets to ride around in the back of a Rolls, too?"

I lean against the arm of the couch and watch her laugh. She's smiled for me before, but this vision of her is new, a Maggie filled with unrelenting happiness, if only for a few minutes. So I let her laugh, let myself watch, enjoying that I played a small role in making this beautiful girl snort.

What if

"Is that your second question?" I ask. "What I'll name my offspring should there ever be any?" The question is meant as a joke, but inwardly I flinch at the idea, at the thought of someone small and vulnerable relying on *me* to show them the way.

She shakes her head. "Okay. Um…favorite TV show."

"Current or canceled?"

"Either."

"Easy. *Firefly.*"

"Good one. I would have guessed *Game of Thrones.*"

"Reading the books first. Are you a watcher before a reader?"

"I don't have the attention span for long books anymore." She fidgets with the cards after she says this.

"Anymore?" I ask and wish I hadn't. Because to know the answer means to dig deeper into who this girl is, and to know her—to really *know* her—would mean *something*, and what if I'm not capable of giving back?

She gives her head another shake, and a teasing smile takes over whatever it is she didn't mean to admit with that last remark. "It's not your turn to ask me a question yet. That was a freebee."

I cross my arms. "I see how it is. Okay. Two questions left, and I promise you I'll pick a WILD card."

"Why do you deflect? I'm not buying the whole judgment thing."

Well, I guess we're going there.

"With my family?"

Her shoulders rise and fall. "In general, I guess. That's a deflection, right?" She nods toward the empty beer bottle on the coffee table and then up at the breakfast bar, empty bottles from the week lined up to take to the recycling bin. My gut wrenches.

"I'm not a drunk, Maggie."

"But it's a good diversion, right? And what you looked like last week when we met…your eye? What happens when you go home to Griffin Cartwright…I mean Carrington…shit!"

"Caldwell?" I ask, trying to get her to smile, to get whatever is going off the rails back on, but she keeps going.

"Yes, Griffin. Yes. What happens when you go home to Griffin *Caldwell* Reed Senior looking like that?"

Her green eyes burn, and this whole line of questioning—I don't know where it's coming from. It's like she's trying to make me angry. And it's fucking working.

"Jesus, Maggie. You act like there's an easy answer to shit you know nothing about. I think it's time to deflect."

Maybe it's an overreaction, but this isn't what I signed up for. Intimacy leads to judgment, and Maggie just proved that. I get enough of that at home. That's what I was trying to make clear. But she's just like everyone else, and she doesn't even know me yet. So I drop the card on the couch and head to the kitchen. Looks like I won't be leaving the dishes until morning.

I turn the water on hot and at full spray, busying myself with anything but looking back to where she sits alone, flipping a card around in her fingers.

Of course it's a diversion. It's all a fucking diversion, the only way to prolong the inevitable, to avoid living a life that's not mine.

With the water on high and the steam in my face, I don't notice her leave the couch until she's standing beside me.

What if

She turns off the water and pulls my wet hands to hers, drying them with the towel on the counter.

"I was out of line. I'm sorry. I just, I have a hard time watching other people make harmful decisions, physically harmful decisions to a body…and a mind…that's perfectly healthy."

"I don't understand," I say. "I've had a few slipups here and there, but you accuse me of something I don't have—choice."

"I'm sorry," she says again. "It's me, and you didn't deserve that. I have no right unloading my baggage on you. I'm not looking to scare you off…yet." The corners of her mouth attempt to turn up, but the smile never really comes. She reaches into her back pocket and takes out a card, placing it in my now dry palm.

WILD.

"One question?" I ask, already knowing what it will be.

She nods.

"Can I kiss you?"

"Please."

So I do.

Deflect.

Chapter Twelve

I wake to the sound of running water. My eyes fight to adjust to the darkness, the lack of visual confirmation adding to my disorientation.

My phone. I need my phone.

On instinct I check the unfamiliar bedside table next to me, and it's there—plugged in and charged. The time reads eleven-thirty-two, the day still Saturday, and as my eyes find their way in the darkness, I recognize the space because I've been here before—Griffin's room.

I remember the WILD card and the kiss and then… blank.

Griffin emerges from the bathroom, towel drying his hair and shirtless while sporting a pair of flannel pants. For a second I forget my confusion and admire the view while he doesn't notice me looking.

What if

"You're up," he says, his face still obscured by the towel, and I gasp at being found out. "I thought you were gone for the night."

He drops the towel to show his face, an affectionate grin accompanying a weariness in his eyes, though I'm pretty sure he didn't do anything too taxing today.

"When did I...fall asleep?" I bank on the normalcy of one falling asleep without remembering when or how. It happens to the best of us when we're exhausted, though normal I am not. "It wasn't when we were..."

I don't want to finish the question because if the answer is yes, then I'm the *worst*.

His radiant smile brightens his eyes, lit only by the escaping light from the bathroom doorway. "No. It wasn't when we did a terrible job of cleaning the dishes, or an even worse job of kicking the Uno deck to the floor once we got back to the couch. It was..."

"I fell asleep on your chest!" I interrupt with delight, the memory starting fuzzy, but the edges quickly solidify. I remember our kiss beginning in the kitchen, soft and unsure after the shitty things I said to him. Then the couch, his continued kisses, soft and gentle, telling me what I said hadn't ruined the evening.

Then total and utter exhaustion. I forgot, but it wasn't permanent. Somehow with Griffin, memories return.

He sits on the edge of the bed next to me. "I hope it's okay. I walked you in here so you'd be more comfortable. You didn't want me to take you home."

I sit up, suddenly aware of what the time means.

"I missed the last bus."

He brushes my hair, wild from sleep, out of my face and

behind my ear.

"I can take you home whenever you need," he says, and I shake my head. The thought of him in my apartment, of him seeing who I really am—that's when whatever this is will be over. Because he has no idea what he's really getting himself into with me, and the longer I can keep him from seeing, the longer we can pretend that none of it matters. That nothing outside of what we let each other see exists.

"Or, you could stay. It's late. You're wiped out."

He grabs a book from the nightstand, *A Storm of Swords*, book three in George R.R. Martin's *Game of Thrones* series. He wasn't kidding.

"I have some reading to do, so your snoring won't bother me."

"I don't snore!" I slap him lightly on his stomach, and a flash of heat runs through me. Independent of thought, my hand walks up his torso to the healing wound on his chest. For a second I go blank but then brush it off as sense memory kicks in. My hands have been here before, and their recollection picks up the slack of my own.

I press my eyes closed, giving myself a beat to collect my thoughts, trying not to read into this momentary lapse.

"Your fence attack is healing."

He smiles, placing his palm over my hand so it lies flat against his skin.

"Skin-deep shit heals quickly."

I know, I want to tell him. But I say nothing, letting the thought linger for only a second before I push it away, before my eyelids grow heavy with sleep again.

"I'll take the first morning bus," I tell him through a yawn, and he climbs over to the other side of the bed, book

What if

in hand, and I realize I must be on his side of the bed.

"We can switch," I say, propping myself up on my elbow to face him.

He reaches over me to the nightstand again. "Don't worry. Just need these."

And there he sits, no shirt, flannel pants hugging his hips, and wire-framed reading glasses perched on his nose.

Suddenly I'm not so sleepy.

I look down to the floor and find my bag, retrieving my camera.

"Can I?" My face grows hot, and I can't finish the question. Because I don't take pictures for any reason other than necessity, to help me focus. But this. It's not simply that he's fun to look at. It's the intimacy of the moment, a piece of him that's more than skin deep. I don't want to forget this.

He opens the book and starts reading, or feigns reading. Either way, I take his silence, his hint of a grin, as permission.

Click.

As soon as the photo appears, I pull it free and watch his figure develop, first as a blur of rainbow colors, then the outline of him crystalizing into focus, bit by bit, until he's there, fully formed and complete.

More than skin deep. That's what you are.

He rests his forearms on his knees and watches me watching him in photo form. When it's too much, when I can't look away, I set the picture gingerly on the nightstand and crawl over the inches between us, resting my head on his chest.

"Thank you," I say.

He strokes my hair. "For what?"

"For tonight. The pizza. The games. All of it." I let my lips brush his skin. "For a non-date. It's one of the best nights

I've had in a long time."

My eyes are heavy again as my breaths move in time with the rise and fall of his chest.

"Come home with me tomorrow," he says, his voice hoarse and low. "Don't answer me now. Sleep on it. It's only Sunday brunch. We do it every week. But I think…" He says nothing else for several seconds, and I wait, not letting sleep in until he finishes. "I think I'd like it if you were there with me."

He slides down so I lie flat, his body my pillow, one hand stroking my hair, the other propping his book open against his knees. When he dips his head to kiss mine, that's when I surrender, letting sleep—and thoughts of Griffin—take me.

No headache plagues me this time, no excuse to run. When I wake in the morning, I know where I am and who I'm with, and I don't want to leave. We've barely changed positions since last night. I lie in the nook of his arm, my face inches from his.

He's still asleep, so I watch him, waiting, wondering if his offer still stands, if what he asked of me last night was because of the moment or because it's what he wanted. I haven't believed in something more with anyone for so long, waiting for the right time, until I could handle it—until someone else could handle me.

His eyes flutter open and meet mine, an adorable sleepy grin lighting up his features.

He angles his face so our lips align, and I gasp and cover my mouth.

What if

"Not quite the reaction I was hoping for," he says, his voice raspy with the day's first words.

"Morning breath," I say, the words muffled in my hand.

His fingers wrap around my wrist, freeing my face from its protective barrier.

"Then we'll cancel each other out," he insists, and while I know he's full of shit, I don't argue. Because I want him close. I want his mouth on mine. I want too much, so I'll settle for whatever I can get, even pre-Colgate kisses from a guy who wants no complications.

He laughs at my feeble attempt at resistance, and without hesitation, he kisses me. The moment our lips touch, I forget any objections I had because I'm an idiot for putting this off for even a second.

He smells of soap from his shower last night and something else inherently him—apples. I remember his shampoo, remember in my haze of a waning migraine last week the scent of my own hair, how it reminded me of him.

His lips trail the line of my jaw to my neck, and down. Somewhere in the middle of the night I must have removed my bra and jeans because only my T-shirt and boy shorts remain.

Propped on one arm, Griffin's hand glides to the hem of my shirt, and then it slips beneath.

A breathy sigh escapes my lips, and he groans lightly against my neck.

While his hand finds its way to my breasts, mine walks up his flannel-covered leg, to the drawstring of his pants.

"Wait," he says, his voice full of need. "Before anything happens, I need to say what I should have said last night."

We pause, his hand still under my shirt, mine ready, so ready, to help him lose the flannel.

"Okay," I say, trying to hide the rawness of my need.

"Whatever last night was called, you need to know I feel the same, that it was my best night in…let's just say in a long time."

I think of the implications of this, of the guy who drove to his parents with a bruise under his eye and a phone number on his hand. Maybe that guy was the act, the one who was pretending, and this one, he's the real deal.

"And I meant what I said last night, whether this morning's activities go any further or not. Come home with me, only for a couple hours. If it's a disaster, we'll get out of there and, I don't know, do other things."

He tries to hold back a grin, but it breaks free. Who the hell can say *no* to that? Still, I take a *little* pleasure in teasing him.

"Other things like…see a movie? Ooh, or go bowling? How about painting pottery? I hear that's a fun *thing*."

He wraps a lock of my hair round his index finger. "If you want to paint pottery, Pippi, we'll paint pottery."

A shiver of delight runs through me at the sight of his playful grin, the teasing of his voice when he uses his nickname for me. I slide my leg over his, straddling him and feeling him beneath me, ready and wanting. And I want him, too. In so many ways.

I lift my T-shirt over my head. I am without the cloak of night or the distraction of the shower. Just me, bare but for my underwear and Griffin's eyes, watching.

"You know what *I* want?" he asks.

I try to sit still, so still, because the anticipation of his touch is almost too much to handle. "What do *you* want?"

"To kiss every one of your freckles."

I draw in a breath. "That will take a very long time."

He places a hand behind me and maneuvers me to my back, now straddling me.

"I'm a patient guy," he says, and he kisses the tip of my nose. "There's one." His lips find my shoulder. "Two." The next one on my neck. "Three."

"Yes," I say, sounding as composed as I can when I'm minutes from oblivion. "I'll come home with you today."

His face is the picture of happiness, a smile all the way to his eyes.

"There must be hundreds of freckles on and around your lips," he says.

"Then you better get to work." I pull him to me, and he obliges.

His mouth finds mine again, and we abandon any pretense that we don't *need* this. His hand fumbles in the nightstand drawer and produces a condom. He slides my underwear to my ankles, and I kick free. His hand drifts between my legs, and I shake my head. I want to be filled up with him in a way that scares the shit out of me, but I crave it anyway. The flannel pants are history, and in seconds he's inside of me. For once everything is clear and focused, and I know without any doubt that I'm falling.

I let the hunger take over, let it obliterate the emotion, and I kiss him, taste him, devour him with my senses, my chest pressed to his and our bodies entwined.

"Maggie." His voice is ragged but with a twinge of emotion. "Maggie…I…"

I kiss him again before he has a chance to finish, rocking my hips to his, bringing him deeper, bringing us closer, every thrust and every kiss keeping him from saying more.

When we reach the edge, and he collapses next to me in exhaustion, I think the words back to him.

Griffin...I...

I don't finish the thought, and he won't finish the phrase.

Ground rule number three, and this is one that only exists in my head: Never let emotions get in the way of what's best.

We lie in silence, wrapped up in his tangled sheet, in each other. But with every second, I slip further away from ground rule number three. Whatever we call this, dating or not, every second I'm with him I want more seconds...minutes...hours...days. I want, but wanting isn't what's best, for either of us.

I sit up and swing my legs off the bed, tracing the trail of my clothing throughout the bedroom.

"Oh shit," I say once I have my T-shirt back on. "I have nothing to wear!"

How could I say *yes* to this stupid idea? I'm going to meet his family in a day-old coffeehouse T-shirt and jeans? Plus I smell like a stale pot of coffee. I can change my mind. I'm a master at making up excuses. This isn't part of the plan, and it's only going to make things harder. I'll fake a call from Miles that I need to fill a shift. But he cuts me off before I get the words out.

"You can wear that," he says, pointing to a Minnesota hoodie draped over a chair. I peel off my wrinkled Tee and swap it for the sweatshirt, and hell if it doesn't smell like apples.

"Thanks."

My tone is clipped, and his eyes narrow at the sound of it. In a room where we should have released every bit of tension along with a few yelps of pleasure, a tightness fills the air,

What if

one that is my fault. The anticipation of brunch—and what it means that he wants to bring me home—isn't part of our deal.

He *wants* to bring me home, and I said yes, which means he doesn't deserve the fallout from my heightened anxiety.

DEFCON 1 blares from my bag. *Meds.*

"Just…give me a second?" I ask, and he nods, brows crinkled as he stares toward the source of the sound. "Forgot to turn off my alarm."

I back into the bathroom and kill the alarm. Once the door is closed, I pull out my backup supply of daily meds, the ones that hang in my bag just in case. This morning counts as just in case.

After rushing through the routine and splashing some water on my face just to snap myself out of this frenzy, I take a deep breath and head back to his room.

"That's one hell of an alarm," he says. "You must be a heavier sleeper than I thought."

My only response is a nervous laugh. Crisis averted, for now. But I maintain my early assertions of this guy. Griffin Reed is a distraction.

Swimming in his garment, I hop back on the bed next to him, putting on the show of all smiles and whimsy, the Maggie he met last week. That's the Maggie he wants to hop in the car. She's fun. Families love her, and maybe I can pull her off for a few hours.

"Come on," I say, nudging him toward the edge. "Let's go have your family scare the shit out of me."

He grins. "You're gonna be great."

I smile back. He's right. Parents love me. They always have.

As long as I can keep up the show.

Chapter Thirteen

GRIFFIN

Violet opens the door before I have a chance to grab the door knob and throws herself into my arms.

"You're early! Mom owes me five dollars! Hey, Mom, you owe me five bucks!"

I lower my niece to her feet and plant a kiss on her forehead.

"You guys are placing bets on my arrival?"

Maggie stands next to me, laughing under her breath.

"Hey," Violet starts. "I bet in your favor. It's Mom you should be angry at. And Auntie Megan and Auntie Jen." She looks at Maggie, noticing for the first time that I'm not alone.

"Who's your friend?" Violet extends a hand in Maggie's direction. "I'm Violet."

"I'm Maggie."

The two shake hands, and it's only now I realize what I've done by bringing her here. Sure, she gets to see the best parts of my life, like Vi and my sisters, when they aren't betting against me. But she's going to see the other parts, too, everything I've always hidden from anyone who knows me, one of the reasons I keep everything outside of the Reed family simple, easy. Scotland was also a good lesson—in the art of pretending. Letting myself fall for Jordan, someone who loved someone else—I was such an asshole. No. The show I put on suits me better, enough that I've started to believe it. How could I be anyone other than who I trained myself to be?

I know better now. Self-preservation wins every time. So what am I doing letting my life outside these doors collide with what lies within? Self-preservation in the form of self-sabotage? The me of only a week ago wouldn't have called her after the first night. Up until now, I thought I knew my own agenda—to let her get a glimpse and then send her running. But that's not it.

Last night when I asked her to come here, all I could think about was wanting her with me for a few more hours, for another day. To soak up whatever time we had before everything went south, as it always does. As I know it will.

I lace my fingers through hers and squeeze her hand. She squeezes back.

I want her here because I want her here. That's the only conscious reason I can think of, and my chest constricts at the thought of it. *I want her here.*

The second our hands relax, Violet pulls her from me and toward the kitchen.

"You need to come meet everyone else," she says.

Maggie moves away from me, looking back over her shoulder, and I shrug as she flashes me a confused-but-resigned smile, waving with her free hand, the one that was just in mine. My imagination twists the meaning of her look—as if she knows me so well already—into one of pity.

I shake my head free of this thought, forcing myself to remember her in my bed a little more than an hour ago. No such pity existed then.

"Griffin." The voice comes from my right, the foyer entrance to the great room.

"Hey, Dad." I shove my hands into my front pockets—my automatic response to seeing him—to avoid the awkwardness of feeling like our greeting should include some sort of familial gesture like a hug or a handshake when neither of us has the inclination to do it.

For a second I think he's about to do it anyway, his right hand leaving his side, but instead his fingers rake through his thick mix of sandy-gray hair. He almost looks younger when he does this, something I know is a reflex of mine. But I tell myself our similarities end there, at the surface.

"Did I hear Violet say there was someone to meet?"

I open my mouth to answer him, to tell him about Maggie, but he doesn't want an answer.

"I was hoping you'd stay for a bit after your sisters leave so we could talk about your applications. I know you haven't received any responses yet, but we should start prioritizing, strategizing where we can get you some internships based on where you'll be getting that MBA."

I free my hands from my pockets, clasping them behind my neck as I muster my best apologetic grin.

"I'm really sorry, Dad. Maggie needs to be at work in a couple hours, and I promised I'd drop her off." And there it is, my out. As much as I tell myself I wanted Maggie here because I *wanted* her here, a part of me cringes at my selfishness, at how I just used her without her knowledge. Even though she's not a witness to it, I want to take back my deflection, to fucking say what I should have said two years ago.

This isn't what I want. It's never been what I wanted. Oh, and by the way. I don't actually know what I want since I've always been expected to be you. But thanks for the thousands of dollars you've thrown at me to keep me in place. Much appreciated.

Instead I say, "Maybe next week, Dad," knowing it will never happen because Black Friday is reunion day, and for some inexplicable reason, I decided to spend Thanksgiving weekend with Jordan and Noah. I'll exchange standing up to my father for spending an evening with the girl I fell for and the guy she wanted instead of me.

There will be a hotel and a bar and everything I need to blot out the memories when they get too real. And maybe, just maybe, I won't have to do it alone.

• • •

MAGGIE

Jen, Megan, Natalie. Jen, Megan, Natalie. I repeat the silent mantra in my head, his sisters' names in birth-order sequence, over and over while silverware clanks against dishes, while Griffin bears the constant ribbing of his siblings, yet all in fun. And love. *So* much love between them all. Even his dad—about whom he hasn't said much beyond that night in the parking garage—softens whenever his granddaughter looks his way.

Her name isn't part of my mantra, so I've already lost it.

"Won't you try the mimosa, Maggie?" Griffin's mom sits

across from me, the pitcher raised and ready to pour.

"No, thank you. I don't drink." The words come out like an apology, and I want a do-over. But when I look around the table, Griffin to one side of me, his niece on the other, everyone's glass is filled, the young girl's flute containing only OJ, I assume, but she drinks from the flute, modeling the adults.

The silence means they're waiting, as if what I said needs to be explained.

"I get migraines," I tell them, hoping the half truth will suffice. "Alcohol is a trigger for some people, and I'm one of the lucky ones." I shrug, like it's no big deal, like I never went to a frat party for the cheap beer or Jell-O shots. Now that's not even an option. I'm the girl with the ready-to-go syringe for when the headache comes on too fast, the daily blood thinners I take increasing the effect of alcohol in my system at an exponential rate.

"Dude. That sucks." This from the young niece at my right.

"Vi?" Griffin half chastises her from the other side of me, and I try to file away her name, or nickname at least. What did it stand for?

This isn't the place to whip out an instant camera and start snapping pics. It's not something I do with strangers. Griffin was different. I was able to take that first shot under the pretense of safeguarding my life from a would-be Saturday-morning serial killer. After that it just felt okay to do. It felt right.

"Are you a student?" The question comes from the end of the table, from the oldest sister. Megan. No, Jen. Nat has the daughter. *Jen, Megan, Nat.*

"Yep. I'm a Gopher."

What if

"What are you studying?"

I turn right, to Megan at the other end.

"I'm double majoring in art and psychology."

Griffin's hand moves under the table to rest on my knee. He gives me a reassuring squeeze, a tacit *You're doing great.* I wish there was some way to say back, *You have no idea.*

"What will you *do* with that double major?" Straight across from me, Griffin's father asks the question nicely enough, minus the hint of condescension in the word *do.*

Griffin interrupts. "Something fantastic. From what I've seen, she's an amazing artist."

My breath catches in my throat when I let my eyes go to his, warmed by this interjection, but for a few long moments unsure of why he would say this. Of how he knows.

"Art therapy," I respond absently to Griffin's father. Then I turn back to Griffin. "But you've never seen my work," I say, feeling the heat rise up my neck as my palms begin to sweat. Maybe he's seen my sketches at the coffee shop, but he doesn't know they're mine. Does he?

His head angles toward mine, and he whispers in my ear, "Right. Our little secret. I think I'd call your work fence-hopping amazing."

I force a nervous laugh, but then slide my chair from the table.

"I'm sorry. Can someone point me toward the nearest bathroom?"

"Maggie?"

He stands with me, and the worry in his eyes must mirror the same in mine.

"I just need a minute. Please."

I feel the entire table of Reeds staring at me, but I only

look at Griffin.

"Through the kitchen and on your right," he says, and I'm gone as soon as he says the words.

I must hold my breath for the whole walk to the bathroom because once I'm closed inside, I'm hyperventilating.

I fumble in my bag for my phone and text Miles.

Me: *Talk me down.*

As always, he replies immediately.

Miles: *Do I need details?*

I shake my head, but then realize he can't see me.

Me: *No. Just tell me Griffin's family doesn't think I'm crazy for bailing in the middle of a convo to hide in the bathroom.*

This time there is a delay before he responds.

Miles: *Griffin's family??? Okay. Right. No deets. Just talking you down. Here it is, Mags. You're impossible not to love. Get the hell out there so they can fall in love with you.*

I sigh, my breathing less labored now.

Me: *I thought he was different. Thought things were clearer with him, but I still forget. I forgot *him*.*

Miles: *What about a trigger?*

Miles knows about triggers, something that jogs my senses into remembering. Yes, Griffin's words were all I needed,

What if

fence-hopping amazing. He brought me right back to that night, to every piece of an evening I never want to forget.

Me: *Yes. Freaking triggers. Don't want to need them or lose my shit in front of a table of seven when I have a little trigger event. It's been two years. Can't my brain just work like everybody else's already?*

Miles: *7 ??? Fuck it. Go back out there. Stop hiding. And trust me when I tell you that you don't want your brain to work like mine. ;-) Love you.*

Three light knocks sound on the door.

"Maggie?"

Not Griffin. That much I know. And how long have I been gone that I'm getting the worried knock?

I drop my phone in my bag and take one more long, slow breath.

Fuck it. Right, Miles. Easier said than done. But I open the door anyway, since I can't really stay in the bathroom for the rest of time.

I open my mouth to greet her. "Hi..." Then I freeze. Here I go again.

She lays her palm on her chest. "Natalie."

"Right. Of course. Hi, Natalie."

"I wanted to apologize for my parents...and maybe for my little brother not quite letting you know what you're in for. All of us at once can be a lot to take in."

She moves aside, allowing me to step out into the hall next to her.

"No, it's not that. I mean, you guys are all great, but it's just…"

She gives me a knowing smile, and my shoulders relax, releasing the tension.

"Okay. Yes. It's a lot to take in. I'm sure you can tell my appearance wasn't a planned one."

Natalie laughs. "We're always up for surprises where Griffin is concerned. Whatever happened out there, it's nothing in the grand scheme of what my little brother has done today."

"What's that?" I ask.

"He brought you here, and he hasn't taken his eyes off you since you walked in the door, save for the few times you weren't in the same room. Something's different with him—good different. And I'm pretty sure we have you to thank for that."

I can't help but smile. I want to tell her that it's the same for me, that something's changed this past week. But saying it makes it real, and I'm pretty sure I just proved that I don't handle real that well.

"Thank you," I say, and leave it at that. Then I let Natalie lead me back to the dining room. Maybe the overstimulation got to me, but this I could get used to—having a sister, someone like Natalie looking out for me. I wonder if Griffin knows how lucky he is, regardless of how tough on him his father may be.

Back at the table, everyone makes a concerted effort *not* to stare at me this time, but it's no use trying to play it off like nothing happened.

I take my seat next to Griffin.

"I'm one of a family of three—well, formerly three. Now we're two. This is all new to me. I guess I need some practice

What if

in the large family setting."

"Well, shit!" This comes from Megan. I remember Megan, the little one. "Griffin should have done a better job of warning you about us, honey. I don't blame you for needing a few minutes to yourself."

I smile, and Griffin chuckles. Natalie rolls her eyes.

"I'm not taking all the blame for corrupting my daughter's vocabulary," she says.

Soon everyone is laughing, everyone except Mr. Reed, that is.

"Maggie," he says over the quickly fading mirth. "Tell me about this art therapy. How does that work?"

"Jesus," Griffin says under his breath.

"You can use it for lots of different things," I say. "There are so many ways for the creative process to explore the psyche." If there's one thing I'm sure of, it's the therapeutic qualities of art. Griffin Reed Senior won't trip me up here.

"So you'll need to get your master's, I assume, or some other higher degree to be able to practice."

"Yes. Of course."

Griffin's hand finds mine under the table, and he pulls it to rest on his knee—his knee that bounces in obvious agitation.

"Do you know where you're headed for your post-graduate degree?" Mr. Reed asks, but his eyes shift to Griffin, and I realize the conversation is no longer about me. I'm not sure if it ever was.

"No plans yet," I say. "I'm only a junior." I don't mention that I'm also part-time. It doesn't matter, not anymore.

"Well," Mr. Reed says, "at least you sound committed to your path." His gaze shifts to Griffin.

I squeeze his hand, and this time I'm the one reassuring

him.

"The food is delicious." I search the table, and it's Nat again who throws me the bone.

"I can only vouch for the soufflé. Anything either of my sisters makes is questionable."

"Hey…" The other two respond in chorus, and I look at Griffin, the only one at the table not wearing a smile, false as some of the others may be. I'm in the middle of something bigger than I anticipated. Maybe running for the safety of the bathroom wasn't such a bad idea after all.

Griffin's jaw tightens, but he says nothing, his eyes far away, not focused on his senior counterpart across the table, not focused on anything. Then I understand what we are.

Strangers.

Foolish. That's what it is to think I am falling for a guy I've known for a week.

Yet something inside me tugs, keeping my eyes trained on him until his concentration breaks, bringing him back from wherever he was. He turns to me, eyes dark, fierce—and sad.

Then they soften, resting on mine, the cacophony of female voices filling the space around us.

"Boo," he says, the ghost of a smile tugging at his lips, but I shake my head.

"Can't scare me that easily," I tell him.

"Liar."

"Maybe."

Not like he hasn't already seen me run. They all did. Because strangers or not, I *am* scared.

And foolish.

And falling.

Chapter Fourteen

GRIFFIN

Megan sits on the porch, e-reader in hand as she rocks on the glider. My parents and my other sisters play Bridge in the living room. In the resulting quiet, I stand in the opening that separates the kitchen from the great room, watching from a distance as my niece observes Maggie sketching the bowl of fruit perched on the table, one meant to be viewed but not eaten.

"She's lovely," a voice says from behind, and I flinch, as if caught doing something I shouldn't.

"Geez, Nat. Keep some Tic Tacs in your pocket or something so I know you're approaching."

She whacks me on the shoulder. "Explain yourself," she demands.

I know what she means to ask, but I buy myself a few seconds by playing dumb.

"Explain what?"

My reluctance to face her coupled with not taking my eyes off the pair at the far end of the kitchen table gives me away.

"You have *never* brought anyone other than Davis to brunch before. I gotta say, I prefer Maggie, but it still doesn't explain your motives."

"My motives…" It's not a question but more of a challenge, to see how far she'll go figuring it out on her terms before she gets me to speak.

Then she's quiet.

For over five seconds. The silence builds until I have to face her, knowing she'll hold out until I do.

"No answer I give is going to satisfy you," I say. She grins.

"I'd accuse you of being self-serving," she says, "using her as your latest distraction." Then she waits a beat. "If it wasn't for the way you look at her."

I sigh. Or maybe it's a groan. Whatever it is, it's joined with the word "fuck" under my breath.

"Didn't I just use her, though?"

Nat shakes her head.

"I don't think you meant to, sweetie. That wasn't your intent."

I study the slats in the wood floor, the hint of guilt still there despite my intent. Not only guilt for letting her be a distraction, but for wanting her to be something more when something more has never been what I'm willing to give.

Nat pokes me in the chest.

"Hey. When are you going to give yourself permission to be happy? I'm not only talking about her." Nat inclines her head toward the kitchen.

"I already freaked her out by bringing her here today," I say. "It was way too much way too soon."

Nat shrugs. "*Happy,*" she repeats, and I laugh.

"Says the girl who's been on her own since, I don't know, always? Didn't I learn from the best? Didn't I learn from all of you where rocking the boat will get you?"

Nat's the one to look away now because she knows I'm right. She knows how things work around here.

"You're going to enlighten me on happiness?" I ask. "You play the system as well as I do."

"Vi makes me happy, asshole. Vi is enough."

She's right, about the asshole part. "Who are you trying to convince?" I ask. "Me? Or yourself?"

I never said my power of deflection didn't get others caught in the wake. She turns to walk away, to rejoin the card game in the living room.

"Wait." I grab her shoulder, and she stops, her eyes dark — not with anger but with pure, raw hurt…and something else I can't identify. "I'm sorry. You know I love Violet more than anything. I *know* she makes you happy."

Then I recognize what else is there beside the pain — acceptance.

"I knew the choice I was making when I had her, Griffin. And the consequences that came with it. But the joy of being her mom, the unfathomable depth of love I have for her, it absolutely obliterates *everything* else. It has to. She comes first, and every decision I make has her best interest at heart. She *is* my happiness and always will be. It doesn't mean I don't want more. It means more will be harder because of what's at stake."

She looks at me for a long, hard moment and then says,

"I accept my choices and what they mean for me, but you take yours for granted. You *have* choices, Griffin. They might not be easy ones, but they're there."

I don't respond because she doesn't wait to hear it. Instead of heading back to the living room, she opts for the far end of the kitchen, the table where Maggie and Vi sit sketching fruit. I watch as she sits down next to her daughter, Nat's face transforming when Violet's eyes meet hers. Then Maggie looks up, too, her gaze meeting mine, and I feel the transformation, wonder if she can see it on me—the hope, the possibility, the start of something more. Not easy, but more.

When we leave, it's under the pretense of Maggie having to work. But it's two in the afternoon, and Maggie and I have nowhere we actually need to be, except back at my place where a co-ed shower promises to rinse away any immediate worries.

"Your sisters are great," she says as she removes my borrowed sweatshirt, letting it fall on my bedroom floor. "Thank you for wanting me there today."

I move toward her, and she stands unmoving as I let my hands fall onto her waist.

"I want you…" I say, my words trailing off as I find a freckle to kiss, "…everywhere."

She lets out a shaky breath. "And I'm sorry for, you know, kind of losing it at brunch. Sometimes I forget…"

I unclasp her bra, and her head falls back, a soft hum escaping her lips.

"Let *me* make it up to *you*," I say. I kiss her neck, help her as she finds the hem of my shirt and begins to lift it above my head. "I should have warned you better about the Reed family brunch. I didn't anticipate my father giving you the

What if

third degree. I thought he only saved that for me."

More kisses, my mouth finding its way to one breast and then the other, and everything else falls away.

"I want you, too," she says, her voice soft but insistent. Her gaze holds mine, and for several seconds she just looks at me. I wait for her to break the silence.

"You're different," she says. "Is it possible for someone to be so different after a week? Or have I had it wrong from the start?"

She reaches for my face, lets her fingers trace over my once-bruised eye and then trail down the disappearing wound on my chest. The physical markers that were the start of this change. *My* change.

"I think, maybe," I say, "that I see things differently now. That can happen in a week, right?"

She nods, her green eyes turning glassy.

"I think so." Her voice trembles, and she clears her throat. "How about I start the water?" she asks and backs away before I can respond.

Seconds later her voice echoes along with the sound of the water splattering against the tiled walls.

"Are you joining me?" Maggie peeks out from the shower door, her auburn waves drenched against her milky skin, and I can't get out of my jeans fast enough.

My phone vibrates in my pocket with an incoming text, and curiosity gets the best of me. It's Nat.

This shouldn't be a big deal. Vi had a great time with Maggie. Totally hit it off. But after the bathroom incident, I thought this was a little strange so wanted to tell you. When they were hanging in the kitchen,

Vi said Maggie asked her what her name was three times. Maybe something's going on with her, Griff. Maybe you should ask.

I stare at the screen for a few seconds.

"Hey there, Fancy Pants." She opens the shower door wide, and the sight of her knocks the wind out of me. "I'm getting lonely in here."

It's *not* a big deal. Who wouldn't need help remembering everyone in my crazy family?

I drop the phone on the counter.

I can ask Maggie about it, add more anxiety to what was already an intense day, or I can continue on my quest to kiss every freckled inch of her skin. Besides, I've gone down this path before. If I ask for an explanation, I run the risk of ruining the moment, like I did in the library when I saw that random guy's picture.

This choice *is* easy.

Seconds later I'm right where she wants me and right where I want to be, no questions asked.

• • •

MAGGIE

Miles bangs around in my excuse for a kitchen while Paige walks through the door with giant throw pillows piled above her face.

"You can't see where you're going," I tell her, and she drops the stack on the floor in front of her. Her blonde hair is piled on her head in a messy bun, but something about the appearance of it tells me she put time into the

What if

I-seem-like-I'm-low-maintenance look. Despite the near-freezing temps outside, she sports a black, ribbed tank, fitted in all the right places, and multicolored harem pants, the perfect combination of exposed skin and snuggle chic. I glance down at my attire: Griffin's Minnesota sweatshirt that he insisted I wear home, but my jeans have been swapped out for black yoga pants. Snuggly—sure. Chic—not even a little bit.

"If I fall down, at least I'll have these to break my fall." Then she gracefully collapses on the pillows anyway. "Is Miles done yet? I'm hungry. And I want to see my *Gilmore Girls* boyfriend."

Miles steps around the corner from the tiny kitchen to tiny living room-dining room—basically, my couch, coffee table, and TV stand. He sets the bowl of homemade guacamole on the table, and Paige perks up, ripping open the bag of lime-flavored tortilla chips as Miles joins her on her pile of pillows.

"I will fight you for Logan Huntzberger, and you know I will," Miles tells Paige. "I am fiercely possessive of my pretend crushes."

She huffs out a breath and swats his hand away from the chips.

"It's so not fair that you challenge me on this when you're the *only* one here who crushes on the female characters, too. Can't I have him tonight? Please?"

Paige draws out the last word, and I laugh, abandoning my lone spot on the couch to join the party.

"Sorry, sweetheart," he says. "But when it comes to Stars Hollow, I prefer the gentlemen."

Paige whacks him with a giant pillow, and Miles obliges by wrestling it from her and arranging it so he rests against the foot of the couch, lounging in his fitted jeans and equally fitted black T-shirt. His inky hair and lashes are almost too much. The guy is a specimen to be reckoned with, adored by guys and girls as he adores both as well, and tonight the flirtation between him and Paige is palpable.

When I told Paige Miles was coming over, as he does most Sunday nights to binge-watch *Gilmore Girls*, she made it clear she had no plans this evening, either. While the two have met in passing, I've never mixed neighbor life with, well, Miles life. Right now I wonder if I should have thought twice about my invitation for her to join us.

Don't break my neighbor's heart, Miles. I kinda need her.

Instead of letting on about my misgivings, I shake my head at both of them. "It's my choice tonight, and we're not watching a Logan episode. We're watching a Jess one."

The two of them groan in stereo, but then a spark alights in Miles's blue eyes.

"You want fucking 'Swan Song,' don't you?" he asks, accusation in his tone and a grin on his face.

I don't answer him. Because, damn it, he's freaking right, and I hate when he figures me out before I mean him to.

"'Swan Song?'" Paige repeats.

I stuff a guacamole-covered chip in my mouth and let out a tiny moan of pleasure before returning to mock surliness.

"Yes, I want to watch a Jess episode, and yes, I want to watch 'Swan Song.' But why do I get the feeling this choice of mine is about to come with a dose of analysis?" They can crush on Logan all they want, but my fictional heart belongs to Jess—troubled, closed-off Jess who could have held on to Rory Gilmore if he was only emotionally capable of letting go of his pride.

Miles sits forward, commanding Paige's attention, ever the know-it-all grad student.

"Because it does, darlin'. Are you new? What's the one class we had together?"

I roll my eyes because I know what he's doing. Laying it on thick, as if he needs to, and all for Paige's sake.

"You were a T.A. in my Intro to Psych class sophomore year." Now he's a doctoral student, working his way through school while earning his PhD in psychology.

Paige's eyes widen, and she bites back a smile. *Shit.*

Miles nods in my direction. "Let's take a look at the lovely Margaret's attire."

Paige directs her gaze, reluctantly, at me.

"Margaret, Miles? Really?"

He doesn't falter. "The size of her university attire tells us one of two things—either the campus store was plum out of women's sizes or even a small or medium in men's, and our dear Margaret was desperate to represent the Gophers anyway. *Or*, this sweatshirt belongs to someone else, someone who, like our friend Jess Mariano in said episode, came into our lovely friend's life with a shiner…and probably as much emotional baggage."

I'm rethinking my wardrobe now, not only from Miles's astute analysis. Maybe Paige was on to something with her choice of attire because the room feels much hotter than it did a few minutes ago.

"I'm not following," Paige says. "Whose sweatshirt is she wearing?"

"Maggie?" Miles's voice loses the taunting tone, and it's all warmth now. "Tell us how the date that wasn't went last night."

I bring my knees to my chest and bury my face so I can hide the evidence that will give me away. When I come out of hiding, I can't disguise the flush of my cheeks or the uncontainable grin that comes with remembering where I was only a couple of hours ago—back in Griffin's shower. Then back in his bed. I smile because it's him. I smile because I remember.

Then, because I really never wanted to hide this, not from Miles—and now not from Paige, either—I tell them everything.

Miles walks Paige home…to her next-door apartment, and I try to trust that he won't make things difficult for me in the one place where I have the most control—home. When he comes back, he finds me in my room, pushing a thumbtack through a photo. Not on the bulletin board with the photos I *need*, the ones that serve a practical purpose, though there is a photo or two of Griffin there. No, this one goes on a small board that leans like a picture frame on my nightstand, the top edge balancing against the wall. On it are only two other photos—one of me and my grandparents from my high-school graduation, the other of me and Miles posing with my first piece of latte art. And now this one.

Miles drapes his arms over my shoulders from behind, his chin resting on my head.

"Are you sure he's not for me?" he asks, though there's no authenticity in his teasing, not now that he knows the extent of my week since meeting Griffin. A pang of guilt settles in my chest at the realization that Miles now knows more about me and Griffin than Griffin does. Because he knows me. All of me.

"Maggie." My name comes out as a sigh, and I don't respond, knowing he'll continue. "You know the reason we never would have worked isn't because of this, right?"

He steps back, gesturing toward the bulletin board that takes up most of the large wall in my room. Like his analysis of "Swan Song," he's right on the money with what I'm thinking now. He sits on the edge of my bed, eyes still trained on my *photographic memory*. I perch next to him and exhale, long and slow.

"I know," I say with as much conviction as I can muster. Miles knew me before, and he knows me now, and everything about us has always screamed *friends* instead of *more than.* Sleeping with him had been wonderful, but we both felt the same when it was over. We were just sharing loneliness. That wasn't where our relationship was supposed to go. But a tiny part of me, the only part I've never shared with him, still thinks about *What if?* What if I was still the girl in that Intro to Psych class? What if I didn't have to worry about what I eat or drink, about getting enough sleep, about anything that could be a new trigger, that could turn a good day into one that ends with my head on a cold, tile floor begging for the throbbing to stop? What if I didn't live in fear that all of it would happen again, that if it does, I might not be so lucky?

Lucky. What a subjective word.

Miles nudges my shoulder with his own.

"Now say it like you mean it," he says, and I laugh.

"Did you know that ten to fifteen percent of people with diagnosed aneurysms will have more than one?"

This is our thing. When Miles has to talk me off a ledge, I throw statistics at him. He's relentless with his hope for me, but I keep a wall full of reminders that say otherwise. Tonight, though, as I spout off my anxieties, I realize my fear isn't for me alone. It's for him—Griffin. When I think of what I put Gran through, of how much she lost before she almost lost me—how could I set someone else up for that possibility? Wanting him feels too selfish, too soon. I owe Griffin more than that.

"I'm proud of you," he continues, and I peel my eyes from the vision in front of us, questioning him with raised brows.

"For what?" I add.

He kisses my forehead.

"For trying out this living thing. It looks good on you, sweetie."

I sigh. "I feel good. But for how long? How long can I keep *this* at bay?"

I motion back to the wall, but Miles keeps his eyes on me.

"Why do you have to?" he asks. "The guy is crazy about you. And this is only a piece of you. It doesn't define you, not if you don't let it."

"Yeah, well…"

But he doesn't give me a chance to argue. Miles pulls me in for a hug. I think about tonight, about what attracts bad-boy Jess to straight-laced Rory, and vice versa. He's broken, and she wants to fix him. But in the end, Jess is the one to fix himself. Because he's not fixable until he wants it.

What happens when both parties are a little bit broken, though? Griffin has to want to fix himself. I can't do that for him. And me? No one wants fixing more than me, but part of me may be beyond repair. How do I offer that to someone else to take on, someone who hasn't taken on himself yet?

I don't ask Miles this because he'll find a way to argue against me. Mr. Sunshine, the guy with the positive spin on everything, he'd try to convince me that two wrongs actually do make a right, that somehow broken plus broken can equal fixed. But I don't want to argue. I don't want to prove what I know is true. I want to sail as far as I can get before the boat rocks me hard enough to throw me overboard.

"So Paige, huh?" I ask, perfecting the art of subject change, and Miles releases me from our embrace. Leave it to me to call Griffin out on his talent for deflection only to use it to my advantage. Hello, pot. Meet kettle. "No more Andrew?" I add.

"I don't know," he says. "Andrew wanted to get serious. And, well, you know me. Paige, though. She's funny. And smart. Do you know she's not only a bartender? She manages the place she works at. She has a degree in restaurant management and hospitality services."

I didn't know that. Paige and I have the perfect neighborly relationship. She locks my door when I forget, comes over for coffee every now and then, and never asks what I do beyond work and school. Simple. Easy. And, at the same time, not at all a friendship. But it could be. Tonight it was clear Paige is a great ally to have in my corner, for more than merely swapping keys in case of emergency.

"You got all that from walking her five feet down the hall."

He shrugs.

"She's hot, too," I add, and his grin turns a certain shade

of naughty.

"And tastes delicious even after devouring my spicy guacamole."

I push him away and stand up. "Ew, Miles! That's just...I don't need to picture you and Paige like that yet, okay?"

He stands, too, his broad shoulders shaking with laughter.

"You're going to see him again, right?" he asks, backing out of the room.

I shrug. "We still haven't exchanged phone numbers."

"You're not pulling that serendipity bullshit, are you?" he asks, and I push him out my bedroom door and toward the main door of the apartment.

"He knows where I work, and he knows I hang at the library on Monday afternoons. So no. No serendipity."

Just hope, I think. And *want*. I *want* to see Griffin again.

Chapter Fifteen

I give up hope at four-fifteen Monday afternoon. With my classes done, any and all studying complete, I take ten minutes to unwind, to remind myself we had no plans to meet at the library today. Just because he came looking for me last Monday doesn't mean we have some sort of standing arrangement.

I take my sketchbook out of my bag, opening to the bowl of fruit from Griffin's parents' house. On the opposite page is my unfinished portrait of Griffin's niece, Vi. My finger traces over the letters, *V-I*, and the same relief floods through me as it did yesterday when she asked if I would draw her, and I asked her to sign her name to the unfinished piece when I was done. I can differentiate between all of them now, Griffin's sisters, his mother, and his niece. Despite the similarities in genetic makeup—I've never seen so many women look so much alike—a couple hours with this family was enough for me to distinguish, to pick up on some of their nuances once the overstimulation of such an unfamiliar environment subsided.

I tell myself it's all part of the continued healing process, but that's not the only reason. It was Griffin, too. Being there with him helped drown out the extra noise, the parts of a strange experience that would normally distract me. It's these thoughts distracting me now, easing the anxiety brought on by false hope. So when the chair across from me slides out with a hasty scrape across the wood floor, I startle to see Griffin, wide-eyed and out of breath, sitting across from me.

"Are you okay?" I ask, forgetting my disappointment at almost being stood up for a date that didn't exist.

His fists clench and unclench on the table in front of him, and then he slaps both palms down with a crack, much to the annoyance of patrons surrounding us. Griffin Reed was not made for library subtlety.

"I'm gonna need your number," he says. One of his hands leaves the table only to return with his cell phone and with it a folded-up piece of paper. He slides the phone across to where my hand rests on Vi's name in my book.

"What?" I ask, his urgency still a mystery.

"Your phone number. And I mean *your* number. Not the coffeehouse number, and not a landline, if for some crazy reason you still have one. Type your mobile number into my phone. Please. I'll wait."

I do as he says, stunned by the turn of events. I don't ask what brought this on until I hand the phone back to him.

"I'm gonna ask again, now," I say. "Are you okay?"

He eyes the screen, and his breathing slows, the frantic

What if

nature of his entrance morphing into calm. He breathes out a silent laugh, and when he looks up from the screen, there it is—the grin that threatens to melt me into a puddle.

"Pippi," he says. "You fucking wrote Pippi."

The unmasked joy in his voice startles me more than his entrance does. While I wouldn't trade having him show up when I feared he wouldn't, now I fear something even bigger. A phone number. Such a small thing, a tiny gift to give. But what does it mean?

"My Poli-Sci professor ambushed me after class, no doubt set up by my father, and I've spent the past two hours having phone and Skype interviews with three different business schools—interviews I wasn't prepared for and interviews I had no intention of ever setting up in the first place."

"Why would he do that?" I ask. "Why set you up to fail?"

He shakes his head. "That's the thing. I'm a master bullshit artist, especially under pressure. Learned from the best. He knew I'd pull it off rather than make him, or me, look like an asshole."

I still don't understand, and the expression on my face must tell him this.

"I've been dragging my ass in terms of what I'm going to do next year, and my father has apparently had enough of it. To quote him, 'It's time I start giving back.' Because I guess I owe my parents for my *easy* upbringing."

"Why?" I ask. "Why are you dragging your ass?"

He shrugs. "Because everything I've worked for since my education mattered has been for a life I don't want."

I sigh, wanting to fix this for him but knowing this problem is not mine to solve. But I can still ask him the unanswered question.

"You're good at so many things. Languages. Cooking." At the mention of the last word, my eyes fall closed as I smile at the memory of our non-date. "Bullshitting," I tease. "You have so many talents, Griffin. So much you could do. What do *you* want?"

His posture loosens as he sags in the chair, and he looks down at his hands before bringing his eyes back to mine.

"I don't know," he says. "I never considered what I wanted because I *thought* I wanted this. I made myself believe I did until it got too close, too real. Now I guess I'm just—lost."

I smile against my sadness. "I can understand that."

I pick up the folded piece of paper he must have had in the pocket with his phone.

"What's this?"

I start to unfold it, and he doesn't stop me.

"It's stupid," he says. "Just something on the job bulletin board in the business building. Kinda ironic, isn't it?"

When I flatten the paper, I bounce in my chair, then look up at him with the biggest, goofiest grin.

"AmeriCorps? Griffin, this is fantastic!"

He shrugs and looks down, but a small smile tugs at his lips.

"My father does want me to *give back*…"

I read through the description on the flyer.

"Wow," I say. "An anti-hunger coalition. This is amazing, but it's a huge change."

His eyes fall to the table. "You're right," he says. "It was a stupid thought. I wouldn't know what the hell I was doing."

"No." I reach for his hand. "That's not what I meant." He meets my gaze, his eyes unsure and searching. "This is amazing. *You'd* be amazing. All the stuff you've never done before, you'd learn. And the food part of it? You grow basil on your freaking windowsill. You just caught me off guard." I smile at him, hoping he knows how much I mean what I'm saying. "I can tell you want this, Griffin, and that's all that matters. If you want it, I know you'll be great at it."

He raises his head, his brown eyes gleaming.

"I could be pretty good at it, couldn't I? There's no money in it, though. I mean, there's a stipend, but it's not enough to live on."

I slide the flyer back to him.

"Maybe not the way you're living now, but you're creative. You'd think of something."

He folds it up again and sticks it back in his pocket.

"It's an option," he says, the unsureness creeping back into his voice.

"Consider it," I say. "For real."

"I will," he says. "You want to know what the most fucked-up part of the day was?"

I nod.

"This girl I wanted to see, who maybe wanted to see me, too…" He pauses, then relaxes his features into a revelatory smile. "You're still here," he says.

I don't try to hide my shared happiness. "I'm still here."

He clears his throat, attempting to get back into his overconfident character, but it's too late. The masks are off, and this silly thing—me waiting for him in the library and him hoping I'd be here—it makes me feel bare, more so than that first night in the shower, so very different than removing our clothes for each other.

"I don't ever want you to think I'm not showing up again, okay?"

He waves his phone between us, an explanation for his initial strange request.

"Okay." I take my phone out of my bag, ready to make the same request, when it vibrates with one of my alarms. "I need to catch the bus," I tell him.

"Wait for the next one," he says. "Come have dinner with me."

I purse my lips in contemplation. "This isn't a date, is it, Mr. Reed?"

He shakes his head. "Impossible. We're not dating."

"That's a relief," I say, ignoring the butterflies dancing their betrayal in my belly.

"But I want to ask you something," he says.

I lead him outside and down the street, to a small Chinese take-out shop that makes any dish I ask for without MSG. We bring the food back to the library basement to eat, since I don't want to be far when the next bus comes.

Griffin asks his question, and for reasons I still can't comprehend, I say yes.

Chapter Sixteen

I load my suitcase into the truck and start her up so it's warm when Maggie gets here. While I wait, I reread my most recent text. It's from Jordan Brooks, the girl I met in Scotland. For so long I've seen her as the one who got away, but that label doesn't seem to work anymore, not since Maggie.

> Jordan: *Can't wait to see you! It's been too long. SO excited you're bringing someone. Was starting to worry about you.*

She sent the message an hour ago, and I haven't responded. Because I still haven't officially decided I'm going on this trip. Not until Miles pulls up in front of my building in his hundred-year-old Nissan do I make my final decision. Maggie saved me once before, at my parents' house a week ago. Having her with me now has the same effect. When I'm with Maggie, I get the feeling—or maybe delusion—that I can do things I didn't think I could. Though she said yes when I asked her to come with me, I haven't let myself believe it. Not until I see her emerge from the car and watch Miles hoist her suitcase out of the trunk do I let myself admit this is real.

Me: *On the road in a few. Text you when we get there.*

I take Maggie's bag from Miles and deposit it next to mine in the trunk.

"So…" he says.

"So…" I answer, extending my hand to him, and we shake.

"Take care of her," Miles says, a note of authority in his tone, enough to show he cares but not make him sound like an asshole.

A throat clears, and we both look at Maggie, who bounces to keep warm in the late November chill.

"I think someone is forgetting his own ground rule," she says pointedly, her eyes fixed on me.

I let out a laugh, remembering. *I always kiss hello.* I back up so I'm sitting on the edge of the still-open trunk. Then I grab the belt of her wool coat and pull her to me without hesitation as I position her between my legs and my lips find hers.

Fingerless gloves cup my face, and delicious, warm lips spread their heat to mine.

"Oh, for fuck's sake," Miles says to us both, but laughter colors his words.

Maggie steps away from me, enough time for her to

What if

say good-bye to her friend, and then she's back, her mouth opening this time to let me in, and our tongues tease, and taste, and somehow forget we're sitting half outside a parked car until we hear the Nissan's engine start, after two tries, as Miles leaves me with this girl, the girl who said *yes.*

"We should get on the road," I tell her. "We'll hopefully make good time since it's still a holiday, but who knows what the Black Friday traffic will be like when we get to the city."

Maggie pouts, and I almost throw her down on top of our suitcases, but I decide to be patient and hope she can be, too. It's been a week since we slept together; Maggie had to work or study every night since Sunday, except last night when she spent Thanksgiving with friends, and I spent it with my family. Though we kept our standing library meet-up on Monday, that's been it. On more than one night this week I wanted to make use of her number, but what right do I have to call her to come over? How do I tell a girl I'm *not* dating that sleeping with her next to me is better than not? So I splurged. We have a suite waiting for us at the Four Seasons. And hell if I'm not going to get us to the city in time to make use of it before we have to head to the Signature Lounge for the reunion.

I catch sight of her in my peripheral vision as I drive, her head leaning against the glass of the passenger-side window, eyes lazy but watching, observing. The corner of her mouth creeps up toward her cheek, and I wonder if she's lost in thought rather than watching the road go by.

"You still with me?" I ask, and she blinks, her eyes seeming to focus on something in front of her.

"Hmm?" Her head turns toward mine. "Yeah. I'm here. Can't really get too far away. How long's the drive?"

I give her a quick look, thinking she's messing with me, but she grabs her bag from the floor and opens it to show me a slightly crumpled paper bag from Royal Grounds.

"I brought breakfast, but if we get hungry for something other than pastry, I can Google some restaurants that are on the way. If you want."

She's not messing with me.

"Uh...a little over six hours," I tell her and choose my next words carefully, gently. "Didn't we just have this conversation, except instead of food we were talking about where and when we'd stop to use the bathroom?"

Her ivory cheeks turn a shade of pink, and she looks away, her eyes back to the window.

"Pippi?" I ask. "Are you okay?" Something is off. Maggie's always so focused. I think about that text from Nat after Sunday brunch, Maggie not remembering Vi's name. Now she's blanking on a full conversation. Maybe she doesn't want this. I pressured her into that brunch, right? Made it seem like it wasn't a big deal, but how could it not be? I brought her home, let her see what no one else sees—me. The realization is a punch to the gut. What this weekend means to me is beyond the confines of our agreement, and I let my hope blind me to the possibility that Maggie might not want what I'm starting to admit I do.

She waves me off but doesn't look at me when she speaks. "I'm fine," she says. "I'm sorry. I guess I'm...nervous?"

I glance in her direction and catch her reflection in the pane of glass. I expect something along the lines of a shy smile, something that tells me no matter how nervous she is—and shit, I am, too—that she wants this, whatever this is we're doing. But her eyes are closed, no trace of a smile on her face, so I focus on the road and try not to read too much into the look, or her questions that keep repeating. Because if I do, I'll tell myself she's having second thoughts, that she's filling the silence with random chitchat in order to avoid anything else.

I have to say something, so to escape any further complication, I grab her hand from her lap and give it a squeeze.

This, at least, separates her from the window as her eyes go from our hands to my face.

"It's okay," I tell her. "I'm nervous, too."

She releases her grip, and I exhale, prepared for her to pull away completely, to ride the hours we have left in silent contemplation of interstate cornfields. Instead she adjusts her grip, threading her fingers through mine and squeezing tighter.

"Oh thank God," she says. "I mean, it's not like it's any different than spending the night at your place, right? We've done that before. But somehow it's…"

"Different." I finish her thought because I've been thinking the same thing.

I bring our hands to my mouth and press my lips to her fingers.

"And…" She hesitates. "This girl, Jordan, she's kind of important, right? You haven't told me much. Not that it's my business because it's not. I mean—"

This is why I haven't said much. Because what do I say that doesn't make me look like an ass, that doesn't remind her who I was a couple weeks ago—and in her eyes, who I still might be?

"Shit," I say, and now she does take her hand back.

"Oh." It's her only response, but the sound of the word says enough. *Oh, you had feelings for this girl. Oh, it wasn't important enough to tell me.*

Oh, we don't share important things because we aren't... What the fuck are we?

So I tell her the truth because—why not? Maybe this is what we need, proof of why, when it comes down to it, I've always chosen easy.

"She's from Chicago. We dated while I was in Scotland. Our agreement was we'd keep things casual, stay in the moment rather than worry about the future, because what kind of future is there with someone you meet in a foreign country and who lives in another state?"

She says nothing at first, only watches me, her top teeth dragging slowly over her bottom lip.

"So that's a bunch of bullshit, right?" she asks, an impassiveness to her tone, as if that could hide her judgment.

"What? Maggie, you asked, and I told you." Which was obviously a mistake, the reason I didn't say anything in the first place.

"It's bullshit, Griffin." Her voice stays calm but is peppered with anger. "We're on our way to Chicago right now to see her, a trip that would be easy enough to make monthly, weekly if you really wanted to. It's your stupid deflection—'Hey look over here at these stupid reasons why we can't be serious so I don't let myself get invested.' God. How happy you must be with all your casual relationships. It doesn't sound like a lonely existence at all."

Her voice trembles on the last sentence, and I veer across the three lanes of traffic to the exit ramp on the right.

What if

"What are you doing?"

I don't answer, only watch the road, exiting the interstate and pulling into the first gas station I see.

"Griffin. You're freaking me out. What are you doing?"

Once stopped, I throw the car into park and turn off the ignition. When I face her, the fear in her eyes dissipates when she sees what's in mine—not anger, not sadness. Just regret. Her hand reaches for my face, cupping my cheek.

"Did you fall in love with her anyway?"

I nod, the first time I've admitted this to anyone, including myself. Not saying the word, not acknowledging how I felt, helped me get back to old habits. Safe habits. But I thought I was safe back then, and I wasn't. With Maggie, I knew that first night the danger I was in, but I lied to myself anyway.

"She was in love with someone else," I tell her.

She shakes her head. "The guy with her at the reunion." I nod again. "I'm sorry, Griffin. It wasn't my business, and I…I shouldn't have gotten so angry. That had nothing to do with you."

My hand covers hers, holding it there, the heat from her palm warming me as the temperature in the car slowly drops.

"It *is* bullshit," I tell her. "But it's all I've ever known, and it's always been enough."

She keeps her eyes locked on mine when she asks the next question.

"Do you still love her?"

I shake my head without hesitation.

"No. I don't. It's been two years already. But I remember what it was like, her kissing me when I knew she wanted to be with him. I'm the asshole for letting it go on as long as it did. I don't want to be that asshole again."

She lowers her hand, and I loosen my grip.

"So the anger that you said has nothing to do with me? Anything you want to tell me?"

A long, slow breath exits her lips, and for several seconds she says nothing.

"No," she says, a finality in her tone. "We should probably get back on the road if we want to check in before the party."

With that she straightens in her seat, her head finding its resting spot on the cool glass of the passenger window.

We've kept ourselves closed off enough since the day we met that I realize I know nothing more about her beyond what she's let me see. Little by little she has cracked my resistance, slipped into the parts of me I tried to hide as well. And she's still here. But for every space I let her fill, she bottles up another one of her own.

She's right. It's bullshit. All of it. When it comes to Maggie, it's no longer enough.

Chapter Seventeen

MAGGIE

If there was a third person on the trip with us, her name would be Awkward Silence. And yes, she'd be a girl because, well, she's me. We made it through the rest of the drive with ample small talk about tastes in music and playing the alphabet game with road signs and license plates. But that was simply noise to fill an ever-widening gap. One that I created, have been creating even as Griffin and I have been seeing each other more.

Now I follow him in that same silence down a hotel corridor, wheeling my suitcase behind me to the room we'll share tonight, wondering if we'll really share anything more than the same space, the same pocket of time.

When he unlocks the door, he holds it open, ushering me through first, and when he follows behind, we both stop short at what lies before us. Thirty-six stories above the street, a picture window looks out over Lake Michigan. Griffin whistles while I gasp, and our shared reaction brings laughter from him and from me, and somehow the distance lessens, if only by a fraction of space, but it lessens nonetheless.

"Pretend you drew a WILD card," I tell him, searching for a way to stitch the gap even tighter.

"What?" he asks, his eyes abandoning the view for me.

"The Uno deck," I say. "A WILD card means you get to ask me anything. Pretend you drew a WILD."

Once the request is out there, I walk from the entrance across the elegant room to the window seat. The setting sun has the city ablaze in lights, their reflections dancing off the water. I sit, and wait, the promise—or maybe threat—of a question hanging in the air.

I hear him move, his footsteps padding across the carpeted floor. In the reflection of the glass I watch him perch on the edge of the king-sized bed, listen to his exhales, sounds that denote thought. And I wait.

"Tell me about someone *you* were in love with."

It's not a question, but his request asks so much. I spin around on the bench, let my back rest against the tall window. My lips press together in a line, and I shake my head, giving him what he asks for—the truth.

His brows rise in challenge before he reacts with words.

"You've never been in love with *anyone*?"

I laugh, though my expression feels like anything but a smile.

Now his brows pinch together. "I don't get it," he says.

I shrug, having answered his question. I don't have to tell him that in high school I was too focused on AP classes, on earning a full-ride to college so I wouldn't break my grandparents with loans. I don't explain that once my grandfather passed away, I started working at the coffee shop, even before starting at the U, to help offset my living expenses. Anyone I'd met, anyone I could have fallen for, wasn't enough of a distraction to warrant the time away from more important endeavors. I sure as hell don't let him in on how I lost my scholarship after sophomore year, when I could no longer attend classes full-time…or at all for what would have technically been my junior year.

And now—now there's this guy who is more than a worthy distraction, and for weeks I've been keeping him at a distance, but the pull is stronger than my push. Because for weeks, I've also been falling, and all it would take is one more tug from him, and I'd have no push left.

"Is that it?" I ask. "Because you can draw another card if you want." He leans forward, his elbows on his knees as he contemplates my invitation to ask more, to mend the ripping seam between us.

He stands and makes his way to the bench next to me. He angles his head toward mine, and I suck in a breath, waiting for his lips to be his response, and they are. Just not on mine.

Warm breath tickles my ear before I hear his voice.

"That depends. If I had another, could I ask you if you could fall in love with…*this*?"

His tongue flicks at my earlobe, and his teeth follow close behind, grazing and tugging, and a sigh of pleasure trickles off my lips.

"Or this?" His tongue trails the length of my neck to my collarbone, and this time a word forms.

"*Oh*." In my head I scream my response. *Yes! I could fall in love with…this.* But the answer will not form. Nor will the mounting question of *Why?* and *What does this mean?* and *How could you still want me when I keep doing everything in my power to push you away?*

As if he can hear inside my messed-up head, he answers my questioning thoughts.

"For this weekend only, shut everything else out… except me."

His ragged voice, filled with need, only has to ask once because my answer is a resounding, "Yes."

I wriggle out of my coat and, without further pause, rise up on my knees as I face him, lifting my top over my head and unclasping my bra, needing his mouth on me. One quick glance to my left assures me, despite the wall of windows we're up against, we are hidden in the privacy of our height above the city, nothing but the lapping waves of the lake to see us. I don't hide my need. He obliges immediately, after he lets out a soft but hungry groan.

His tongue tastes and then lips close around me, his hand making sure my other breast isn't left out of the fun. My fingers tangle in his hair as he licks and pinches and devours, and in my head I hear myself say again, *Yes! I could fall in love with this.*

Because of course it's more than *this.* It's always been more than this. But I can't say it, can't give him the three words I'll take back once we leave this fairy tale. So I return to that night at his place, when I stopped him before the words were too much to reciprocate, and I think it.

Griffin, I…

I let the thought dangle, unfinished, unsaid. If saying it aloud makes it real, thinking it plants the seed of reality, and

What if

I don't know how to make it grow.

I can shut it all out for a night. That much is true. I can wrap my arms around his neck and climb forward, my legs straddling him as I lower myself to his lap, his lips dragging up my collarbone, my neck, my chin — until they meet mine. And then — fireworks.

Chapter Eighteen

GRIFFIN

Chicago winters, brutal as I hear they can get, are nothing compared to Minnesota, and certainly not in November. So we walk the two blocks to the Hancock, Michigan Avenue ablaze now in holiday lights.

I check the time on my phone, a quarter after seven, and see a text I must have missed when Maggie distracted me on the window seat. Not that I'm complaining. She gave me an opening to ask her anything. Then she offered me more, which is exactly why I didn't take it from her. All I needed to know was that she was willing to let me into her secrets, if only for a small peek. And to touch her. God, I needed to touch her. Just thinking about it stokes the need, so much I'm almost willing to say *fuck it* to this whole reunion thing. Then my phone *buzzes* again.

It's Jordan, as was the previous message. Though her

What if

texts have lost their effect on me since Maggie came into the picture, there's a sort of twist in my gut, a knot in my throat, at the thought of seeing her again after so long.

Jordan: *You're late! Did you get my other text? We have a surprise for you!*

We have a surprise for you. *We* have a surprise for you.

"You okay?" Maggie's voice cuts through the memories, reminding me it's not Jordan I miss but the *What if?* What if someone like her could have fallen for someone like me? How different would I be now? Would Maggie trust me enough to let me all the way past her walls? Would I let her past mine?

I look away from the screen and into Maggie's green eyes and realize Jordan Brooks is not my *What if?* It's this girl in front of me right now, nose red from the cold and fingertips poking out of the openings in her gloves to grab the lapels of my coat.

I drop the phone back into my pocket, text message unanswered. We're late. And I don't give a shit. My hands cup Maggie's cheeks, and I tilt my head down, forehead resting on hers.

"What if?" I ask her, and she doesn't respond with anything more than the warmth of her breath mingling with mine, the air between us the only source of heat on a Chicago winter night.

"What if?" I ask it again, quieter this time, because maybe the question is only for me. Maybe this step is mine to take whether she's with me or not, because either way the risk is huge, but I don't want to walk into that building pretending. I don't want to face the person who didn't see me as a real option without proving to her—no, to myself—that I can be real. That I can want something fucking real more than my own self-preservation.

"Griffin, I don't understand…"

She doesn't finish because my lips are on hers, soft and questioning at first, until she answers by letting her mouth fall open, inviting me inside. And the hunger returns, not only for lips touching lips or the surrounding air warming with our exhalations. It's the hunger for *more*. More with this girl who hitched a ride with a stranger and still hasn't run for her life. That has to be *something*.

We break apart, but only because of the whistling and clapping from some of the Michigan Avenue passersby.

"Oops," Maggie says through a giggle. "Guess we have an audience."

"Guess so," I say, pressing a gentle kiss to her puppy-dog cold nose. I'm not ready for my lips to *not* be touching her skin.

"Maybe that's our cue to leave?"

I want to kiss her all over again for making her words a question rather than a statement, which can only mean she doesn't want to stop, either.

"Maybe." Her hand slips into mine, and she tugs me forward. Or maybe I lead her. Either way, we're moving again, the Hancock right in front of us and, therefore, the Signature Lounge.

"Quite the tourist location, huh?" I ask.

"It's beautiful," she says, eying the skyscraper from head to toe, her gaze landing on the massive Christmas tree that stands outside the building's exposed lower level.

What if

Her hand still in mine, I lead her down the steps to the base of the tree where tourists amass taking pictures with one of the city's most popular holiday decorations.

"Do you have your camera?"

She takes it out of her bag, brandishing it as her answer. I pull her closer to the tree and tap a picture-snapping tourist on the shoulder, a man taking a photo of what must be his wife and kids in front of the tree.

"Would you take one of us, and I'll get one of you with your family?"

He thanks me and hands me his camera. After getting a couple good shots of him and his family, we trade cameras so he has Maggie's, and we position ourselves in front of the tree.

"So…uh, this is awkward, huh?" she asks, and I understand. She's taken a few photos of me, but we've never been in one together.

"How about if we just smile?" I suggest.

She nods, but it's her next action that gets me. Standing on my side, she wraps both arms around my midsection, leaning her head on my chest. I wonder if she feels my heart hammering against her, an admission I'm still scared shitless to make.

My head dips to kiss the top of hers before posing for the camera, and tourist dad yells, "That's a great shot! How about one more?"

Maggie's shoulders shake with quiet laughter, and it's contagious. Whatever our photographer captures now, it's anything but posed.

"Thank you," I tell him when he hands Maggie's camera back to me, his wife and two boys standing next to him.

"You're a beautiful couple," she says, and then looks at

her husband with a grin. "Remember when we were in love like that?"

They both laugh and head back up the stairs. Maggie's hand sits in mine, but for a long moment we avoid eye contact, letting the woman's comment fade along with the flush of heat in my cheeks I know will give me away.

When I think enough time has passed to allow us to look at each other again, I turn to face her, asking a question I can't believe I haven't asked yet. "Is this your first time in Chicago?"

She nods. "Sort of."

My brows crease in question. Her smile fades, and her eyes do that far-off thing they did in the car, like she's looking past me or through me. In seconds her focus returns, and she sighs.

"My grandmother and I came for a girls' weekend early spring of my freshman year. We took tons of selfies everywhere we went, not caring that we looked like tourists."

She pauses, taking a couple of slow breaths, and I wait because she's gearing up for something.

"The trip itself is hazy, but those selfies are my best memories of anything she and I have done together. Because I can see my happiness in those photos and try to relive it. Hers, too, even though it was after we lost my grandfather." Another pause. "Griffin. I want to tell you something."

"*Oi!* Griffin, mate!"

The voice comes from up the stairs, and though it's been two years since I've heard it, I recognize it all the same. This is Jordan's surprise.

I let Maggie's hand go and turn toward the voice. Duncan. He barrels down the stairs toward us, embracing me *and*

What if

Maggie at once.

"For fuck's sake, man. We've been upstairs in this bloody fancy place waiting for you and your Maggie." He lets us go, backing up to look at us. "Jordan's been going on about you bringing a girl. I think part of it is for Noah. He's a little nervous. But she's happy for you, mate. Really happy. Anyway, I wanted to come outside, see all the lights now that it's totally dark, and here you are!"

Maggie's expression is wide-eyed, a mixture of shock and most likely delight because *not* smiling in Duncan's presence is an impossibility.

"Maggie, meet Duncan. We lived in the same dorm in Scotland."

"Neighbors, actually!" Duncan extends a hand toward Maggie even though he's already full-on embraced her.

As they shake, Maggie's surprise morphs into a smile. She beams all the way to her eyes, and I have to catch my breath at the sight of it. Of course Duncan brings this out in her. He brings it out in everyone. But I want that power, to make her smile like that again.

Duncan's dark hair has grown from the buzz cut he sported a couple of years ago, though he still keeps it short. I laugh when I realize he's not wearing a coat, only a navy sweater and dark jeans.

"No coat?" I ask him, and he shrugs.

"You're lucky I've got jeans on. I'm only wearing 'em because Elaina said I couldn't walk down Michigan Avenue in a kilt with this wind." He leans in, lowering his voice. "I think she's afraid the other lasses will see my legs and not be able to keep their hands off."

I raise a brow, and Duncan blurts out a "Shite! I ruined

the rest of the surprise. Okay, not all of it. I'll let Elaina tell you we're getting married."

Maggie and I look at each other and burst out laughing. Then we look at Duncan.

"Shite!"

We ride the elevator up to the ninety-sixth floor, the whole time Duncan pleading with us to act surprised not only to *see* Elaina but also when she tells us the big news. When Duncan gets distracted by a text he missed from the future missus, I take it as a moment alone in a space with no privacy.

"You wanted to tell me something downstairs, before Duncan showed up. Didn't you?"

She shakes her head. "It can wait. This is your night. Let's enjoy it."

Her eyes shift to Duncan, who furiously types a message into his phone, one that probably won't get to Elaina before we do.

"I will," I say. "*We* will, but on one condition."

"What's that?" she asks.

"One more WILD card, when we get back to the room tonight."

The elevator rocks to a gentle halt, the three of us emerging into the Signature Lounge. Duncan leads us to the small section cornered off for the Aberdeen representatives and alumni. I look for the unassuming, pixie-haired girl I knew two years ago but don't see her. Instead I'm greeted by a beautiful, vibrant woman with long, dark, wavy hair, brimming with confidence. Her arms are around me before my brain registers that it's her.

"Jordan? Holy shit. Look at you. You're beautiful." I speak the words into her hair, returning her embrace. It feels good to hold her, all my uncertainty melting away. Because while I can't believe this is Jordan Brooks in my arms again, the only feelings I have are those of gratitude and joy at seeing my friend again. My *friend*.

So fucking much has held me back from Maggie — my history, my family, any excuse I could come up with to look for an easy way out because I've always known, even growing up where so much seemed handed to me, that everything has its price. But it's always worked for me, never investing myself one-hundred percent — anywhere — so I've never risked the pain.

I was so sure coming here tonight would ignite old feelings, feelings I risked for Jordan that weren't returned, that couldn't be returned. Instead, holding her like this, it's fucking clarity.

Jordan and I release each other, a mutual letting go of the hug, and I grab Maggie's hand, hoping she can read something new in my touch — a promise that she's worth the risk, the potential for pain. I'm not letting go this time.

"Jordan…this is Maggie."

Jordan scoops Maggie into a hug. "I am so happy to meet you," she says.

Over Jordan's shoulder, Noah approaches, a slight tension in the set of his shoulders. If this meeting had happened a month ago, I may have responded the same way, apprehension in seeing the guy she chose instead of me. The one who gave her every reason to run, to say it wasn't worth the pain.

I get it now, enduring the pain for all the good that comes with it. And here they are, two years later. Together.

Okay, so the sting of rejection might still linger.

"Hey, man," he says, his hand outstretched.

"Hey." We shake, and that's when Duncan and Elaina swarm in on either side of us.

"No. No. This will not do," Elaina says, yanking our hands apart.

"Not a'tall," Duncan chimes in. "I can't spend the bloody night watching you two wankers act like you're still in Aberdeen. It's been two years, *aye*?"

Neither Noah nor I respond, and Elaina continues, her thick Greek accent emphasizing her insistence that whatever is between us doesn't go any further than right now.

"Noah, are you and Jordan happy? Remember, my offer still stands to kill you in your sleep if you hurt her. You can see that I am not above traveling long distances when the reason is important."

At this, Noah cracks a smile, and Jordan materializes next to him, her and Maggie somehow forgotten by us for the moment. Maggie stands to my right, hesitating.

Jordan wraps her arms around him, edging Elaina out of the way, and the glint in her eyes says it all. She *is* happy, a type of happy I wasn't capable of giving her, not then. Any doubt I had about Noah, about what he was willing to give to her, vanishes when I see him return her look, like she is the only person he sees, even after two years. And that's all it takes for the tension to vanish.

"I'm really happy for you guys," I tell them, ending Maggie's hesitation by grabbing the belt loop of her coat and yanking her close, so there's no more visible space between us.

"I'm Maggie," she says, beating me to the introduction, her words coming out with a laugh.

"Maggie," Jordan says, "this is Noah, and the bossy one is Elaina."

Elaina's brows shoot up, but then she says, "It is true. I am the bossy one." Elaina glances pointedly at Duncan, then back at us. "Why does no one look surprised to see me?" But she doesn't wait for an answer.

She wraps Maggie in a hug and kisses her on the cheek.

"He is a good one," Elaina says, nodding her head at me. "He drank my coffee, the first time I offered." She crosses her arm and huffs out a breath. "Jordan never drank my coffee. Where I come from, it is a great dishonor to refuse food or drink offered to you."

"What?" Jordan interrupts. "You never said...dishonor?" Her expression looks crestfallen.

Elaina smiles. "I am fucking with you, pussy lightweight. Let's see how you can hold your alcohol after two years of practice, yes?"

Jordan pouts, but a smile hides underneath the expression.

"No snakebites here," I say. "You have to have one of their specialty drinks even though they cost, like, a hundred dollars."

"Or..." Duncan says, resting his head on Elaina's shoulder from behind. "We could all share the bottle of expensive champagne I ordered. Because Elaina has something she wants to tell everyone."

Elaina pats his cheek lovingly, and I do my best to forget what she's about to say so I can act surprised.

Her smile takes over her entire face. "I am going to wear

a dress to my wedding…and the groom is going to w₍
skirt."

Maggie nudges my leg with her knee, reminding me t.
is where I'm supposed to say something, to react, but I a
ready know I won't get anything past Elaina's radar. When
do open my mouth to finally speak, Maggie beats me to the
punch.

"You're getting married?"

The question is tinged with sweetness, with joy, and I
know Maggie means it, despite her already knowing the
news. While I want to hug her for rescuing me, I realize that
no one is any match for Elaina.

Her eyes narrow on Maggie, who flinches at her stare.
When Elaina's gaze shifts to me, I'm positive she reads the
word *guilty* stamped on my forehead. It's when she cranes
her neck to look at her fiancé that I want to run for cover.
Nobody should watch what's about to happen to Duncan.

"You told them?" Elaina's voice is a low tremble. Then
she does the strangest thing. She…smiles. "Who the fuck
cares? I am getting married, and I am happy, and I want to
share it with all of you. Let us drink the champagne and then
decide if Jordan is still a pussy lightweight!"

"She is," Noah assures us.

"I am," Jordan adds.

At that, all of us burst into laughter as a server brings
over a bottle and champagne flutes.

"Let me take your picture!" Maggie says, attempting
to line us up in front of the unbelievable floor-to-ceiling
windows.

"No fucking way," I tell her, grabbing the camera from
her hands and then tapping our server on the shoulder as

ɔack to the bar.

ان you take our picture?"

says, taking the camera and backing up while
.ated.

ى my arms around Maggie, her back against my
ɩen I lean down, intending to say something in her
ᴉe's the one who speaks first.

"This isn't my place, Griffin. I don't belong here, as part
ıf this special moment."

Her voice strains, and it's more than a need to keep the
conversation private. She believes what she's saying.

I start to answer, and she cuts me off again.

"These are your friends, from this amazing year that I
wasn't a part of, and…"

"Pippi," I interrupt when she pauses for breath. "Can I
say something now?"

She exhales and nods against me while we face the server, who waits while Elaina decides which angle best shows
off her ring.

"You are here with me tonight because it's exactly
where I want you to be…and where I hope you want to be,
too. That means every part of tonight includes you—with
me. *Every* part. Because this *is* where you belong."

She stills against me, which means she's not running
away, at least from the picture.

Our server clears his throat. "I'm really sorry. I have
another table's order I was about to pick up. I can come right
back…"

Duncan stills Elaina against him in an embrace, placing
her left hand, ringed finger and all, on his right shoulder facing the camera. Jordan and Noah stand, arms locked around

one another, and I straighten, my hands clasped around Maggie's middle, enjoying the rise and fall of her slowly steadying breaths.

"*Aye*," Duncan says. "We're ready, mate. Sorry for that."

"Take three pictures, if that's okay," I tell him. "We're all going home to different places tomorrow. I think each couple would like a copy."

I don't realize the implication of the word *couple* until it comes out of my mouth. For years it has scared the shit out of me. But here I am, saying it and not wanting to swallow the word back up before anyone registers any meaning.

"Sure thing," waiter guy says, and I squeeze Maggie against me. She yelps with laughter, and I'm not far behind. He snaps three photos, waiting long enough for each to spit out the front of the camera. Each of the girls grabs her copy to watch it develop while waiter dude rushes off to his next table.

"See?" I ask, as the image of our combined laughter jumps off the face of the photo. "Right where you belong."

Chapter Nineteen

Watching Griffin with these four friends, he's the most comfortable with himself I've ever seen. This is him removed from the bullshit—the real Griffin. And it hits me. He can be who he wants to be if he can get out from under the crap he lets weigh him down. He has choices I don't. It's not that I begrudge him this, not one bit. But when I look at him, at the smile shining in his eyes, I want to think he can be more than the expectations he lets others put on him. What scares me is wanting to be a part of it all. If he chooses happiness, does that mean me? Could I give him what he deserves?

Most of the other attendees of the small reunion are Aberdeen representatives and students from years other than when Griffin was there. The only people he knows are the ones we are already with, so we crowd around a small table, ready to toast the newly engaged couple.

"Who's celebrating?" Duncan holds up a bottle of champagne, foam bubbling over the top. "I just spent one hundred fifty American dollars on this, so it must be good. But if it's rubbish, I won't know the difference because I've never had champagne."

We all stare at him.

"What? They don't have the bubbly stuff on tap where I come from."

Elaina laughs, patting him on the cheek with her palm.

Everyone holds up a flute. My hand rests on the stem of the glass in front of me, and when Duncan's brows raise in question, Griffin answers before I can.

"Maggie doesn't drink." He says it so matter-of-fact, like it's no big deal. So why does it feel like a big deal? Like maybe I was finding a place where I belong only to be reminded of all my restrictions, of not being like everyone else—like I was before all of *my* bullshit.

My doctor never told me I couldn't drink, only to avoid foods and beverages I thought could trigger or worsen a migraine. Sometimes I get one even when avoiding triggers. I'm well-rested, well-hydrated, and in case of emergency, I have my injection cartridges ready to go in my bag. All signs point to stepping out of my safety zone.

"Tonight I do," I say, raising my flute. "It's a celebration. I can't say no to what probably costs more than a dollar a sip." I smile at Duncan, and he beams. When I look to Griffin, he does the same.

"And here I thought you judged me when I drank," he says.

"I don't judge you. But I can't stand to see you abuse your body in a way that's self-destructive instead of celebratory."

What if

"Hmmm…" he muses, his grin turning wicked. "Abusing my body for celebration. I kinda like the sound of that, especially if you're involved."

"Stop," I say, sliding my glass of bubbly toward me, waiting for everyone else to get filled and for what I expect will be a short toast from Duncan.

"Stop talking about it, or thinking about it? Because I can do one, but not the other."

I snort, and thank God Griffin is the only one who hears, but then he says, "You're sexy when you make barnyard animal sounds," and my skin catches on fire, both with embarrassment and with the thought of his bringing out sounds and sensations in me I've never experienced before.

He leans in, making sure I'm the only one who hears him. "You're sexy no matter what sound you make, Maggie. Everything about you drives me crazy."

I suck in a breath, unable to respond, relief flooding me when Duncan begins his toast.

He stands, framed by the window and lights of the city, a sentimentality in his expression that seems out of character for the short time I've known him.

"When Jordan told me about this Aberdeen reunion, I think she was half taking the piss when she asked if we'd come. But when I realized it meant we'd all be here together, it wasn't even a question. I may have been pissed as hell on my birthday two years ago, but Elaina gave me the only gift I wanted — a kiss from her. The only reason she made good on her promise to give it to me was because Jordan and Griffin talked her into it."

Griffin's eyes meet Jordan's, and they share a conspiratorial grin. There's this whole life he has, and I know nothing about it. I envy her for having shared more of him than I've been given. But something shifted with us back at the hotel and then in the elevator here. For nearly a month we've been only what the other needs, an escape from who we are. What if we could be more? What if after we leave the city Griffin could be the guy he is tonight? My coat hangs over the back of my chair, and I shove my hand in the pocket, my fingers poking on the edges of the photograph of the six of us, of the names and faces too ingrained already to forget because they welcomed me like I fit. Griffin makes me feel like I fit. Me being here? This already is something more.

"So this toast is not only because she said yes." Duncan looks at Elaina seated next to him, his eyes shining with the threat of tears, and Elaina's cheeks already covered with them. "It's because we wouldn't be here without the two of you." He nods to Jordan and Griffin, and they both raise their glasses. "Now it's time to show I have the bloody testicles to share a secret with my soon-to-be wife."

Elaina blinks her tear-soaked eyes, and they widen. "Did you just use *testicles* in our engagement toast?"

Duncan laughs and continues. "Elaina." He clears his throat. "A year and a half ago, when the four of us traveled Europe for the summer—you, me, Jordan, and Noah—we flew to Greece when the Americans went home."

"Yes, I know this," she says. "But you still said *testicles* in our engagement toast."

"I told you I didn't know any Greek, but I lied." Elaina's mock annoyance fades as her eyes lock on his. "I was happy your dad spoke some English, but I wanted to do it properly. And one night when your mum and you were having a coffee with a neighbor, I asked him, '*Boróona pantrépsei tin*

What if

kóri sas?' I said I didn't know when but that someday I was going to ask you, and I had to ask him in person. So I did, a full six months before."

Elaina's tears flow freely now, and she stands on her toes, meeting her lips with his. Then she turns to us to translate. "He asked my papa for my hand eighteen months ago!" Her eyes go back to Duncan. "Okay then. My turn," she says. "Jordan and Griffin never had to talk me into it, not that I would have admitted to that. I was always going to kiss you on your birthday…and every night after that."

Duncan gasps, the first I've seen him lose his composure tonight, and the two kiss again to the applause of the four of us and quite a few patrons nearby.

"Don't mind us," Duncan says between kisses.

Jordan holds up her glass next, keeping the toasts going, a look of hesitation in her eyes I know is for Griffin's sake, but when I look at him, he smiles at her without holding back. His hand finds mine in my lap, and he squeezes it softly.

"I love you, Noah. I know I've said it a thousand times before. But what I've never said is thank you. I am grateful for your patience, for always putting us first even with your teaching, and when this master's program kicks my ass and I feel like the most selfish person in the world. Thank you for loving me through my self-doubt as a writer, through my crazy weekends of too much coffee, not enough sleep, and probably one shower too few. There's no one I'd rather navigate the crazy with than you."

Noah cups her cheeks in his hands. "You're welcome, Brooks." He kisses her. "I plan to navigate the crazy with you for a long time to come. I know it's not our time yet, but I *am* going to marry you."

Jordan nods and whispers almost too soft for me to hear, "As you wish."

As much as my heart is filled by watching these couples express their love for one another, I'm starting to feel less like I fit and more like an intruder, not on their lives but on Griffin's. We don't have these things to say to each other, at least not that I can admit. Not until he knows what it would really mean to be with me. I look at Jordan and measure myself against what seems an unattainable sort of perfection. Of course Griffin fell for her. I don't expect he'd have words like that for me. But with less than a beat, he turns to me, glass raised.

"I'm sensing a theme here, Pippi, so I want to tell you something." A sweet but nervous smile takes over his features. "I've barely known you for a month, but a part of me swears it's been years. I know what we said, what we agreed. But I want more than a WILD card. I want new ground rules."

My breath catches at his words, at both of us thinking we could avoid complication yet neither of us being able to do it. Because I want what he wants, too. I want to give to him what he's asking. So that's what I choose to tell him.

"Rule number one," I say. "You can have the whole deck."

The apprehension doesn't leave his smile, but it's joined by something fierce, a determination that makes me believe maybe I'm not fooling myself. That I can believe Miles and his trust in my readiness to take something for myself.

"Oh will you two snog already so we can drink?"

So we follow Duncan's orders, my lips rushing to meet Griffin's as we collide in a kiss that is the start of something.

"*Sláinte!*" Duncan yells, and Griffin and I separate.

Everyone holds a glass up high, and we repeat the word, one of the few in Gaelic I actually know.

Then we drink, the bubbles of the liquid popping on my tongue, down my throat—my first sip in two years. My eyes drift shut as I hold on to the taste, the memories that go with it.

"Hey, slow down there, Speed Racer."

When I open my eyes, Griffin raises a brow at my glass. Without realizing it, I drained three quarters of it on my first swig. A different kind of heat floods my cheeks now, one filled with bubbles that rise and pop at the top of my glass as Duncan tops me off.

"I'm good," I tell him. "I feel...good."

Duncan and Elaina fall into conversation with Jordan and Noah, but Griffin keeps his eyes on me.

"Did you really mean it?" he asks. "The whole deck?"

I nod and take another sip, my inhibitions crumbling with each one—and along with it the wall I've kept between us.

"Well, that depends," I say, threading my fingers through his free hand. "Does it mean no more phone numbers on your palm?"

I expect him to laugh or maybe look surprised at the forwardness of my question and what his answer would mean. Instead his brows knit together. Then he shakes his head like he's pushing away his thoughts.

"What?"

He untangles his hand from mine and places it on my cheek, heat adding to heat.

"Tell me you see me differently, that you trust I'm not the guy I was before I met you."

"Yes," I admit. "That's the part that scares me. You're willing to give me something I never asked for, and what if I can't do the same? What if you find out *I'm* different than you think I am?"

"I don't understand."

"Something happened," I start. "I had to take a year off, and now I'm part-time and…"

"Food!" Duncan yells. "I was getting bloody hungry! Thanks, mate."

The same server who took our picture arrives at our table with loads of appetizers, compliments of the reunion committee. Our pocket of privacy dissolves as everyone turns to the table and digs in to the array of dips—hummus and pita, black bean dip and plantain chips, and my favorite, guacamole.

Griffin's eyes search mine for a moment, but I shake my head. We'll have to finish talking later, and I realize I want to be sober when I tell him, and each sip takes me further from that possibility. Tonight can be fun without complication. We have six hours in the car tomorrow to unload baggage.

So we eat. And we drink, the set of Griffin's shoulders relaxing with each new conversation and each pour of the second and modestly less-expensive bottle of champagne. I surprise him when I pull an Uno deck from my bag, something I found buried in my nightstand drawer, a reminder of one of the hardest times in my life. But after the second night I spent at Griffin's, the date that wasn't a date, seeing the deck evokes new memories. Memories that include him. Memories that, despite the constant threat, have yet to fade.

"Uno! Oh my God, I love that game!" This comes from Jordan who bounces in her chair with excitement.

What if

"You guys want to play?" I ask, my words slow and methodical as I consciously try to avoid a slur.

Duncan and Elaina shrug in unison.

"We'll teach you," Noah assures them. "It's easy. And really competitive if you want it to be." He smiles, and Jordan pushes a dark wave of his hair from his forehead before she plants a kiss in the same spot, and he starts explaining the rules to our foreign friends, like the girl he's head over heels for touches him like this, shows her love for him in this way, all the time. And I realize she must.

"Perfect," Elaina says when Noah finishes. "I will kick all of the asses."

We laugh as Griffin empties the deck from the box and begins shuffling.

"How about teams?" he asks. "Couple against couple?" He pushes back his chair, patting the spot on his lap. I don't think twice about abandoning my chair for a more preferable seat.

But something about the jarring movement rocks my brain between my ears.

No. No, no, no, no, no.

I felt great. One-hundred-fifty percent fine. Better than I have in years. Yet when I look at my glass, my perpetually filled glass, I don't know how many I've had. What I do know is champagne is the *only* beverage that's passed my lips. Meaning no water, nothing to cut the speed of the alcohol's effects, which I knew had the potential to be stronger than usual because of my blood thinners. I thought I was handling myself well enough without diluting. But the dehydration. I forgot about the dehydration.

"I'll be right back," I tell Griffin, attempting to stand

from my position on his lap. The words don't sound right, though. Too slow. Definitely slurred, and spots like sunbursts form in the corners of my vision.

My elbow gives out, and I fall back onto him. I bury my face in his neck and try to articulate the words, my palms sweating against his shoulders. The words don't come, so I squeeze my eyes shut, blocking out any light that threatens to speed the progression.

"Maggie." Griffin's voice. I love that voice but right now wish he would just shut up. Quiet. I want quiet.

"Damn it," he says, but he's not talking to me. I can tell his head is turned. "She told me one of the reasons she doesn't drink is because alcohol triggers her migraines. I'm a fucking idiot for not slowing her down."

"You need to get her back to the hotel." Another male voice, unaccented. Noah, then. "My mom gets migraines. She needs dark, and quiet, and water. Maggie needs to get some water in her."

I nod my head against Griffin and find my voice.

"Good idea." I breathe against him. And then, "I'm so sorry."

Minutes later I'm propped in Griffin's arms in the elevator, and then he helps me into a cab. I'm too drunk and too close to losing my lunch all over the cab that I don't bother to ask why we're driving two blocks. Because duh. I'm a fucking mess. That much I know.

Somehow I make it back to the room without hurling all over the cab, but the second we're in the door, I run for the bathroom, slam the door behind me, and make it to the toilet with zero time to spare.

The experience is sobering but in no way a relief.

What if

"Maggie? Are you okay? Please let me help you."

Griffin's voice is soft behind the door. He doesn't knock, and this tiny gesture tugs at my insides...as does a bout of dry heaving.

His voice sounds again, but he's not talking to me.

"I don't know what to do. She locked the door." A pause. "I don't know how to deal with this."

Translation: He can't deal with this. He can't deal with me.

I flush the toilet when the dry heaving subsides and I'm able to make it to the sink, my eyes open in the pitch darkness. After splashing my face with water yet having no clue what he'll see when I emerge, I open the door enough let my head and arm through.

They're all here, sitting in wait on the window bench, but Griffin is at the door seconds after it clicks open.

"I need my bag. I have medication to fix this. You all should go back and enjoy your night."

Griffin hands me my bag. He must have carried it home because I have no recollection of even putting on my coat, let alone grabbing my things.

"Thank you," I say, closing the door without another word.

More than once my grandmother had to perform this duty. Even Miles has done it once. Yet despite the state I'm in, I can't ask for Griffin's help. As much as everything in his eyes said he wanted to give it, he's right. He can't handle this. *I* can't handle this. I'm not ready. I can't get out from under the bullshit like he can. If he stays with me, I'll only bury him further.

Sliding down the wall opposite the sink, I silently rescind

my offer to change the ground rules or to offer him the full deck. The cartridge in my hand lays the foundation for new rules. Or rather, a return to the old.

A clean break. No bad feelings. We walk away. That was the deal for when things got complicated. And I just complicated the fuck out of everything.

I roll up my sleeve and press the injection cartridge to my upper arm. My thumb presses down on the blue button, and the needle enters my skin.

One. Two. Three. Four. Five.

I pull the cartridge away and unclench my teeth, depositing the medical waste back into its case to dispose of at home.

Then I curl up on the rug and wait, eyes squeezed shut against the throb, and hope they'll all leave, return to their night and their lives that I got to be a part of for at least a few hours. Tomorrow it'll be nothing but a memory. Or this time, if I'm lucky, not even that.

Chapter Twenty

The four of them watch me pace in front of the bathroom door. I'm helpless. She's in there, in pain, alone. And I can't do a fucking thing about it. Scratch that. I could have done something. I could have *remembered* why she doesn't drink in first place instead of enjoying her drunk and flirty and *fuck*. She was ready to trust me, to give me something more, and I blew it because I thought she was sexy when she let herself go.

"Hey, mate," Duncan says. "You want me to go downstairs and grab you a pint? Help ya calm down and deal with…" He points to the bathroom door.

"I don't know what's going on," I say. "I don't know how to handle this."

"Griffin." A hand grabs my shoulder, and I stop moving, her voice soft in my ear. Jordan.

My eyes lock on hers, desperate for some sort of

reassurance.

"Griffin, you *can* handle this. Whatever it is, you can do this."

I shake my head. "This isn't the first time something strange has happened with her. Last week, at my parents' house…" Jordan's brows pull together, and I realize there's too much to explain, especially since I don't know what's going on myself. But the text Nat sent after brunch, the one I ignored for my own selfish needs, replays in my head. I don't deserve this girl, not when I seem to keep putting myself first. "I already fucked up. She told me about the migraines, and I didn't think. I was having too much fun. I didn't think about the consequences of what she was doing, that she was putting herself at risk to make everything go well for me. That's not handling shit. In case you haven't noticed, I'm not big on responsibility. She needs someone better."

"We're going to go play Uno in the lobby," Noah says, leading Duncan and Elaina to the door.

"No good-byes yet, *aye*?" Duncan asks, and I nod.

"Maggie doesn't need us all here when she comes out." Noah sneaks a kiss from Jordan. "You stay. We can have a drink in the bar here when you get back down," he tells her. "You, too, man," he says to me. "She's going to want to sleep. We're happy to hang at the hotel for the rest of the night so we don't have to cut the visit short."

"Thank you," I say. "Are you sure it's okay if Jordan…" I don't know how to finish the question, and luckily I don't have to.

"No worries. You guys need to talk."

Jordan squeezes him in an embrace. "Yawp," she whispers to him.

What if

"Yawp," he whispers in return, his head buried in her hair. Though I have no idea what the word means, I know what it means to them.

When the door closes, I call quietly to Maggie again, but she doesn't answer. Jordan heads back to the window bench, tapping the spot next to her. Because pacing does nothing to calm me, I sit.

"Do you remember," she starts, looking out at the star-speckled sky, "when you told me I could have reformed you?"

I sigh, leaning my head against the glass. "Thanksgiving two years ago."

"Mmmm-hmmm." She spins so her back is flush with the window like mine, her legs dangling over the end of the bench. "But you never looked at me like you look at her."

She says this not with jealousy or anger but with a smile and something that sounds like hope.

"I know," I say. "Could you have, though? If things had been different, could you have seen me as someone who was worth it?"

Maybe the question isn't a fair one, but it's one that's always lingered at the back of my mind, if Jordan saw me as anything different than what I let rise to the surface—if Maggie could really see past the guy I was when she met me.

"Is that what you think? That I never saw you as worth it? Griffin, I should have fought harder to show you how I felt. I'm the one who messed up. Not you. You're worth everything, and there's a girl in there who's been looking at you all night like you're the freaking air she breathes. She needs you."

Needing her is what scares the shit out of me.

She spins to face me, one leg still dangling. "You know, in some ways Aberdeen was both the most painful year of my life and the best one. I think that's where you are now, sweetie. The good is *so* good. It really is. But you'll miss out on it if you don't also accept there will be some pain."

My eyes meet hers, and she smiles. Again I'm taken aback by how much she's changed, how much I can tell she's grown since I saw her last.

"When did you get so wise?" I ask her.

She laughs. "I surprise even myself sometimes with my endless fountain of wisdom."

"Can I hug you?"

"Most definitely." She slides closer and wraps her arms around me, this stranger I thought I knew. "Tell her how you feel," she whispers to me. "Let her in, and she'll do the same for you."

"You make it sound so easy," I say.

"It's scary as fucking hell to tell someone you love them, Griffin. But you want to know what's worse?"

"What?"

"Never saying it at all."

She kisses my cheek, and the bathroom door creeps open. Maggie stands, framed in the blackness of the unlit room. She is pale. That much I can see. As she emerges into the lit bedroom, her usually vibrant green eyes are blood-shot, dark circles underneath. The left sleeve of her shirt is pushed high above her elbow, and a small circle of dried blood shows on her upper arm.

I want to go to her, ask her for answers, but something in her stance tells me to keep my distance.

"I'm...I'm so sorry for ruining the night. I'm going to

What if

take a quick shower and then go to bed." She smiles at Jordan. "It was so nice meeting you all. Please take Griffin back to the party and enjoy what's left of the evening."

Jordan ignores the stay-away vibe and heads right for Maggie, hugging her.

"We're so happy you're okay. We'll head back down for a drink or two. We're hanging at your swank hotel now. But only on one condition, that this isn't good-bye yet. There's a Starbucks across the street. Meet for coffee in the morning?"

Maggie nods, and I'm filled with relief. Because I'm not heading back down with Jordan, not yet. I'm not leaving this room until I know Maggie is okay, and if that means waiting until she showers and falls asleep, so be it.

"I'll be down in a bit, then," I say, and Jordan flashes me a look of understanding.

"See you soon," she says, wrapping her arms around my neck.

"See you soon."

"And you..." Jordan looks at Maggie as she backs toward the door. "I'll see *you* in the morning."

Maggie forces another smile. "Sure. See you in the morning."

When Jordan's gone, I follow her lead and ignore whatever it is Maggie is doing to keep me away, and as soon as my hands cup her cheeks, her tears begin to fall.

She opens her mouth to say something, but I don't let her apologize, not again, not for something that is as much my fault as it is her own.

"It's my turn," I tell her. "My turn to say I'm sorry. You told me this could happen. You told me, and I didn't take it seriously. I'm so sorry, Maggie. God, if this weekend was some sort of test for us, I fucking failed. I should have been there for you, and I wasn't."

The tears keep falling, and I kiss them as they do, the word *sorry* spilling from my lips over and over again. Maggie makes no move to kiss me back.

Finally she's able to talk through the tears.

"I need to clean myself up." Her voice is flat aside from the tremble of the ebbing sobs. "Then sleep. You should go be with your friends."

She pulls free, grabbing her toiletry bag from the top of her suitcase, and then she retreats into the bathroom again, closing the door while I stand there alone.

My first instinct is to follow Jordan downstairs. To run. When a girl heads to the bathroom in tears, that's always my sign for an exit. It would be so much easier. If Maggie doesn't want me here, then I don't need to *be* here.

But even if she doesn't want me, she sure as hell needs me — needs *someone*. And I'm her only choice. So I sit on the foot of the bed and wait, and when she emerges in a T-shirt and shorts, hair wrapped in a towel, and her red eyes evidence that she spent the whole shower with tears streaming, I still don't move.

"I'm not going anywhere," I tell her.

She lets out a long breath and joins me at the foot of the bed, unraveling the towel before resting her head on my shoulder.

"Okay."

On the rare occasion I stay the night at my parents' house

What if

and Nat's around, she sometimes goes out on her own, leaving Violet to spend the night in the room my parents have made for her. I don't know what Nat does when she's *out*, but it's nice to see her take time for herself. Watching Violet is beyond easy. The girl can practically take care of herself. And when I tuck her in at night, I always know Nat is a phone call away, or my parents are down the hall. The responsibility of taking care of Vi has never been solely placed on me. Not for real, anyway.

But as I tuck Maggie in now—groggy from her medication and the aftermath of the migraine—I'm struck with an awareness. If I fuck up with Maggie in any way, I have no back-up, no support. I'm on my own.

I lie behind her on top of the blanket, my finger tracing circles on her shoulder.

"You're going to go downstairs with them, right? I won't be able to sleep if I know you missed the rest of the night with your friends."

Even as she says them, her words slur with a heaviness of sleep I can't begin to comprehend.

"I'm not drunk anymore," she assures me with a small but painful laugh. "The migraine and the meds knock me out."

I kiss her cheek, and she sighs, her eyes closed and her breaths deepening.

"Thank you," she says dreamily. "It was a really good night until it wasn't. I don't expect you to know how to handle…" The rest of the sentence drops off, and I want her to stay awake long enough for me to convince her.

"It still is a good night," I say quietly, but she doesn't respond. "Maggie? Are you awake?" Again, nothing. "Nothing's changed. I want the full deck," I say, my lips brushing her temple.

It hits me how much I want it, how much I want more not only with Maggie, but *more*.

I look at the clock on the nightstand. Eleven-twenty. If I know him at all, I know my father is awake, catching up on paperwork in his home office or enjoying his Jack on the rocks on the screened-in porch.

Full deck.

If I'm going to be all-in with Maggie, I have to do the same with the rest of my life. I have a choice. I've just always opted for the easy way out, even if it means sacrificing what I want. I have to stop hoping my family will get sick enough of my bullshit to not want me to fulfill this plan they've set out for me ever since I was born with the one piece of anatomy my sisters didn't have. I thought it sentenced me to a life of becoming not only my father in name but in everything else. It's what I've been raised to believe and what I've been trying to escape. For the first time I need to choose what *I* want. Even if I have no idea what that is. Even if there's risk. And fucking hell, there is risk.

I stare at his cell number on the screen of my phone. All I have to do is tap send to change everything.

He answers on the first ring.

"Hey, Dad. We need to talk."

Chapter Twenty-One

MAGGIE

Coffee with the Scotland gang isn't as mortifying as I expect.

"We missed you last night," Jordan tells me. "I'm so glad you're feeling better."

"Thank you," I say.

"I once got so drunk I woke up on a round-about in the middle of town." This from Duncan, and with it Elaina rolls her eyes while the rest of us laugh.

"And you wonder why it took me so long to kiss you. *That* is why. You were a boy. I had to wait for you to become a man."

Elaina sips her espresso like it's water, and Duncan whispers to the rest of us, "Probably shouldn't tell her it happened after she snogged me, *aye?*"

She smacks him on the shoulder. "I can hear you!"

Again the laughter and Duncan telling her, "I know!"

This is how our short and final visit goes until it's time to leave. Duncan and Elaina are staying a few more days with Jordan and Noah, first at Jordan's family home in the suburbs, then in Ohio, where Jordan's in grad school and where Noah teaches.

"You guys should come to my parents' place. It's less than an hour away."

Jordan's invitation is sincere, and had last night not gone the direction it did, I might hope for Griffin to accept. But I'm relieved when he shakes his head.

"We should get back," he says, with no further explanation, but Jordan offers us both an understanding smile.

She hugs me tight. "He's worth the fight," she whispers.

I swallow hard at her wish because less than twenty-four hours ago it was mine, too. But it was a silly wish, a silly wish for a girl who's way more of a handful than any guy could bargain for, especially this one. Griffin has enough to deal with without having to worry about the next time I disintegrate in public. He said so himself. And let's face it, my track record for the past couple weeks has been shit.

Something is up with him, though. He gave me space this morning because he could tell I needed it, so we haven't talked much. He should be sad to say good-bye to his friends. Maybe he is, but for some reason he's beaming, an unwavering smile on his face despite Elaina and Duncan tearfully embracing him. He and Noah even hug, proof they must have smoothed over any strain they may have felt in each other's presence.

"Why does this seem more difficult than it was two years ago?" Jordan asks as she wraps her arms around Griffin. "We'll do this again, right? Tell me this is proof we don't have to wait two years again."

I watch his smile waiver. Long-distance relationships of any kind aren't easy, friendships included.

Griffin grabs my hand before answering her. "I think last night was proof of a lot of things, one certainly being that I don't want to go this long without seeing any of you again."

Somehow we all end up in a huddle of sorts, and Duncan addresses the group.

"Did I forget to mention the wedding's next December… in Greece? I think you'll be needing one of those fancy cards to remind you of the date so you can buy your tickets!"

Griffin smiles, but it's not entirely sincere, as if Duncan's news isn't what he wants to hear. It's funny, the things you learn about people. It's in this moment I realize I know his smiles—when they're real, when they're not, when they're only for me. Something isn't right, but he doesn't want them to know.

"I wouldn't miss it," he says.

"Don't you mean *we*?" Elaina asks. "Your invitation will have a plus one." I flush not only with the heat of embarrassment, but of rejection, too. Because his first instinct was to think of himself alone. Not us.

"Right. Of course. We," he says, his hand loosening its grip on mine.

A minute ago he couldn't hide his smile if he tried, and now he plasters on a grin so fake I wonder how he can be the same person.

"We should probably get going." I nudge his arm with my elbow. "I mean, if you're ready."

We've all been standing on the verge of leaving for close to ten minutes now.

"Yeah. I'm ready. You all ready?"

The rest of the group responds in a chorus of "readies."

"So we'll see you next December!" Jordan says, giddy as she hugs us both again, and Griffin and I nod, not because we'll be there but because it's the only response we can give for now.

Then the mass of us moves out the door with final good-byes before we head to our respective cars. And as much as part of me doesn't want to ask, doesn't want to be rejected outright even though my mind about us is already made up, another part of me wants to know what could have turned off the gleam in his eyes so quickly.

"What was that all about?" I ask him as he opens my door for me. I'm not going to let him distract me with chivalry.

"What are you talking about?" But his voice is flat, his incredulity unconvincing.

I wait for him to round the truck to his own door, till he sits in his seat and slides the key in the ignition.

"Let me try this again," I say. "I saw you in there. Something had you all, I don't know, giddy. That is, until Duncan mentioned the wedding. In *Greece*. Because doesn't that sound like a shitty place to go in winter?"

He sighs, shoulders sagging in defeat. He rests his hand on the clutch, but we remain in park as he readies himself to speak.

"I graduate in May," he says.

I nod. This isn't news to either of us. So I wait for him to continue.

"And as soon as I have that degree in hand, my parents are kind of done with me financially. I can't afford one ticket to Greece, not to mention two."

He says all of this to the steering wheel. I don't understand what he means because all it takes is one look at the truck he drives, the clothes he wears, and, shit, the house he lives in to know this boy comes from money. If anyone can swing a couple tickets to Greece, I'm pretty sure it's the guy sitting next to me.

"That doesn't make any sense," I say, knowing his relationship with his father is strained but also knowing when it came down to it, he planned to do what was expected of him.

He turns to me now, the heat from the vents fogging the windows.

"I wanted to wait until we were alone to tell you. I wanted you to be the first to know, but now I guess I'm realizing the limitations of my decision."

Reason tells me not to succumb to the uncertainty in his eyes, to the plea in his look. But my body ignores reason when we are this close, and I lift my hand to his cheek. Was it only last night I undressed on the window seat for him, promising him something more? The possibility in that moment feels so far away, yet I can't ignore the charged air between us now, if only from a touch meant to comfort.

He leans into my palm and smiles softly, but the smile is real enough to tug at my insides, to fill me with an ache for what I am giving up.

"You're right. There's a lot I'm good at, and I'd be really good at joining my father's company. But it's not what I want."

I let my hand fall away, and my fingertips skim his jaw and neck. The charged air crackles to life, but I ignore it, push it down.

I ask him the question I asked in the library again. "What do you want, Griffin?"

He shrugs. "I don't think I really knew till I met you. Hell, I'm still not sure I know, but I'm getting closer. While I'm figuring it out, I applied for the AmeriCorps coalition. They have them in all major cities across the U.S. and I can handle staying in Minneapolis for a little longer." He lets out a breath, and I hang on the words, *till I met you*. "I want to tell myself it's okay to be lost, that it's okay to still be figuring it out because I've never tried to figure it out before."

At this I smile, and he returns the expression. *It's okay to be lost.*

A light laugh escapes his lips before his smile loses its easiness. "Bottom line is I've been waiting for my dad to give up on me, to see I wasn't capable of being his carbon copy. Instead he waited me out until I realized I couldn't live up to his expectations and be happy, too."

I grab his hand. "Griffin, this is big. It's huge, and amazing, and wonderful, and I'm proud of you."

He looks down for a second, and when his eyes meet mine again, they shine with pride.

My stomach flips at the sight of it, at him so happy with himself. The moment is short-lived.

"My apartment, my car, letting me travel and take time off—all of that was conditional. As long as I took the GMAT, got into a good business school, and actually enrolled in said business school, none of that would have changed. It was all a means to an end."

"But you changed the ending of your story," I tell him. "Isn't that what you want?"

He nods. "Now, yeah. But it wasn't always. Having my

future laid out before me like that? It was kind of nice. I didn't have to worry about what I was going to do with my life. I didn't have to make any big decisions. I could just… be."

I see the appeal of a life like that. It's the part of my life that will always be missing—a guarantee. But is a promise of the wrong future better than no promise at all?

"Was he angry?" I ask him.

Griffin sighs. "That's the part that kills me. No. He wasn't. But he was disappointed that I wasted all this time, all this money on an education I'm not going to use the way I was supposed to. He sounded…tired."

Like Griffin sounds right now.

"But no money," I say.

"No money. He said it's time I figure it all out. On my own. Should be interesting on a government stipend, but you said I'm creative, right? But it means there's no way I can make it to Duncan and Elaina's wedding. No way I can take you. And I'd want to, you know. If money wasn't an issue, I'd be asking you right now to promise you'll be my date."

At this he inches to the edge of his seat, his hip pressing into the gear shift. His hands find my cheeks, and I close my eyes, not able to deny the effect he has on me, his skin on mine.

"Shit happens, Maggie. So you got sick. No big deal. You met me on a not-so-spectacular morning after, and for reasons I can't begin to imagine, you're still here." Then he kisses me, his lips soft while day-old stubble tickles my chin. "I'm still here. I'm all-in. Full deck." More kisses, his warm mouth tasting of coffee and possibility. "Tell me you're still here," he says, pulling away for air. When he kisses me again, before I give him my answer, I open my mouth, letting myself taste him without holding back, and my resolve crumbles.

"I'm still here," I tell him. Because I want to give him something in the wake of all this uncertainty. I want to give myself a chance at a guarantee. At one for both of us. I thought we were supposed to be each other's escape. Maybe I was wrong.

We drive, the trip filled with conversation about Griffin looking for a job, finding a cheaper apartment, figuring out if he's going to stay in Minneapolis now that the possibilities are endless. We both avoid any talk of last night, which means I get to avoid dropping any bombs about my health, about last night *not* being an isolated incident. The day belongs to him, and I let him talk, let him process his new life. When we get back to his place, Miles waits in his car to take me home.

"I texted him," I say. "When we were getting close."

"Oh. Okay. I guess you want to get home and regroup. Can I see you later?" he asks. While there's nothing I want more right now than to forget about talking and instead find myself in Griffin's bed, I don't think he'll let me off the hook that easily. He's right. I need to regroup, get back into my routine. We don't need to rush into whatever this next phase might be. At least not today.

"I have a paper due Monday morning. Is it okay if we wait until then? Library at one o'clock?"

He bends toward me, his lips finding mine again, a kiss that is good-bye for now but says *There's no way we're finished*. This kiss is long, and soft, and achingly sweet.

When the kiss ends, he doesn't back away but rests his

forehead on mine as he speaks. "Library at one." He lets out a breath. "When do I get to be the one to take you home? Why do I feel like I'm in competition with someone else for your trust? I thought maybe, after this weekend, I had it."

When he backs away, his eyes rest on mine, intent and unwavering.

"There's no competition. Miles is my friend."

"Who gets to take you home."

He doesn't try to disguise the bitterness in his voice, and I can't blame him. I never asked Griffin to let me in, to open himself to me like he has. He did it anyway, and I took what he gave without giving back.

"You're right," I say. "He gets to take me home because he always has. It's second nature. I don't have a car, so when I need a ride, Miles is there because he's my friend. And you're…you're…" How do I come up with the words when this is all so new? What *am* I to him and him to me?

"I'm what?" he asks, the hint of a teasing smile on his lips.

That's all the encouragement I need. "More," I say without looking away. "You're—more. And letting you take me home means I have to be ready for that. I need to gear up to it, okay?"

A full grin takes over his features. "Okay," he says. "I'll take more."

I jump at the sound of knuckles rapping against glass and turn to see Miles outside my window. I open the door, and he greets us with an apology.

"I'm covering a shift this evening and need to get back to the shop. Otherwise I wouldn't, you know…"

"No problem, man," Griffin says. "Let me get her bag."

We all know the gesture is unnecessary, with Miles and me already headed to the trunk, but no one mentions it. No one stops us from one more minute of good-bye. And when Griffin hoists my bag from the truck, Miles grabs it before I can.

"I got it," he says to Griffin and then turns to me. "If I didn't have a shift…"

"Don't apologize again," I say. "I'll be there in a sec. Thank you—for coming to get me."

Miles nods, his soft smile an unspoken *I'm sorry* regardless of my request. When he heads toward his car, I close my eyes and let out a long breath. A beat to collect myself. A small pause to decide to get out of my head and into the moment. When I pivot back to Griffin, an easy grin is all it takes for me to rise on my toes and crush my lips to his, nothing gentle about it.

"Ow," he says, laughter mixed with genuine but hopefully minor pain. He brings a hand to his lip, and his finger comes away with a tiny smear of red.

"Shit. Leave it to me to seize the moment and draw blood instead."

His brows rise. "Seize the moment?"

"Shit," I say again. "That wasn't my inner monologue? My stupid inner monologue I decided *not* to listen to, and look how that turned out." I huff out a breath. "Yes. Seize the moment. I wanted to kiss you one more time, and normally I'd over think it, tell myself why I shouldn't kiss you again, that twice in the car should be enough, that I don't want to give you the wrong idea, that I'm not even sure what the *right* idea is. I just—I wanted to kiss you. So I did, and now we can add drawing blood to my list of fails for the

What if

weekend."

I cross my arms, and he laughs. A car horn gives a tentative honk, and I look past Griffin to find Miles's eyes on mine. That honk is meant for me.

"Pippi," Griffin says, his palms finding the small of my back, pressing me into the diminishing space between us. "At this point, you couldn't fail me if you tried. I'm too far gone, migraine or not, vampire or not."

Despite my annoyance—my fear—I let him finish the kiss, let his tongue slip gently into my mouth while the taste of him consumes me straight down to my toes.

Another honk of the horn, this one not holding back.

"I...I have to go. Monday."

"Monday," he says. "Though I'm not sure I can wait that long. I could come over tomorrow, tide us over until the library."

"Monday," I repeat.

I back toward Miles in his car, Griffin's eyes on mine the whole time. When Miles and I pull away, I give voice to those silent words.

"I'm going to tell him," I say, and Miles's face loses the intensity it wore when I first got in the car. I thought it was because he was going to be late for work, but it was for me.

"Things went well, I take it?"

I shake my head, huffing out a laugh. "No. I mean, that's not entirely true. At first it was perfect, the drive there—the hotel room."

I study Miles's profile as he drives, a dark brow rising along with the corner of his mouth.

"His friends were great, but there I was with this girl, *the* girl. Like, the one person he's fallen for, ever. She was with her boyfriend, and they're clearly in love, like *bonkers* in love, and they were all celebrating Duncan and Elaina's engagement with champagne, and the energy was crazy and charged, and I wanted to be a part of it, to show Griffin I *could* be a part of it, and…"

I stop for a breath as Miles brakes at a red light, not sure if I'm making any sense. When he shifts his eyes in my direction, I flinch at his darkened irises, at the immediate disappearance of his previous grin.

"Maggie, please tell me you didn't drink."

Because I can't give him the answer he wants, I look away and say nothing at all. We drive the last couple minutes to my place in silence.

Miles shifts the car into park but doesn't turn it off, so I release my seat belt and open the door to leave.

"You can't fault me for trying, Miles. And for fuck's sake, you better not judge me for it, either." At this I twist to face him again, and he blinks, his dark eyes closing and opening in what seems like slow motion.

Finally he says something, his tone soft and careful. "I'm not judging you, Maggie. I'm trying to make you see you don't have to play a role. You're not the same person you were three years ago. But guess what? I still love you. Because the real you is in here."

He rests his palm over my heart, and I roll my eyes despite his gesture tugging at my insides. I guess Griffin's not the only master of deflection. Miles is the closest person in my life other than my grandmother, yet I hold him at a distance, too—self-preservation as much as it is my attempt to keep him safe as well.

"You're a pain in the ass sometimes. You know that?"

What if

I smile at this. "You mean beyond the Jess-Logan debate? Because you'll lose that argument."

He sighs. "It's not an argument, only who has the magnetic pull. Logan's pole happens to attract mine. Jess attracts yours."

I let out a wild laugh followed by a snort. "You did *not* just talk about poles attracting poles."

Finally he grins, the mischievous one I'm sure attracts many...poles.

"Innuendo aside, think about it, Mags. Rory thinks Jess needs fixing and wants to be the one to save him or fix him or whatever. But that never works, trying to make someone who you want them to be—who you think they *should* be. It's not your job to fix *him*...or protect him, and it sure as hell isn't your job to fix *you*. You're not broken. You're who you always were, only different. Stop trying to be who you think you *should* be and be who you are. That's the Maggie I want. And I'm pretty sure it's the one he wants, too."

I grab his chin, letting it rest in my palm while I plant a kiss on his lips.

"You think you're pretty smart with your *Gilmore Girls* psychoanalysis."

"You're welcome," he says, as I start to exit the vehicle. "You know, for the ride and reminding you how amazing you are."

I slam the door and walk around to the trunk, rapping my palm on it so he'll pop it open.

"Lemme help..." he starts, but I interrupt him before he's out of his seat.

"I got it," I tell him. "You know, because I'm amazing and everything. I think I can carry my own bag."

The trunk pops open, and I grab the small suitcase without a problem.

"Thank you," I say when I make my way to his window. "For the *ride*."

I head up to my apartment, realizing I never gave Miles the rest of the details about last night. It doesn't matter. What happened, happened, and I can't change that. But Griffin's still here. He saw a hidden piece of me, and he didn't run. *That's* something.

So when my phone buzzes with a text, I'm only a little shocked that it's him.

Griffin: *Nat found out about my phone call and wants to throw me a 'Finally Growing Up' party. Can't say I like the title, but a party is a party, right? Say you'll be there? It's Friday night.*

I laugh at Nat's name for the party, but it takes nothing away from the pride spilling from the spaces between Griffin's words.

Me: *Wouldn't miss it. Just tell me where and when.*

Griffin: *I can pick you up.*

Me: *I'm working, but Miles will let me out of closing. Means I'll be a little late. But you can take me home. If you want.*

His reply is immediate.

Griffin: *Deal. Don't be surprised if I'm ready to leave*

as soon as you arrive, then.

I bite my lip, but the grin is too big to hold back.

Me: *Deal.*

For the first time in a long time, I can't wait for Friday night — or to show someone my place. To show *him* my place. To show him me.

Chapter Twenty-Two

GRIFFIN

The Kitty Cat Klub is a place where a crowded party can masquerade as something more intimate. I picture me and Maggie tucked away in the corner of one of the plush sofa booths, ignoring the throngs of people. It's not like anyone else gives a shit that I'm pissing away parental support in search of who knows what. They're all here for the open bar.

"Why are you empty handed?" Davis collapses onto the booth next to me, his signature Tanq and Tonic in hand. Though after one sip, he's left with a glass full of gin-flavored ice.

"Because you're drinking enough for both of us already."

He crunches a sliver of ice and sets the glass on the table in front of us.

"Wrong answer," he says and waves Nat over, who's busy with the server assigned to our little gathering.

"Is he sick or dying or something? Or maybe this is an intervention?" Davis looks at me and shrugs. "I mean, I never thought you'd go through with it, but I at least wanted in on the gig."

Natalie's eyes narrow at my friend, and I silently revel in the reaction I know is coming.

"What the fuck is wrong with you, Davis? No he's not dying. And who cares if he's not drinking? Is it some sort of badge of honor to slur your words by nine o'clock?"

God I love to watch her hate on Davis, have loved it for years.

Davis keeps his eyes trained on her as he speaks. "Reed, did you know your sister is hot as hell when she's pissed at me? It's a passionate sort of pissiness, don't you think? Did I mention she's hot?"

I ready myself to take another lap to make sure I haven't missed saying hello to anyone my sisters invited.

"Watch it, man. She's my sister. I can't be responsible for the irreparable damage she can cause to parts of your body I'm sure you cherish."

This does nothing to deter him from waggling his brow at her. "That's kind of what I was hoping would happen."

I slap him on the back before standing up. "You're on your own, man."

I kiss Nat on the cheek. "Cut him some slack," I whisper to her. "He did just get dumped."

She sighs. "Two months ago. I'm surprised she lasted as long as she did. A pretty package can only fool someone for so long before they figure out that this"—she gestures toward Davis, who swirls the ice in his glass—"is what lies beneath."

"Keep an eye on him for a few. Will you? I want to check in with Jen and Megan and see if—"

"She's not here yet, Griff. It's not even ten. What time is her shift over?"

I shrug. "She said hopefully she'd be off by nine, depending on how busy it was."

"Then she'll be here soon. And I don't mean to sound like Davis, but are you sure you don't want a drink?"

I shake my head and smile. "Nope. I want to remember tonight."

"I don't," Davis says, butting into the conversation with an outstretched hand brandishing an empty glass. "Grab me another while you're up and about?"

"Sure," I tell him, my sympathy overruling the need to give him shit for his behavior. I hope Nat can muster an ounce or two herself.

Jen is busy chatting up a fellow grad student, and Megan hides in a quiet corner on her phone with, most likely, the guy we've never met. I scan the place with false hope, not so much for Maggie but for the two people I never expected to show their faces but who I still wish would: my parents. The thought bears no logic other than them most likely being the ones funding the evening. A small part of me thought they'd come around, that they'd even be proud of me. But their absence overrides their financial contribution. I think about all the functions I've been expected to attend for them, all the times I showed up not quite on time or in top form and realize they must know how I feel.

When I belly up to the bar, I remind myself I'm grabbing a drink for Davis, despite the underlying desire to have a beer.

"The guest of honor, huh?" The animated voice greets me from across the bar—a blonde-haired girl, tall and trim.

"Uh, yeah. That's me."

She crosses her arms on the bar and leans in my direction.

"What can I get you, gorgeous?"

. . .

MAGGIE

I sniff the shirt I've been wearing all day. Coffee. I do the same to the one hanging in the back room, the one I brought for tonight. Coffee. My hair reeks of it, too.

"What are you waiting for, beautiful? I clocked you out ten minutes ago."

Miles hovers in the doorway, a package of filters in hand. I gesture at my attire and groan.

"What was I thinking agreeing to this after a shift? I'm all gross and coffee-smelling. You've seen the people he hangs out with. They're, like, fancy."

Miles convulses with laughter.

"I'm glad you're enjoying yourself at my expense," I say.

He shakes his head. "Since when do you give a shit and a half about what someone thinks of your clothes? Honey, most girls work to get your hippie-hipster-coffeehouse chic going. But that's you when you roll out of bed. He sees *you*, Mags, even though you hide. I think that's what's freaking you out."

I nod. "I'm good at hiding."

He peeks out into the shop, checking for customers no doubt, before striding in my direction. He drops the filters on the desk and wraps me in his strong arms.

"I know you are. I've been trying to find you for years." His voice bears no bitterness, merely a statement of fact. Because it's true.

I sigh, letting go of the tension as my head falls against his shoulder.

"You're closer than anyone else has gotten," I tell him. "And I'm grateful you're still trying."

He lowers his chin to my hair, resting his head on mine.

"You trust him?" he asks, and I let out a shaky breath.

"I think I do."

His arms loosen, and he backs away to look at me.

"Then get yourself to a party. At a bar. Where you will not drink."

"Where I will not drink." I don't need to learn that lesson twice.

Miles lifts the long-sleeved black peasant top from the coat rack and holds it up for inspection.

"So, you gonna wear the top that smells like coffee or the top that smells like coffee?"

I laugh and look down at my Royal Grounds T-shirt. Then I reach for the one in his.

"Gimme the *fancy* one," I say, and he releases the garment into my hand before turning back to man the counter.

After changing and letting my hair out of its ponytail, I swipe on some deodorant and lip gloss and head out to the front of the shop.

"Are you sure I can't drive you?" Miles asks. "You know Jeanie and George can hold down the fort if I need to run out."

This is true. Jeanie and George know the owner, and they've helped in a pinch before, but this isn't a pinch.

"I have the name of the club and the address on my phone. It's a quick bus ride, and then Griffin is taking me home."

A lightness fills me at saying this aloud, and I don't try to hold back the grin. Griffin is taking me home.

"Look at you," Miles says. "Fancy or not, you're stunning. You know that, right?"

My cheeks hurt as my grin widens. Tonight I let myself believe in possible.

"I'm leaving," is my only response, and I wave as I make my way to the door, bundled to battle the elements.

My wool coat and hat are nothing against the biting wind of an early Minnesota December. But the bus stop is close, and I've timed it perfectly. Within seconds of my arrival, I climb into the toasty vehicle and pull out my phone to double-check time and location. It's only nine fifteen, and I should be there within ten minutes. The Kitty Cat Klub. 315 14th Avenue.

My stomach fills with a butterfly dance party, and I giggle out loud, a mixture of nerves and excitement because tonight marks both an ending and, hopefully, a new beginning.

I look back through a week's worth of texts on my phone, each one a different form of Griffin double-checking that I'll be there tonight, as if I didn't already feel the pressure of how important this is to him—the importance of *me* being there. I'm still having a hard time digesting that and what everything about tonight means, which is why I never answered him with more than *I'll be there*.

As we approach my stop, I stand and hoist my bag over my shoulder, proving that while Griffin may have started as a distraction, thoughts of him—of us—are now a motivation, and I'm the first off the bus as soon as it comes to a halt. Scratch that. I'm the only one exiting at this stop, so there's no delay as I head in the direction of the party. It's only when I slip my hand into my pocket to retrieve my phone that I realize the best laid plans...

No phone in my pocket. I check my bag. It's not there, either. Because it's on the bus. And now, no bus.

I can do this. I remember the name of the club and the street it's on. Fourteenth Avenue. Wait, maybe it's Fifteenth. There was a fifteen in the address for sure.

No big deal. I can do this. It's only two blocks to Fifteenth and then at most a few blocks to the club. But my senses overload, and I second-guess myself. I'm already moving, though, so I keep going.

Only when I turn onto Fifteenth, the first two blocks are purely residential. Block three begins to populate with more commercial properties, and by the time I'm several blocks in, I decide that I fucked up. So I pop into a restaurant, the entrance packed with waiting patrons.

"Excuse me." I tap a stranger's shoulder, an older woman, and she raises a brow at me in response. "Um, do you know where the Kitty Cat Klub is? I think I made a wrong turn."

The woman rolls her eyes under a veil of severe salt-and-pepper bangs.

"Do I look like I know where a *club* is?"

She turns away from me and back into her conversation. *Way to be helpful, lady.* At least I caught sight of her watch. Nine-thirty-two. I need to go now before Griffin thinks I'm not coming.

The noise of the crowded restaurant reverberates in my

ears, disorientation affecting my equilibrium.

Come on. If I can get there, get some caffeine in me, I'll be fine.

I decide to cut through an alley that looks like it connects with the next block, Fourteenth Street, which is where the club must be. In my head Miles asks me what the fuck I'm doing, but I rationalize the alley as a shortcut and remind myself a can of pepper spray lurks somewhere at the bottom of my bag.

I don't recognize the alley when I enter it, but once a few feet in, I know exactly where I am…or at least that I've been here before. Because there it is, our wall. My silly mantra, *What If?* and Griffin's three memories, each in its own language. Forgetting for a moment the perils of a girl hanging out in an alley alone, I approach the wall, hand outstretched, and run my bare fingers over the words, his words: *Souvenir. Memoria. Cuimhne.* Griffin's memories for me, and a wave of recognition hits, knocking the cold air from my lungs.

I haven't forgotten anything about our time together. Not really. I had a couple lapses, but being with him triggered the familiarity I needed to remember. For the most part, the whole past month is crystal clear. *He* is crystal clear, even as the throbbing between my ears begins.

I feel around in my bag for the can of paint that's still there, and I add our names—*Pippi and Fancy Pants.*

Then I reach for what I need, the prescription bottle. Because caffeine won't be enough, and I can't let tonight end like our night in Chicago. But the flashing red-and-blue lights to my right tell me I won't make it farther than the distance I've already gone.

As the officer approaches, I back away from the wall I

was lovingly stroking seconds ago.

"Miss, did you paint this wall?"

I close my eyes and shake my head, futile gestures since the can is still in my possession.

"May I look inside your bag, please?"

Laughter comes without the accompanying smile. What would Griffin say if he saw me like this, ready to lose my lunch and a cop about to restrain me if I don't dial down the hysteria? If he couldn't handle me ruining our night with a debilitating headache, how would he handle this? He told me he was all in, but I never let him know what he was really in for. All I had to do was make it from point A to point B, to be there for him when he needed me, and instead... The hysteria morphs to tears. No one should have to *handle* this.

His hand rests on the cuffs at his belt.

"Those aren't necessary," I say. "I'll go with you."

He sighs, a look of resignation on his tired, aged face. "Follow me, then. The building owner has been on our case to find the person responsible for *defacing* his property. I gotta take you into the station."

The tears flow freely, but I still try to swallow back the knot in my throat, the rising bile resulting from the growing headache and my realization of what a mess I still am. I wanted to be ready for the full deck, to be what he saw in me. How can I let him see this?

"Of course you do," I choke out, knowing that with these words I'm also giving him my last semblance of hope.

We made the decision to walk away when things got too complicated. Well, it doesn't get more complicated than this.

Chapter Twenty-Three

GRIFFIN

"Come on. Let me buy you *one* drink. It's *your* party after all."

I check my phone. Ten-fifteen and no text or missed call. So I bite the bullet and shoot Maggie a text to make sure she's still coming.

> *Looking forward to your arrival so I can take you home.*

I set the phone on the bar to watch for her reply and decide to take Heather up on her offer.

"Aren't the drinks already paid for?" I ask.

She offers a coy smile and shrugs.

"I guess one couldn't hurt," I say.

She drops two shot glasses on the bar and fills them to the rim with Jameson's.

I raise a brow as she clinks my shooter and offers a "Cheers" before throwing hers back like it's water.

"Impressive," I say, following suit, my insides heating as the whiskey blazes a trail down my throat, chest, and stomach. She holds up the bottle, gesturing a second pour, and I shake my head. She's not deterred.

"So, who's taking you home tonight?"

Her tongue trails across her bottom lip as she fills our glasses again. This time she shoots without hesitation, no form of *Cheers*. And because my answer to her question is the one she doesn't want, I respond by taking my shot instead.

"I don't live far," she says. "If you need a place to stay."

She walks around the bar to join me on the paying side, bottle of Jameson's still in her hand.

"Another shot?"

My eyes shift to the phone sitting next to me, the one the whiskey made me forget. No missed calls. No waiting texts.

Damn it, Maggie. All day I ignored the doubt, pushed it away because tonight was not only going to be the start of something for me. It was going to be the start of something for *us*. But ever since we came back from Chicago, she's kept me at a safe distance all the while promising she'd be here.

"Gimme a second," I say. I try her cell again. This time it goes right to voicemail. At the risk of looking desperate, because—fucking hell—at this point I am, I call the first number she ever gave me, Royal Grounds. The voice that answers is female but sounds much older than Maggie's lilting tone.

"Royal Grounds. Can I help you?"

I need to know she's okay before I let the truth sink in.

What if

"Uh. Hi. Is Maggie working tonight?" I ask.

The woman inhales, a sharp sound I hear through the phone. "Oh. Yes, I mean. She was. She's with Miles now. I'm sorry. That was sort of a roundabout way to answer your question. I guess it would have been easier to say, 'No. Maggie's not here. Can I take a message?' I'm a little new at this. Sorry. Can I?"

I try to shake away the fog, but the whiskey fills every empty space inside me. It marinates with my words. "Can you what?"

"Take a message for when she gets back. Shouldn't be long."

My head droops, and I let out a long breath.

"No message," I say before ending the call.

I nod at Heather and shift my eyes to my empty glass.

"One more," I say and watch her pour. I don't notice until I've drained the glass that she has slid off her bar stool and currently stands against mine.

"Now," she says, inching closer. "Who's taking you home tonight?"

And her lips are on mine.

My eyes widen but then close on instinct. I'm not kissing her back yet, but I'm also not pushing her away. Because I fucking did it again. I let myself think a girl could see me as more than I was, that I could *be* more than I was. Maggie saw through the bullshit and stayed, until now.

How easy it would be to let this girl's soft, willing lips drag me back. To fall into a growing haze of the liquor, into the taste of whiskey and strawberry lip gloss.

"Shit." The word comes out as a whisper, a realization, and my hands are on Heather's shoulders, pushing her from me. Have I not changed at all?

"I need to go," I say. Nat's eyes meet mine from across the bar, and she strides toward us.

I bring my gaze back to Heather. "I'm sorry. I shouldn't have let you think... I'm sorry."

"Griffin, what's going on?" Natalie approaches us, the seething look in her eyes illustrating her judgment of me. "I thought Maggie..."

"She's not coming. She never was," I tell her.

I grab the bottle from the bar, pour one last shot, and throw it back.

"I'm sorry for being a dick," I say, handing the bottle to its rightful owner. "But I have to get out of here."

I push past her and my sister, making my way for the door, but Nat follows me outside.

"What the fuck, Griffin? What happened in there?"

Nat blows into her palms as soon as we hit the outdoors, but I don't feel a thing. Logic tells me I should be cold, but the growing heat of the alcohol warms me from the inside out.

"It was all bullshit, Nat. All of it. Fucking hell, you had the right idea all along. It's you, and Vi, and no one to fuck around with your sanity."

She wraps her arms around her midsection, her shoulder-length sandy waves lifting in the wind. "You mean with your heart. No one to fuck around with your heart. You can't even say it, can you?"

No I can't say it. But I don't say this. Because admitting it makes it real. It means I gave her my goddamn heart, and she lied to me. Maggie made me believe she saw something in me no one else could, but I guess she's a better bullshit artist than I am.

"She knew how important tonight was, Nat. I know you planned this big party, but it only mattered to me that one person was here—her. She couldn't even text. Just a big *fuck you* by not showing up."

Nat backs through the door and into the bar again, dragging me with her, and for some reason I let her.

"Can I drive you home, then? You'll freeze out there."

Her eyes, soft with pity, say it all. I see me the way my family does, the way Maggie must have seen me the day we met, the way she still sees me now.

"Look at me," I say, holding my hands up as if to say *ta-da!* "Look at what I almost did in there! I'm still that guy. I'd have stood my ass up, too. But…why now? Why like this? I need to know why she let me hope if it was always going to end like this."

I kiss my sister on the cheek and back out the door again. "I'm sorry for ruining the party," I say. I reach into my pocket and toss her the keys to the truck. "Make sure Davis gets home okay. Will you?"

She looks at the keys, then behind her at Davis, who hasn't left the couch. "Fine. I'll get him home. Just tell me where you're going."

"I need to walk."

"You're not wearing a coat," she says, worry tingeing her words.

"I'll be fine. I'm not going too far." Not too far if I was driving, but on foot the statement is a stretch. I'm almost out the door when Nat grabs my forearm.

"It wasn't a choice," she says, and my brows pull together. "To have Vi on my own. It wasn't a choice." Tears pool in her eyes, but she keeps talking. "He left me before I knew I was pregnant. I loved him, and he left, and he never knew he had a daughter, so I never told him. I didn't *choose* this life, Griffin. It chose me. And I wouldn't trade being Vi's mom for anything. Not ever. But you have a choice I would have done anything for back then, if I wasn't too proud to act on it. Don't choose to be alone, Griffin."

If she says anything after that, I don't hear it. I hear nothing but the *whoosh* of the door as it closes and the pounding of my pulse in my ears.

Chapter Twenty-Four

MAGGIE

A dull throb beats at my skull as I lean against the cool glass of the passenger-side window.

Miles unscrews the cap from a bottle of water and lifts it out of the cup holder to hand to me.

"Take something before it gets worse," he says, his voice gentle and reassuring. When I glance at him, his eyes are dark with worry, so I obey, if only to ease his mind.

"Thank you. I already hurled at the police station." I sift through my bag and find the oral meds for the continuing migraine, trying to make a late-night injection unnecessary. The cop let me take one earlier, but I probably lost it along with my lunch in the station's garbage can.

I swallow back the tablet, washing it down with large gulps of water, half of me knowing that hydration is another deterrent, the other half knowing if I'm drinking I don't have to be talking.

"I need to go back to relieve Jeanie and George and make sure everything is set for closing."

I nod, capping the bottle and setting it back in the cup holder.

"I called the bus company. They have your phone. I can swing by and get it on the way home. Paige is meeting us at the shop so you don't have to wait for me."

Again, a nod. Anything else is too much effort. Anything else will open the dam, letting everything spill out. And I can't. I'm too tired, of all of it.

"He'll understand, honey. All you have to do is tell him, and he'll understand."

This time I respond with a violent head shake, one that sets loose the salt-water blurring my vision.

"It's too much," I finally say, my voice a cross between a sob and whisper. "Getting lost would be one thing, Miles. But look at me. I'm a mess. No trigger other than stress and disorientation. I'm not ready. I can't do it." I wipe away the wetness from my eyes. "You weren't there, in Chicago. I heard him telling his friends he couldn't handle me, that he doesn't do well with responsibility. How can I ask him to be responsible for this?" I motion to myself.

Miles extends his free hand to wrap around mine, giving me a gentle squeeze.

"Mags," he says. "Do you know why I came to pick you up tonight?"

I sniffle and ask a reluctant, "Why?"

He kisses my hand. "It's not because I feel obligated or responsible or whatever label you want to call it. It's because I love you."

What if

My head falls against the cool glass of the window. "It's not the same," I tell him. "You loved me before any of this happened. You're grandfathered in. I can't ask him to take this on at the start, not when he's finally choosing to stand on his own two feet."

Miles nods slowly. I told him all about Griffin and AmeriCorps and having to live free of his parents' financial support as soon as he graduates.

"I'm so proud of him," I continue. "But I won't get in the way of him finding a place for himself."

Miles lets go of my hand and pushes a lock of hair behind my ear. "We'll talk in the morning, after you sleep. Deal?"

I force a smile. "Sure. I'll pay you back," I add. "For the fine. And for coming to get me."

Miles waves me off, but I know a thousand dollars isn't an amount he can part with.

As we pull into the parking lot at the Royal Grounds café, I see George and Jeanie straightening up the tables and Paige behind the counter, wiping it down with a rag.

Miles nods at our little helpers and smiles, and the corner of my mouth lifts as well.

"I'll meet you and Paige back at your place as soon as I'm done. We're having a slumber party."

My throat tightens at the thought of going home, where I was supposed to go with Griffin. "Okay," I croak. "Thank you. For everything."

We exit the car without another word and head inside. Paige beams, her smile obviously a reaction to seeing Miles, but when she turns to me her expression doesn't falter.

"I just need to pee," she says, bouncing with adrenaline or urgency or both. She runs around the counter to hug me before rushing to the staff bathroom in the back.

Miles thanks George and Jeanie for covering for him, and they both hug me on the way out, saying nothing more than "You're welcome."

Suddenly it's two years ago, and I'm home after four weeks of hospitalization. Though memories of those first few months are sketchy, I haven't forgotten the kid-glove treatment, the whispers when people thought I wasn't listening or couldn't hear.

She'll never be the same.

What if she doesn't recover?

I read if it happens to you once, you're at increased risk of it happening again.

To those who know me, I'll always be the toy they're afraid to take out of the box in case it breaks. Those who don't know me, they'll run for the hills as soon as they find out. Hell, I would. I am the definition of high maintenance.

My eyes focus on Miles's hand waving in front of my face.

"Hey...where'd you go? I asked if you wanted some caffeine to take with you."

I blink him back into focus and shake my head.

"I just want to go to sleep."

He folds me into his arms, and I sink against his chest.

"Paige and I will be with you, and I'll take you to your appointment in the morning."

"I can take the bus." I try to protest. He's done enough for me already. But he rubs my back, my hair, and squeezes me tighter.

"At some point, Maggie, you have to let others love you and help you without this guilt you carry around. You aren't responsible for what happened to you or how you've had to alter your life to fit your recovery."

He sighs, and I stay in his arms, safe from seeing his expression—safe from him seeing mine.

"No one sees you as anything less than wonderful, as long as you let us in."

"Maggie."

The sound of my name is hoarse and pained, and though I'm in Miles's arms, it's another voice I hear, coupled with a roaring of wind.

I look to the door, and there stands Griffin, brown eyes glossy with what can only be the effect of a drink too many. But his cheeks burn red from the cold, and his whole body shakes.

"Oh my God, Griffin. Where's your coat? How long were you out there?"

I break free of Miles's warmth and move toward him, forgetting for the moment how this night was supposed to go and how very differently it went instead.

"You're freezing," I say, as I raise my palm to his wind-burned cheek. No sooner does my skin meet his than he flinches away.

"I'm fine. I don't feel anything."

I see the anger and hurt and inebriation burning in his glassy eyes. The first two tear at my heart. I did this to him. But seeing him in this state fuels my anger as well. He has a choice, to self-destruct or not.

"You're drunk, too," I say, taking a step back. "Damn it, Griffin. I thought you were done with this crap."

"I thought you were going to show up tonight. I guess we both get a gold star for disappointment." Despite his intoxication, his words are clear, his voice calm. But the underlying ache breaks me. I can't do this. *We* can't do this, be the constant source of each other's disappointment. Griffin hasn't been drunk the entire time I've known him. I won't be the reason he falls back into these habits, not when he is finally turning things around.

Miles strides up next to me, placing a hand on my shoulder, but I shrug it off. "I'm okay," I tell him, doing everything in my power to mirror the evenness of Griffin's voice, to mask my pain better than his. "We have to do this."

A clean break. No bad feelings. We just walk away. We're too far gone for that, aren't we? I'll have to make him believe I'm not. I can't be the one to send him back down this road.

"I texted you," he says. "I even called over here when your phone went to voicemail. I thought something had happened to you." He breathes in a ragged breath, and I want to tell him I'm sorry. That it's my fault he's hurting. I should tell him I'm not ready for this, that I need help, that I'm not okay on my own yet. But his pity will kill me even more than his hurt. So I say nothing to make this easier on him in the short-term. He's better off hurting now before things get too far. Before I admit how much I've already fallen for him.

"I was with Miles." Miles stands only a foot or so behind me, leaning on the counter, and I can feel the tension seeping off his skin. He'll get over his anger at what I'm doing. Griffin will, too. We all will. That's what I keep telling myself. Eventually, I'll believe it.

"I know," Griffin says, his voice low. His body still trembles, and it takes everything in me not to go to him, to throw my arms around him.

"Griffin, you're shaking. Let me get you some coffee or tea. I think I have your Minnesota sweatshirt in the back."

"I don't want a sweatshirt, Maggie." Anger tinges his voice now. Frustration. "I want to know why. Why let it go on this long? Why come to Chicago? Why let me believe..."

"Griffin, I don't know what you're asking. I don't..."

"You knew," he says. "You knew what tonight meant to me—to *us*. I may be a lot of things, but I'm not enough of an asshole to promise you something I have no intention of actually delivering."

I squeeze my eyes shut. Because knowing this has to end, that neither of us are ready for the other, I can't bear him thinking the last few weeks meant nothing.

"I should have called," I say, hating the taste of the lie.

His hands rake through his hair, gripping the waves tight before dropping to his sides. It's then I notice his sandy waves are darker than normal. They're damp, as is his shirt. When I look past him, out the window, I note the flurries that must have started after Miles and I got inside.

"So this wasn't your way of teaching me some sort of lesson?" he asks. "Because obviously I failed, right? I mean, look at me. I'm exactly where I was a month ago. Hell, I'm exactly where I was two years ago, falling for the wrong person, trusting when I should have known better. Did you lie about him, too? Because things look pretty cozy. He does get to take you home, right?"

Miles steps forward. "Okay, that's enough, man." He stands next to me now, poised to move between us. "You're drunk, and you're going to say something you regret. I think you both need to sleep off the events of the evening and talk when you're thinking clearly." Miles turns his eyes to me.

"Before either of you do or say something you can't take back."

I hook my arm through Miles's, letting my hand rest on his elbow. Griffin flinches at the sight, and I pray for the floor to swallow me up so I don't have to look in his eyes anymore and see what I've done to him, what I'm still doing, all in the name of pushing him away where he'll be happier... eventually.

"There's nothing to sleep on," I say, angling to face Miles, but my eyes still on Griffin. "A clean break, right?" I shrug, a failed attempt at making this casual when it's anything but. "We walk away with no hard feelings. That was the deal."

"I thought we changed the rules." Underneath the anger, his voice pleads.

"I changed them back," I say, moving closer to Miles, squeezing his arm in mine.

"Maggie," Miles starts. "Don't do this."

"It's already done," I say, not fighting the tears.

"Are we ready for our slumber party?" Paige strides out of the bathroom but grinds to a halt when she sees the three of us in front of the door. "I'm gonna take a stab at answering my own question and say no."

Miles nods to Paige and motions for her to join us. "Take her home," he says, unlatching my arm from his. "I'll be there soon."

Paige lays a hand on my shoulder and asks, "Are you sure?" I nod, letting her lead me past Griffin to the door. But I can't keep from meeting his eyes one more time.

"I'm sorry," I say. "I really am sorry. But it's better like this."

Better for him, I tell myself. It would only be selfish to

keep this going.

Then I let Paige push through the door and take me to her car. She doesn't interrupt my quiet sobs as we drive through the empty streets back toward campus. She simply lets me cry, her free hand holding mine, no sound but my intermittent sniffles and vents filling the car with what must be heat. But I never warm up, my insides holding on to their chill.

When we get back to my apartment, I am hollow—no tears, no warmth. Paige piles blankets on top of me on the couch, then runs to her place for her giant pillows, the ones that will serve as bed cushions for her and Miles tonight.

But something propels me to move with zombie-like slowness to my bedroom. I stand at the foot of the bed, scanning the wall that spells out exactly who I am—reminding me of who I'll never be. Photographs and captions mock where they should comfort. I spin to face my bed, see the photo of Griffin lying in his on my nightstand—the perfect night and the photo I took just for me. Not to remember his name or a drink order. The picture is simply *him*.

I take a few hesitant steps to my desk where my Polaroid sits, pick it up and look through the eye piece, first at the photo of Griffin, next at my bulletin-board wall. Then I slam the camera down on the desk's faux-wood surface. Again. And again. I'm not sure what will give first, the desk or the camera, and when glass cracks and chips and spills out from where the lens should be, I know the desk has won.

Paige runs back in, a response, I'm sure, to the sickening crunch of plastic parts succumbing to my last-ditch effort at control. My back is to her, but I feel her eyes on me, know she stands in silence in the frame of my bedroom door, waiting for me to speak. I crumple into a heap on the foot of my bed, my eyes stinging from the need to cry, but the tears will no longer come.

"Oh, honey," she says. "Your camera."

She means what's left of it, which is nothing retrievable. I made sure of that.

"No. It's a stupid reminder of my stupid dependency on everything other than myself."

Paige sits next to me now, her arm around my shoulders. "This *is* you depending on yourself."

She motions to my wall filled with photographs and notes.

I laugh, a bitter sound. "I look like I'm either a serial killer or the cop trying to solve the crime."

She giggles, nudging me with her shoulder. "You just made a joke. You should try it more often, laughing at all of life's *Fuck yous*. It's like your own *Fuck you* right back."

I bump *her* shoulder. "I'm okay. But I needed a tension breaker. It's too late for me to scream without waking the neighbors, so the camera had to die." I let my eyes fall on the destruction sprinkled across my carpet. "Fuck," I lament. "My camera."

"We'll clean it up tomorrow." She rises from the bed, her arm still around me, and I stand with her and let her lead me back to the living room, depositing me on the couch before she gets comfortable on the floor.

"Are you sure about all this?" she asks, curling up on the pillows and turning on the TV.

"No," I admit, knowing she's talking about more than the camera. "But it's what's easiest for both of us. We'll get over each other, and we won't have to worry about what kind of mess I'll get into next. If it's too much for me to handle, he doesn't deserve to bear that responsibility as well."

"How long's it been since your gram went back to Florida?" she asks.

"Six months. Why?"

"Honey. If you weren't doing so well on your own, would she really have left? Is it possible you're setting these limitations for yourself because you're scared? I don't blame you. What happened to you is scary, but I think you forget that you survived it, that you kicked some ass to get to where you are now."

My defenses kick in regardless of whether or not Paige is right. "She left because I couldn't bear to see her miss out on *her* life anymore. I told her to go."

"Maggie. I met your gram when she was here. Though I didn't know your whole situation then, I could tell you were everything to her, and there's no way she would have left if she was worried about anything—about you taking care of yourself, about you getting sick again. There's also no way she cares any less about you simply because you needed *more* care. Why don't you see that?"

I shake my head. "You know what they say, right? You can't choose your family. She has to still love me. It's in the fine print. No matter how difficult I am, she has to be there for me. It's not the same with Griffin. You know it's not."

Paige cues up an episode of the *Gilmore Girls.* "Hmmm…" she muses. "Sounds like a load of bullshit to me. When does your life become yours instead of the fear of what it could be?"

My eyes widen, but she never takes her gaze off the TV, which is perfect. She can't see my reaction, can't know for sure that she's right. Fear is a powerful thing. I've lived with it for a long time now.

She doesn't push me any further, and I silently thank her for that. We watch without talking and wait for Miles to get home.

Maybe it is a load of bullshit, but it doesn't matter. The damage is done and, eventually, Griffin and I will both get past it. We'll have to.

Chapter Twenty-Five

GRIFFIN

Miles stares at me, and I realize I haven't moved since Maggie walked out, since she got in her friend's car and drove away. I thought I came here to do what she did, to get the closure I needed and end this. But when I saw her, even with her arms wrapped around *him*—as if I needed more convincing that she was done with whatever we were doing—I couldn't do it. I couldn't be the one to say good-bye.

"Hey, man. I'm really sorry. Maggie told me how important tonight was to you."

I hear him, but the words don't sink in.

"It's a bullshit word," I say, finding my voice.

"Excuse me?"

"*Sorry*. It's a bullshit word with no meaning. And it changes nothing."

Miles shrugs. "You're right. I'm…uh…I'm not sure what

else to say here."

The damp fabric of my shirt and jeans begins to register, as does the tremble of my insides.

"Those are hers, aren't they?" I nod to the framed drawings on the back wall. "Maggie did those."

Miles nods. "Maggie doing what she does best—observing life. I like to think of it as her wall of wishes," he says.

"How are they her wishes if she's not in any of them?" I ask. "I don't understand."

Miles huffs out a laugh. "No, man. I guess you don't." He sighs. "I wish you did."

"I should go," I say, my legs cold and unable to move, unwilling to admit she isn't coming back.

"Let me give you a ride," he says, but I shake my head.

"I need to clear my head. But thanks." I turn to the door, already pushing it open into the flurries, the chill. I comfort myself with the knowledge I can text Nat if it gets too bad. She's got the truck.

"Hey, man. Watch the door. It sticks in the humidity." Miles tries to warn me as I push against the frame, but my haste drowns out the realization as my cheek crashes into the metal lever so conveniently placed at eye level.

"Fuck!" I yell, my hand flying to my face and coming away bloody.

"Shit!" Miles yells. "Didn't you hear me? I said it sticks sometimes, and now that it's snowing—the humidity—shit!"

I back into the shop again. This seems preferable to staying pinned in the entryway. Because I don't know what else I'm supposed to do, and because I really don't want to see how bad the damage is, I collapse onto a chair at the nearest table.

What if

Miles is there with a wad of napkins as soon as I sit, and I take them gratefully, pressing them to the wound. I breathe in, the pain white-hot.

"Shit," he says again. "I don't even know why that thing is on the door. We never use it." He runs a hand through his hair. "Come on," he says. "I need to get you to the ER."

I roll my eyes but don't argue. I knew the second my face made contact with the metal that I wasn't going home anytime soon.

Miles has the place closed up and me in his passenger seat in less than two minutes. He brings a clean rag dampened with cool water for me to hold on my face until we get to the hospital.

"Are you creative?" I ask him as we start driving. "I'm in the middle of blinding—and might I say sobering—pain right now, so I thought you might muster up some creativity as to how I almost lost an eye so I don't have to say I walked into a door."

Miles barks out a laugh.

"Not the reaction I was hoping for," I say.

He shakes his head, his grin giving no sign of disappearing.

"Fucking 'Swan Song' he says. You've gotta be kidding me."

I let my head fall against the seat, closing my eyes to shut out the pain.

"I'm not following. But I appreciate the laughter. That helps."

"It's just. You won't get it. It's a *Gilmore Girls* reference. It's a Maggie thing."

The mention of her name sends a different kind of pain rocketing through me.

"Shit." I laugh with the realization. "Is that the name of the one where Jess gets the shit kicked out of him by a swan? I have three older sisters," I tell him. "Megan, the bookworm, we call her Rory. All three of them are team Logan, by the way."

At this Miles bursts into laughter. "Fucking Maggie," he says, his smile broad and knowing. "In that episode, Jess won't tell Rory how he got a black eye…"

"Fuck," I say, not sure if I'm proud or ashamed at knowing exactly which episode he's talking about, let alone him thinking I'm Jess—too proud to let Maggie see the real me. "I've hit rock bottom. Haven't I?" I try to laugh at the whole situation, but it hurts too much—not just my eye, but everywhere.

Since I can't sink much lower, I decide to lay it all on the table. "Can I ask you something?"

His smile fades immediately. He knows what's coming.

"We're friends," he says. "Me and Maggie. The way she acted tonight, it's self-preservation. I don't agree with how she handled it, but I know where she's coming from."

"But you were more than friends once, right?"

His hesitation is answer enough, and I'm ready to take back the question. But I'd be a hypocrite to judge her when she never judged me. Not until tonight, at least.

"Look," he starts. "Things have not been easy for Maggie. I was there when she needed someone, but it was only one time. We both knew we could only ever be friends, and that's all we've been ever since. Not that it should matter, but it was six months ago."

My shoulders sag with a sigh. I can live with this, but it doesn't change what happened tonight.

"And you like dudes, too?" I remember that first night at the coffee shop, the blond guy he left with.

Miles laughs again. "I like people," he says. "Everyone's welcome in my book."

We pull into the parking lot of the ER.

"I'll come back to get you," he says to me. "If you'll be okay getting yourself inside. I have to make a quick stop at the bus station. Long story, and not mine to tell. And as far as what you should tell them about what you did to yourself? I think I'd start with the truth."

"I'm in love with her," I say. "How's that for truth?"

"It's a start." He unlocks the doors. "You need me to walk you in?"

I shake my head. "I'm good. Thanks for the ride. I can call my sister to take me home."

"Uh-uh," Miles says. "You're not going home. I'm taking you to Maggie. Plus, I need to make sure you're okay—legal reasons since it was the coffee-shop door that attacked you."

Despite the pain, I laugh. "What if she won't talk to me?" I ask.

"She may not. But she'll at least have to listen."

I nod before getting out of the car. Then I make my way through the sliding doors of the emergency room, no creative story planned. Just the truth.

• • •

Maggie

Bang! Bang! Bang!

My eyes spring open, and I bolt upright on the couch. My heart thuds against my rib cage, but when I look at Paige on the floor next to me, she barely stirs.

The sound comes again, not the terrifying bang that must have been a product of drifting off. Only a quiet *tap, tap, tap* against my door. Miles.

"Coming!" I whisper-shout, trying not to wake Paige. When my eyes adjust, I focus on the microwave's clock to check the time. It's after two in the morning. Where the hell has he been?

I have my answer when I open the door, gasping at the sight of Griffin standing next to Miles, his beautiful eye, the one so recently healed, now an angry mix of purple and red. Coarse, unforgiving black thread holds the skin together where it split. The dark patch under his other eye tells of his weariness, and I have to brace my hand against the wall before my knees give out. Everything in me pulls and twists, urging me toward him, but I cement my feet in place and steady myself enough to speak.

"Miles, you didn't…"

"God, Maggie. No. Just, no. I can't believe you'd even think—"

Griffin shrugs and interrupts. "I was drunk, and I don't have the best track record, so I don't blame her for going there. But no."

His eyes shift to mine, pinning me where I stand. Good thing I don't want to move.

"This is a self-inflicted wound," he continues. "Unintentional, but self-inflicted nonetheless. Believe me, I'd give Miles the credit if I could."

Miles coughs into his hand. More like half coughs, half speaks two words, "*Swan Song*," before sauntering into my apartment.

"All you have to do is listen," Miles whispers as he passes, and my heart leaps in my throat.

Griffin toes the carpet with his worn and weather-soaked Chuck. I can't let him in, not when the only privacy we'd have is in my room, the last place I want him to see now.

"Will you?" he asks, lifting his head from the study of the hallway floor. "Will you listen?"

My feet release the lead weights holding them in place, and I move out into the hallway with him, shutting the door behind me. I have to fight my instinct to touch his face, to want to fix him like I tried to do so many weeks ago.

Instead I lean my back against the door, arms crossed, my features impassive. Every bit of my expression a lie.

"I'm listening," I say, hoping he'll make this quick so we can have the closure we need.

Griffin backs up to the opposite wall and proceeds to slide down to a sitting position.

"Mind if I sit?" he asks and then laughs. "It's been a long night."

I do the same, grateful for one less thing to think about because yes, at this point in the evening or morning or whatever we're going to call it, the effort to stand is one I don't want to put forth at the moment. I wrap my arms around my knees. Griffin rests his elbows on his, arms crossed and hands dangling.

"I want you to know that however this ends..." He blinks slowly. "I mean, however this night ends...it still *is* a new beginning. For me, even if not for us."

My tear ducts seem to have replenished because though his words make me smile—for him—my vision starts to blur, and one small stream escapes—for us.

"Whatever made you decide not to show up tonight, it doesn't change how I feel, Maggie. It doesn't change that *I've* changed, and so much of that is because of you. Whatever you thought of me when we first met, I'm not the same person I was then."

I want to tell him the same, that all the parts of me that have grown I owe in some way to him, for wanting me, believing in me, and trusting me when I fought so hard not to let him get close. But letting him in also means letting him get hurt, and I don't want to be the person who hurts him.

"I'm proud of you," I say, smiling through the tears. "You're going to find what makes you happy."

He sucks in a deep breath and lets it out, long and slow.

"I told you I didn't know what I wanted, but that was only partly true. I may not know what I want to do with my life, but I know *who* I want. I want you. *You* make me happy, Maggie."

He scoots across the floor, our toes touching now. His thumb swipes at a falling tear on my cheek, which only makes them fall faster.

"What about tonight?" I ask. "Did I make you happy tonight? Did I make you happy in Chicago? Because this is what it's like to be with me, Griffin. You don't know what you're taking on by saying these things."

"You act as if every moment we've spent together has been as much of a mess as tonight has been. What about those nights at my apartment?"

My chest tightens at the thought of him lying on his bed, glasses on and book propped against his chest—the photo I left sitting next to my bed. *That* was perfect. But he doesn't know about the first one, about me sneaking out because I got sick. So I bring up the obvious.

"What about Chicago?" I throw the question at him like a dare. Because he can't argue against that mess.

"Do you want to know why I loved Chicago?" He inches toward me.

I should push him away, but the nearness of him overrides my logic, so I leave him open to fill the space. And he does.

"I love you, Maggie." His lips brush mine as he speaks the words. Then he's kissing me, and I'm kissing him back. Kissing him and filling with the guilt of knowing this is good-bye when he has to think otherwise. But the guilt will be here for a long while, so I push it down, allowing myself the minute or two of basking in those words—*I love you, Maggie*—hoping he knows with each touch of my lips to his that I'm telling him the same, that I've loved him since the date that wasn't a date, that this is good-bye *because* I love him, too.

When he pulls away for air, I release my head from the cradle of his hands, sliding to my knees, then climbing to my feet. Griffin stands, too, but he doesn't try to kiss me again. He knows. He sees it in my guarded stare.

"You don't know me," I say. "Not like you think you do. You wouldn't feel the same if you did. I want so much for you, Griffin, but I'm not the one to give it to you."

"I'll decide that, Maggie. Don't push me away because you think you know me, too. Let me into your life so I can prove you wrong."

I reach behind me, my hand on the doorknob, ready to run.

"I need to go." The realization hits that he came here

with Miles, that Miles thought I'd let him stay. "I'll have Miles drive you home." His jaw ticks.

"Don't worry about me," he says, his tone flat. "Miles said I can crash at Paige's since it's so late. So that's it? You're going to walk away without giving me a chance."

His voice pleads now, but I'm already turning the handle.

"I don't want to hurt you, Griffin. But I will. If I don't walk away now, I'll only hurt you more."

Because walking away now is hard enough. It'll only get worse if we put it off.

The door opens, and I take a step back over the threshold and into my apartment.

"I'm sorry, Griffin." The tears flow freely. At least I can give him that. I can show him this is anything but easy, but it's for the best.

"Maggie, don't."

"Mags." I hear Miles behind me, the disappointment in his voice too much on top of Griffin's hurt.

"I can't," I tell them both. "Not yet. I just can't."

I let the door swing wide as I head for the only place I can be alone, yet the one place Griffin remains, even if he isn't here — my room.

I don't turn on the light so I don't have to see his face in any of the photos on the wall…or the one on my nightstand of him reading in bed. I collapse on my bed, his words still echoing in my head.

My eyes closed and sleep already winning the fight, I whisper to the darkness, "I love you, too."

Chapter Twenty-Six

When I wake up, the first thing I notice is the partially obstructed vision in my right eye. Then there's the pain, the skin swollen and stretched and stitched together. But the other pain is worse, my insides twisted and knotted and *fuck*. Everything about last night comes rushing in, and I close my eyes, begging sleep to take me for a little while longer so I don't have to deal with today. Today's an asshole.

But the smell of coffee rouses me further, as does the fact I can see from the couch that Paige and Miles left the front door wide open. Her kitchen is empty, which means the coffee isn't here. Neither is Paige.

I find the bathroom and decide to first take care of business and then *not* avoid the mirror. When I meet my own stare in the glass, I laugh, wincing as I do. Sunday brunch is in twenty-four hours.

Tomorrow is the last time you go home looking like you don't give a shit, like your life's not worth wanting something more.

I'm pretty sure that thought comes from my reflection because right now the only thing I have to say to myself is a big old *Fuck you*.

There's that coffee aroma again. And Paige's open door. I know where she must be but am not sure I want to follow.

Cotton mouth along with the hope of something filling my stomach enough to take my pain meds helps propel me out the door and through Maggie's, which also sits wide open.

Paige sits on the couch, mug in hand, flipping through Maggie's DVR.

"She's not here. Neither is Miles. They're at her six-month checkup, and I'm butting in where I don't belong."

My feet stay rooted in the doorway. I shouldn't be here if I haven't been invited. Yet I know being this close means finding out some kind of answer, an answer Paige wants me to have.

"Tell me to leave, Paige." But I can see in her eyes her mind is made up. I only have to step the rest of the way through this door to make up mine, but the violation is too big. I can't do it.

She sets her mug down on the table and strides past me into the kitchen, filling a second mug from the coffee maker.

"My coffee maker is broken," she says, handing me the mug. "I told Maggie I wasn't letting you leave without making you a cup...without letting you in."

She sighs, leading me far enough into the apartment so she can kick the door shut.

What if

"She didn't fight me on it."

"But she didn't ask you to let me in."

"Semantics. Either way, she knows you're here. Do what you will with that, but I suggest you take a quick tour. Then you can be on your way and make whatever decision you want to make."

I let the mug warm my hands, my body still recovering from the time I spent outside last night.

"What am I going to find?" I ask, my throat tightening as reality sets in. All I've wanted is to know Maggie the way I let her know me. But what if she's right? What if what I find changes how I feel?

"You already found her, honey, the real Maggie. What's in there is only the missing pieces. That's all."

And that's enough.

I move through the living room, smiling at the pillows lined up on the floor, extending from either side of the couch. Miles and Paige's *beds*. I would have thought I'd be jealous to see something like this, pillows on a floor an indication of how much more of her they've always been able to see. Instead I'm filled with a kind of warmth, of knowing even without three sisters looking out for her, Maggie has her family.

A narrow hallway boasts two small doors. The one on my right opens to a bathroom much like the one I was in at Paige's place. The other opens to what must be Maggie's bedroom. Blackout shades block the morning sun, so I flip on the light.

The first thing I see is a wall covered by a giant bulletin board. I step closer, looking at one of the many photos pinned to the board, reading the caption: *Douche-bag customer who never tips.* I laugh, hearing her voice in my head. The next one is of an older man, smiling proudly with one of Maggie's beverages in his hand. This one reads: *George: loves my latte art.*

I smile at that one, having heard her talk about George and Jeanie. There are more like this, all of the captions some sort of reminder about the people in each photo. Soon I find myself looking for my own image, some sort of evidence to give me hope. When I find the one she took that first day, all it says is *Griffin/Fancy Pants.* Not much to go on there.

My eyes move next to a section of the board sporting not photographs but articles—one on the benefits of art therapy, another on surviving traumatic brain injury, the lasting and sometimes chronic aftereffects of brain surgery.

Sticky notes adorn the board as well, adding follow-up text to a photo's caption or a reminder of something she doesn't want to forget about one of the articles. I flash back to that night at Royal Grounds, the *trainee's* notes behind the counter.

Maggie. We could have figured this out.

I want to believe we would have found a way if she would have told me. What evidence did I ever give her, though, that I was capable of handling this when I was so good at showing her I could barely handle myself? When I turn toward her bed, I see the first glimmer of hope. On her nightstand are the only pictures without explanations, one of me from that night at my apartment. Our best night. And next to them is a sketch—Maggie and me at a table in the coffee shop, her hands resting on a mug and one of mine raking through my hair. I laugh. She knows me so well. The two people in the sketch laugh, too, a happy version of us in a scene that hasn't happened—yet. *Maggie's wall of wishes.* All I can do is hope that this is one she still wants to come true.

Then I glance at her desk, and that's where I find it—a worn red box of Uno cards.

. . .

MAGGIE

My heel taps the floor of the car, and Miles places a hand on my knee to steady me.

"Tell me again what the neurologist said," he demands, a stupid, goofy grin plastered across his face, the same one I'm wearing, too.

"He said my scan shows no clots. And when I told him about my class-load and my work-load and my grades, he said there's no reason I can't take a full schedule next year."

"Aaaand…" Miles knows this. He sat there when the doctor relayed the information to me, but it doesn't take away from the excitement of repeating those words again.

"He also said I can drive. Any medical provisions have been removed, and I can take the driving test and get a new license any time I want…which means never." Because my doctor would have okayed me to drive a year ago, but all I think about is what would happen if I zoned out in traffic. Or worse. What if I develop another clot, and it bursts while I'm in a vehicle?

Miles reads my silence, like he always does. "Enough with the *What ifs*, okay? What if zombies attacked right
)"

>unch his shoulder, with love of course. "There are
kits and guides for that. It's not the same."

But I can't help the perma-grin on my face. Something about making it this far, about surviving the past two-plus years... I look at Miles, think about Paige trying to set me straight last night, and everything clicks into place. I'm *not* the person I was before I got sick, but I'm also not the girl lying in a hospital bed, relearning how to live. I can do so much now that I couldn't a year ago, and maybe—hopefully—a year from now, I'll be able to do more.

"I've been thinking, and maybe, just maybe everything that happened last night could have happened to anyone. People get lost, right?"

Miles lets out a long sigh.

"Yes, sweetheart. It could have happened anyway."

I squeeze his hand. "And I've experienced the headaches long enough to know that staying up all night or... or hell, drinking—I know better. I can avoid so many of my symptoms if I pay better attention to myself. I'm an idiot. I let him distract me."

Miles shakes his head. "No, honey. You fell in love with him."

I start to laugh. Or maybe it's a sob. I'm not sure.

"I fell in love with him," I admit. "But I hurt him."

We pull into a parking spot in front of my apartment building.

"Not because you're sick or because you're broken or any less of the Maggie you were when I first met you. You hurt him because you're scared," he says, and I nod.

"I'm so scared, Miles. Not just of me losing him."

"I know, sweetie. But making him lose you when he doesn't have to? That's not fair. He deserves better. *You* deserve better."

He kisses my hand.

"We all are scared. But shutting us out? Keeping the people who love you at a distance—it doesn't make it any less scary. Just lonely."

"I don't want to be alone," I admit. He releases my hand so we can get out of the car. "I don't want to let fear win anymore," I tell him. "But it's not going to be easy. I may need your help."

Miles cups his hands around his mouth and hollers to the wind. "Did you hear that, Maggie's fear? Maggie gets to win now!"

I slap him on the shoulder and then steer him toward the building, both of us laughing as we go.

Once inside, we head up to my place in silence. Walking in there elicits a new fear, a fear that I succeeded, that shutting Griffin out last night after he told me he loved me was the final push. I tell myself I'll be okay. Because I have to be. I can be scared and be okay, too.

Paige's door is ajar, which means she's still home. Griffin has to be gone by now. I reach for my keys in my bag but note my door isn't clicked shut, either. I slowly nudge it open to find Paige on the couch alone, drinking coffee and watching a *Gilmore Girls* episode.

She springs up to greet us, coffee sloshing over her hand. "Ow! Shit. Sorry, Mags. I'll clean that up. But tell me, how'd the appointment go?"

She rushes past us to the kitchen to grab a roll of paper towels, and as my eyes follow her they stop at a sight on the counter—another coffee mug.

"Paige..." I draw out her name, the rest of my question catching in my throat.

When she spins around, paper towels in hand, she follows my gaze to the counter.

"Paige, was he *here*?"

I knew she was plotting something when she asked to have coffee over here, but after last night, I expected Griffin to leave without looking back.

"He was here, honey."

Her expression should be sad, right? I fell in love with a guy and pushed him away every time he tried to get close. So what's up with the goofy grin?

I glance at Miles, who wears a confused smile, but a smile nonetheless, and I turn back at her. Then I book it to my room for no reason other than thoughts of Griffin propelling me there.

When I flip on the light, the first thing I notice is my floor, no sign of the camera I destroyed littering the space between my bed and my wall. And then the wall.

A rainbow of Uno cards illuminates the space, all with messages scrawled in Sharpie, the handwriting foreign though I have no doubt whose it is.

The first one is pinned to the photo I took of Griffin the day we met, him in the driver's seat and me outside his window at the café.

I was afraid I'd never see you again after you snapped this one.

Next is the one of him before we snuck into the theater.

This is when I knew you were trouble, that no matter what our agreement was, I was already yours, even if I wouldn't admit it.

All of my captions on the pictures were to remind me of the time we spent together, in case I forgot. Because I knew, too, though I wouldn't admit it, either, that I didn't want to forget him.

But here's the thing — I haven't forgotten any of it, not one single moment of our time together. The photos were a crutch, or maybe a way for me to hold on to him even as I pushed him away.

The one of us in front of the tree at the John Hancock Center, the caption reads: *Aberdeen reunion with Griffin in Chicago*. But the note on the card next to it has me choking back a sob.

> *The guy I was a month ago would have run away so fast, but everything about you pulls me in. All of it, Maggie. When you're healthy, when you're sick. Full deck. I'm in.*

My hand slides across the board to the end where there are no pictures but instead articles. "Brain Aneurysm Recovery: Symptoms and Setbacks," "Short-term Memory Loss and How to Cope," "Statistics for Aneurysm Survivors," "Art Therapy for Psychological Health."

There it is, two years of my life plastered across a bulletin board as I try to make sense of it while at the same time hiding myself from those who matter most. One card sits among the posted articles.

> *I see you, Maggie. I see you, and I'm amazed and scared…and I love you.*

I spin toward my nightstand, where the one photo sits

that matters most. Because it's the night I fell in love with him. Griffin in his bed, shirt off and glasses on, reading a book. I move slowly toward the foot of my bed and slide along the edge, not sure I can take any more once I'm close enough to read. And when I'm there, the photo and the card in my hand, laughter spills out between the tears. Because there is no caption on this photo. I didn't need one because I've always known what it means, and now so does Griffin.

You so totally love me, too.

Paige and Miles are at my door now, staring at me as I sob and laugh, a picture and sticky note clutched to my chest.

"You okay?" Miles asks.

I nod and shake my head as tears pour over my smile.

"I don't know," I say. "I think I will be, though."

"Can I ask you something, then?" he says, and I nod as he produces an Uno card from his back pocket. "Do you always keep Uno cards in the freezer?"

Oh my God. He left them everywhere?

Now I'm laughing, full-on, big-bellowed laughing with the occasional snort.

They leave me then, alone in the room that is a portrait of me and thoughts of the person who saw it all, who saw me, who's scared right along with me and loves me anyway. And yeah, I so totally love him, too.

On Monday morning I go back through my phone's messages, reading the ones he sent Friday night—the night of his party.

What if

But there's been no communication since then. I needed the weekend to collect myself, to build up the courage to face him. That would require him to show up, though, and I have no guarantee he will.

I hesitate inside the library's entrance for a good ten minutes, only moving when the stares from the girl at the information desk make me more self-conscious than nervous. I decide on the stairs, taking them slowly—not only to avoid perspiring but also getting there too quickly—to the sixth floor. Not until someone bumps my shoulder do I realize I'm standing in the door frame of the sixth-floor study room with my eyes squeezed shut.

"Sorry," the girl says as she passes. "I didn't expect you to stop."

I open my eyes because I'm in a public place and am expected to act like an adult. But if I try to respond to the girl's apology, my flip-flopping stomach will leap out of my mouth.

This might happen anyway because as soon as my eyes regain their focus they lock on his. His beautiful chocolate eyes, despite the one that seems to be forever swollen and bruised.

He came. And he waited. And I can't move or else that whole stomach leaving my insides thing is going to happen anyway.

Griffin smiles, and if I wasn't stuck where I stand, I'd stagger at the sight of it. Then he's moving, his chair sliding out behind him, his body hurrying closer to mine.

When he's near enough for me to smell apples, he grabs my bag off my shoulder and repositions it on his.

"Hey, Pippi," he says. "What took you so long?"

Chapter Twenty-Seven

GRIFFIN

I smile when I see the whiteboard calendar in the kitchen… and the girl wearing nothing but my Aberdeen T-shirt and boy briefs standing next to the espresso maker, the first item we bought together. When my lease is up in May, this will be *our* place, not that I don't spend a majority of my time here anyway.

"I have my first AmeriCorps meeting tonight, a sort of meet and greet," I say as I approach her. She takes a lazy sip from her mug before setting it on the counter.

"Bring them some basil, and they'll fall head over heels in love with you." She giggles, and I plant a kiss on her nose. "Here," she says, lifting a mug brimming with foam. When I look at it, I see the heart she's drawn in my drink.

I stand, my palms braced on the counter on either side of her.

"Thanks, Pippi. But I'm not really thirsty yet."

She lets out a soft laugh as she sets my latte down, her elbow bumping the mason jar filled with loose change labeled "My Big Fat Scottish and Greek Wedding." Because we're going to make it to Greece. We're going to make it lots of places, but first things first.

"Nice outfit," she says, eying my only piece of clothing, my boxer briefs. "It goes well with your glasses."

I stifle my own laugh, aiming to win this teasing standoff.

"I'd like it better if we matched," I say, sliding my palms from the counter to her waist, taking great care to lift her T-shirt enough so skin meets skin.

Both of us take in a sharp breath, and my hands glide up her torso under her shirt until they find her bare breasts. At this she hums, and I know I'm a goner.

Maggie lifts her arms above her head, and in seconds the T-shirt is a goner, too.

"There," I say. "Matching."

She reaches for my glasses and folds them carefully before setting them on the counter.

"For their safety," she says.

"You can read me what's on the board," I say. "I don't need them to see you."

I dip my head to her neck, peppering it with soft kisses and an occasional nibble.

"I think I found a few more freckles," I tell her, and again that hum of hers that drives me crazy. "What's on the agenda again for today?" I ask.

Breathless, she says, "Driving lesson. Then coffee shop at three for me."

I squint at the small numbers on the microwave clock. It's only eight-fifteen.

My hands skim down her sides, past the fabric of her briefs until they rest on the back of her thighs. I don't warn her before picking her up and wrapping her freckled thighs around my waist.

She yelps with laughter, and I have to steady myself at the feeling of her breasts against my skin.

"You're going to have to butter me up before I let you get behind the wheel of my car."

"If you're nervous, I can always let Paige or Miles help me prepare for the driving test. I'm sure they won't mind."

She yelps again as I nip at her neck, and then she's laughing and kissing me, and I can't remember what battle of wits I was trying to win because when it comes to Maggie, she's the victor every time.

"I'll mind," I say as I pilot her away from the counter and toward her room.

"We can't have that, then, can we?" she asks, and her head dips to mine so I'm walking blind, her lips on me as we somehow make it through her door without incident.

I lower her to her feet, careful not to let our lips break contact, but she pulls away, fixing me in her stare.

"Wild card," she says, and my brows tug together in question. "Ask me anything."

I cup her cheeks and kiss her forehead, her eyelids, her nose.

"Do you love me, Maggie Kendall?"

Her eyes crinkle as she smiles. "I love you, Griffin Reed. That's all you want to know?"

No, I want to tell her. *I want to know everything.* But she doesn't have to give me everything today.

"Full deck?" I ask. "All-in?"

She bites her bottom lip.

"All-in," she whispers, and I smooth her wild, red waves back from her face.

"Then we have all the time we need."

I kiss her long and slow, tasting her coffee-flavored lips and everything Maggie.

"Because I've got a confession," I say, and her brows rise in question. "I'm yours for as long as you'll have me. Always have been, ground rules or no."

She pulls me toward the side of the bed, her grin transforming from sweet to anything but.

"Have I mentioned the rules about waking up in my apartment when we have hours of free time?"

I shake my head.

"Rule number one—stay in bed for as long as humanly possible."

I kick the door shut behind me. I'm beginning to like following the rules.

Want more Griffin and Maggie? How about that first night at Griffin's apartment from Griffin's point of view and a bonus chapter where Griffin gives Maggie a driving lesson in Miles's Nissan? Leave a review, and you'll get these two bonus chapters!

Email the link to your review to amy@ajpine.com, and A.J. Pine will personally send you those bonus chapters!

Thank you so much for reading!

Acknowledgments

Sometimes you don't even know the book you're meant to write until someone pushes you in that direction. First and foremost I want to thank my editors at Entangled, Karen Grove and Nicole Steinhaus, for wanting Griffin's book as well as helping make my words shinier and prettier than I knew they could be. And big thanks to Brittany Marczak for my gorgeous cover. I'm pretty sure you found the photo the tourist took of Griffin and Maggie by the Christmas tree in Chicago. To my agent, Courtney Miller-Callihan, thank you for joining me on my Entangled journey. Then there's Griffin, the guy I intended as a secondary character in book one, the obvious wrong choice, but he so didn't listen. Isn't that just like Griffin, though? I'm so glad his voice never shut down and that he found his way to Maggie. Griffin deserved his happily ever after, and I'm so happy to have given him one.

Natalie Blitt, this book would not have made it through

the initial drafting stages without your amazing edits and encouraging love notes. I don't know what I did to deserve you, but I'm never letting you go. FYI, you are stuck with me for life. Lia Riley and Megan Erickson, thank you both for falling in love with Griffin as much as I did. Your thumbs-up responses mean everything, as does your friendship. I'm so lucky to have you in my corner. Jennifer Blackwood, my agent sister and mini me, your support via Facebook, Twitter, email, gchat, and phone (plus various forums, groups, and newsletters) is a must in my writing life. Thank you for always being only a form of social media away. Lex Martin, we started this crazy journey together, and I will always have you to thank for saying for the first time, "I wrote a book." Think of where we were when we met and where we are now. Pretty incredible. So much love for all you talented girls!

I've met so many writers on this journey whose work I admire and adore, and one of them is the fabulous and gracious Rachel Harris. Thank you for reading and loving my little book and for taking the time to blurb it. Your support means so much.

I've found some of the best, most supportive fellow New Adult writers in our NA 14 group. I shower you all with BUCKETS of love. I'm so grateful to get to hang with all of you. Without you, I'd never be able to make epically inappropriate teaser images. What can I say? We're a good team. T-Rex hugs for all!

Jen Vincent, thank you for our always focused Starbucks writing dates…and for getting me hooked on Cool Lime Refreshers. Can't wait for our "after" picture!

Thank you to my family, especially my husband and

kids, for forgiving the fact that if I'm awake (which is me most hours of the day), I most likely have writing work to do. You accept my laptop as one of my vital organs, and on top of that, you still think it's pretty cool that I make books. I couldn't make 'em without you. Love you all.

Readers—especially those of you who read all the way to here—thank YOU for showing me it's never too late to chase the dream.

About the Author

A.J. Pine writes stories to break readers' hearts, but don't worry—she'll mend them with a happily ever after. As an English teacher and a librarian, AJ has always surrounded herself with books. All her favorites have one big commonality—romance. Naturally, her own books have the same. When she's not writing, she's reading. Then there's online shopping (everything from groceries to shoes) and, of course, a tiny bit of TV where she nourishes her undying love of vampires, from Eric Northman to the Salvatore brothers. And in the midst of all of this, you'll also find her hanging with her family in the Chicago burbs. Her first New Adult novel was If Only, also published with Entangled Publishing.

51260363R00176

Made in the USA
Charleston, SC
13 January 2016